Frobisher's
Savage

Also by Leonard Tourney

Witness of Bones
Knaves Templar
Old Saxon Blood
The Bartholomew Fair Murders
Familiar Spirits
Low Treason
The Players' Boy Is Dead

Frobisher's Savage

A Joan and Matthew Stock Mystery

Leonard Tourney

ST. MARTIN'S PRESS NEW YORK

Library of Congress Cataloging-in-Publication Data

Tourney, Leonard D.
    Frobisher's savage   /   Leonard Tourney.
        p.   cm.
    "A Thomas Dunne book."
    ISBN 0-312-11437-0 (hardcover)
    1. Stock, Matthew (Fictitious character)—Fiction.
2. Great   Britain—History—Elizabeth,   1558-1603—Fiction. 3. Frobisher, Martin, Sir, ca. 1535-1594—Fiction.
4. Eskimos—Travel—England—Fiction.   I. Title.
PS3570.O784F76   1994
813'.54—dc20   94-21754
                                                CIP

First edition: October 1994

10 9 8 7 6 5 4 3 2 1

For
Shelly Lowenkopf

—

In the name of God in whom we all believe, who, I trust, hath preserved your bodies and souls among these infidels, I commend me unto you. I will be glad to seek by all means you can devise for your deliverance, either with force, or with any commodities within my ships, which I will not spare for your sakes, or anything else I can do for you. I have aboard of theirs a man, a woman, and a child, which I am contented to deliver for you, but the man I carried away from hence last year is dead in England. . . .

—*from a Letter of Martin Frobisher,*
  7 August 1577, to five men lost from his
  first expedition to Greenland

Prologue

Coast of Greenland, 1576

The savage was shorter than the shortest of the Englishmen by a span, and round-faced, squinty-eyed, foul-smelling, as all the savages were. His brown, leathery face peered out with shy, curious eyes from the shaggy cowl of bearskin framing his head. Behind him, mountains of ice rose in the distance like church steeples in the timorous light of the northern sun. All else was a narrow shelf of black rock, the whitecapped sea, bone-wrackingly cold and bottomless, and the sky like none of the Englishmen had ever seen in their own country; a blue so pale and soulless as to cause the heart to break with the very emptiness of it.

Six Englishmen had come in the cockboat: Frobisher, whom the men called "the General," and five who weren't too weakened from sickness to endure the rowing and exposure to the open sea and the treacherous, half-submerged chunks of ice. The General had first spotted the savage making his way along the shore. He ordered the boat toward the rocks, but in the time it took for its prow to nudge the ice and the boatswain to clamber ashore, the savage had noticed the English. He stopped dead in his tracks and stood waiting submissively. Frobisher and four of the men—one having remained to make sure the cockboat didn't float back to England by itself—approached to parley and trade.

Frobisher had declared after the first few encounters with the savages that their heathenish tongue was too difficult even to attempt—consisting as it did of such belly snarling and squealing and mostly, he had observed, of gestures—more dumbfounding than the Welsh of his own ancestors. Perhaps, Frobisher had theorized, the frigid air had paralyzed the natural organs of speech, or perhaps it was due to some deficiency of the brain.

"I am Martin Frobisher," the General declared to the savage in a stentorian voice more suited to Parliament than this icy waste. "Servant of Her Most Sovereign and Dreaded Majesty, Elizabeth, queen of England."

He had earlier claimed the territory for her whom he served and dispensed with the ceremonial words. He was interested in the savage, however, and would have fain claimed him, but already the little man, who seemed but a youth, was backing away, fear having replaced the shy curiosity in his eyes.

Frobisher motioned to the boatswain, who was tall and muscular, and who looked at the moment like a bear in his layers of good English wool. Without a word, the boatswain removed a long chain from the purse at his belt and extended it toward the savage.

The chain was made of base metal and was one of a hundreds of such baubles Frobisher had providently secured to trade with the savages when he should find that northwestern passage and open it to England, let the Spaniards be cursed, but it gleamed like silver in the sun. The savage never looked at it but continued his slow retreat, never taking his gaze from Frobisher's face, as though the General were a basilisk from whose own eyes one could not withdraw, one's will notwithstanding.

Frobisher said, "Take him."

At the sharp command, the savage ran, as though he had understood its import as well as the English had. The savage was fleet over the rock as the English were not, practiced in escaping from the great white bears. Frobisher ran as fast as the others, despite his breastplate and leg armor and despite having almost twice the years of several. Breathing heavily, he cried, "Circle round him, you slaggards. Head him off."

But it was not possible to advance around him. The shelf between sea and rising mountain was as narrow as a country lane. It must have a been a furlong he ran before he slipped, and the boatswain, the strongest runner and endowed with the agility of an acrobat, flung himself upon the savage, wrestled him to the ice, and straddling the little man began to pound upon his shoulders and back, cursing all the while.

Until Frobisher caught up and ordered him to cease, although not to remove himself from the back of the savage, who was making no sound at all but lay as though already dead.

"Great God in heaven," the boatswain gasped, ruddy-faced and sweating. "He smells so. Like betwixt the legs of a Bankside whore. Like a dog's vomit. Like a—"

"To him you may smell no sweeter," Frobisher said, huffing and puffing and filling the air with the fog of his breath. The other Englishmen came up and circled the prey, laughing and pointing. The strenuous exercise had warmed them and dispelled their melancholy. It was a small victory for largely disappointed men.

Frobisher said, "Bind him. We'll take him back to the ship. Since he will not trade our chain for his gold, we shall take him with us to show those at home how far from England these northern climes be."

The savage had a name as had any Christian soul, but none of the men aboard ship could pronounce it, and some were afraid to try. He had already declared his inhumanity in eating his meat raw, in stinking so abominably, in staring at the Englishmen with the leaden eyes of a dead man. Frobisher himself had had some little intercourse with the savages. He had seen how wretchedly they lived, "very strange and beastly." His crew, sons of the sea, were by nature superstitious and would no sooner have polluted their tongues with a heathen word than have pissed into the wind. Both tempted fate.

So Frobisher named the savage Adam, because the savage was the first man of his kind to whom Frobisher had given a name, and the strangest he had observed in all his career as mariner and shipmaster, freebooter, pirate, and now, praise be God, the queen's good servant. And so the name stuck like the tongue to frozen steel.

" 'Tis a great shame he shall have no Eve to be his helpmate," Christopher Hall, master of the *Gabriel,* observed wryly after the name had been bestowed. Another present speculated as to whether the savages mated like normal folk. "Nay," quipped Hall, "no doubt like the Italians, rather."

"Or the beastly French," said the boatswain, who had been given credit among his shipmates for subduing the prisoner. The boatswain gyrated his hips and ran his hands down his flanks provocatively.

All the men laughed, but the savage, who, having been examined in Frobisher's cabin, as naked as his namesake on the day of creation, and found to have parts corresponding exactly to the Englishmen's, stood as still and curiously staring as in the moments preceding his capture.

"He shall dwell a singular man in his new Eden," Frobisher said. "And Eden our England shall seem, after this barren waste where neither God nor the devil can abide for glare or cold."

The men murmured in agreement and were very merry. All knew the capture of the savage meant it was likely they would be returning to England soon, despite the ship's condition.

Until far into the night aboard the *Gabriel* there was more good-natured raillery at him Frobisher had named Adam. But the savage endured this mockery with the patience an old

Stoic Greek would have approved and continued to regard the Englishmen with a mixture of curiosity and loathing, even after they had become preoccupied by a common black stone, which each examined in his hand over and over as though it were a thing of considerable worth.

Chapter 1

ה

Essex, England, 1595

Years after his capture, long ago having given up hope of returning to whence he came, Adam, who had been given the surname Nemo, both in ironic jest and so that he could be like other men with family name as well as Christian, and who had nearly forgotten the name by which he had been known by his own people, still dreamed of ice. He dreamed of the restless, green sea, of the glistening mountains of perpetual snow, and of the sky without clouds and the earth that was forever frozen and knew no change, either in fact or in his memory. He dreamed of his parents, his brothers and sisters, all as vague in his waking life now as the ghostly presences in the big house at Burton Court—except in his dreams, when they were more vividly remembered than Matilda the cook or James the hostler, or the long-faced solemn steward, Jeroboam.

This was after his short-lived career as a human aberration, after Frobisher's voyages were thought to be a stale jest, a notable fiasco and scandal for having yielded no gold, after Adam himself had all but disappeared into obscurity and become no more than a servant, curious in appearance, known to be some kind of foreigner, perhaps a gypsy or Muscovite. Thought to have died, even. Which Frobisher had supposed, and a notion Adam had done nothing to disabuse any man of, for he was profoundly grateful to the Englishman, John Crookback, who had freed him from the staring of curious Londoners and brought him to where he could at least have a modicum of peace.

Adam Nemo was of indeterminant years; his own people had not fussed about such matters. A youth when taken, he reckoned he was now forty or thereabouts. Compact and muscular, he had filled out with age and the more provident English diet of beef and grains. In English jerkin and hose, he did not seem so great an anomaly. Yet his round face, swarthy skin, and Asian eyes betrayed him as no native of English soil. That and his speech, which was colored with a curious accent. Now he was a servant in a great house, Adam, the first man—at least, of his race—in the green, fertile land that was England.

Still he dreamed of ice, even in Essex, even in the great house of Master Arthur Burton, where he was one of thirty or more servants kept around the estate to prevent the sprawling, chimney-sprouting house from falling into a more abject decay while its absentee lord spent all of his time in London, attending plays and currying favor at court.

Adam worked six days a week, like the other servants, and on Sunday attended church under the stern supervision of Jeroboam, the solemn steward who ruled the lower servants with an artful diversity of scowls and threats.

On this Sunday in February, however, Adam stayed home. Two of the serving girls were sick abed with some mysterious fever, and besides, Jeroboam insisted that there be a man about the house in his own absence. James the hostler was normally chosen for this purpose, he being tall, broadshouldered, and a clear match for any sturdy beggar who chose God's Sabbath to beat upon the door and perhaps steal if his begging proved futile. But James had been sent off to Chelmsford to visit a dying father, and as Jeroboam lamented, there was nothing for it but to appoint Adam to the task.

"Let no one in, save him you already know," Jeroboam said. "Give a firm nay to beggars. As for the wenches, if they be sick indeed, let them keep to their beds and not dance for glee that they are excused from the parson's sermon."

Adam nodded, his usual reply to Jeroboam's instructions to beware of housebreakers, of whom the glowering steward had a terrible dread. Adam had over the years ingratiated himself with Jeroboam by ready compliance to every order, no matter how arbitrary. Since the other servants were sometimes insolent, Jeroboam being regarded by them—behind his back, at least—as a stolid, self-righteous knave and fool, Adam enjoyed a position of esteem in Jeroboam's eyes. Adam noticed that over the years his duties had been slowly lightened. The other servants had likewise observed these favors and resented them.

It was a mild day for the season. Rain had sweetened the earth, and the smooth fields of Essex with their occasional copse and hillock offered a pleasant prospect even in the depths of winter. Adam walked down the high road from his master's house, mindful that his abandonment of his station would put him in poor stead with the steward but confident he could complete his errand before Jeroboam returned from church with the other servants and delivered his long, tedious recital of the parson's sermon to those who stayed at home.

He had left the sick wenches behind him, having confirmed the steward's opinion that their sickness was nothing else but a ploy to allow them to sleep late. He had roused them from their slumber in their attic quarters only to find them well enough, teaseful young harlots in their loose-bodiced shifts and their white breasts wagging at him provocatively. "You shall be Adam, but we shall be no Eves," taunted Martha, the older of the two, laughing lustily.

"By God's little body, Martha," cried Sarah, the younger, who was thin-hipped and as fair as a lady and had had two

8

children begot upon her body by the master's unruly son, Harold. "You are so ripe for a husband to plow your furrow that you will have even Adam here for a tiller. Yet he is as black as a Moor and his eyes seem sewn half shut."

"Nay, I shall not," pronounced Martha, standing atop her bed with her arms akimbo as though she was queen and not a simple servant girl. "For I doubt me he has a plow, and it must needs cut a wide swath to pleasure me."

Accustomed to such bawdy talk, Adam made no answer. He turned his back on the two women and went downstairs, satisfied that he had no caretaker's office to perform for these two but was at liberty to do what he willed. He had known no woman in his life, either she of his own people or of the English and had never desired any, and the household females, having perhaps sensed as much, generally treated him as third thing, neither male nor female, and sometimes went half naked in his presence, leering at him with wanton eyes and making salacious gibes, fearless of his manhood and confident of his discretion.

But Adam did have a friend, the young son of the man who had brought him to Essex out of horrid London years earlier. This was Nicholas. Deaf and dumb, Nicholas was nineteen or thereabouts, and because of some crippling disease that had damaged his brain, unable to do much more than feed and milk his father's cows or shell peas. He made gestures, wagged his head, looked simpleminded as well as inarticulate. Nicholas's virtue, in Adam's mind, was his acceptance of Adam. From Nicholas came no cruel jibes, threats, or references veiled thinly or otherwise, to his dusky complexion, exotic eyes, or thick black hair. But he and the boy would find a tree somewhere off by themselves, and under its canopy Adam would tell his friend—who might well have been born without ears or tongue, for all the good they did him—stories from his childhood in the land of endless winter where the sea knew no bottom and the sky no end, and the whiteness of the ice was intense enough to strike one blind.

For years, Adam had regarded his obscurity as a blessing. He had not spoken of his origins, although perhaps the master knew of them and was too uninterested in anything but his own ambition and lechery to care. Adam's history had been one of frequent transfer. Frobisher had turned Adam over to one of his lieutenants, and the lieutenant had offered him to another son of the sea to repay a debt. Adam had found his way at last into the custody of John Crookback, quondam mariner, now yeoman farmer, and finally to the house of the Burtons of Burton Court. Under the auspices of Master Burton, Adam had shed his public identity as an infidel. He had submitted to Christian baptism. He could recite the creed, knew when to stand and kneel, could write his name and could cipher too. He had become just another servant, virtually invisible and contemptible by definition.

John Crookback did not take his son Nicholas to church, for Nicholas would always croon in a high-pitched voice when the congregation sang, much to Crookback's mortification. To have such a defective son could only be construed as a sign of some evil on Crookback's own part. There was a wife, Susanna, a younger son named Benjamin, and three daughters, the two elder from the farmer's first wife. They both had married and lived in Chelmsford with husbands who kept shops in the High Street. The last of the daughters, Magdalen, was eleven. Like the rest of the siblings, she was ashamed of her oldest brother, a blot on the family escutcheon, had the family been of sufficient birth to have enjoyed one.

But what Adam had lost in celebrity and memory he had gained in peace. There were no longer great crowds to gawk at him, to regard him as a freak of nature, only Nicholas, who listened to his stories, with his wide vacant eyes the same color as the English sky.

The opportunity to pass a pleasant morning with his friend was one that Adam could not pass up, despite the risk that Martha and Sarah might complain of his desertion to Jeroboam. He was about to venture forth when he saw the beggar crossing the lawn in front of the house.

Here was a fellow Adam recognized as a regular supplicant. A man about Adam's age with a crutch and a surly manner, the

10

beggar, who was by some called Marsh and by others Sawyer, was notorious in the county for his impudence when his petitions failed and widely thought to be a thief. More than once Jeroboam had threatened to set the dogs on him if he did not leave the master's property, and seeing the beggar, Adam suspected he had waited until Jeroboam and the other servants had gone off to church and had then emerged to make mischief.

"You there, fellow," Adam called out, almost unconsciously adopting Jeroboam's imperious tone.

Sawyer stopped and turned to Adam. "You there, yourself, sirrah. You little dog-face. I am a free man and may walk where I please."

"You may not walk on my master's land if he forbids it."

"Master Burton may tell me then to my face," returned Sawyer. "I have been a soldier in my time, have fought Spaniard and Portugee on land and sea. I take no orders from such as you—some snivelling base groom with a face like a dried prune. Where is Jeroboam, he of the solemn countenance? Gone churchward, to plague the parson with his glower? To fiddle with his codpiece in the church pew? By God's wounds, my curse upon you all, every one, who thinks himself better than a poor man without means or health."

Adam had no stomach for a quarrel with Sawyer, but he knew his duty. He said, "You are known in the town, Henry Sawyer. Be off, or the constable shall know of your trespass. He shall sit you royally in the stocks. You shall have spittle in your lap instead of pennies."

Sawyer glared and shifted on his crutch. He muttered beneath his breath and made a gesture of contempt. "Oh you are a fine Christian, you are," he said. "May God be blind and deaf in your time of need as you are in mine. Curse your heathen heart with cancers and warts, carbuncles and gumboils."

Adam suffered Sawyer's curse to lie on the wind. Dismissing him with a wave of his hand, he watched the beggar turn and hobble off, then resumed the journey Sawyer's arrival had interrupted.

He went speedily across the pasture, forded a small stream,

11

and within minutes was on the high road, his back to his master's house and the morning's share of curses.

Adam was happiest when he was alone, when his mind could settle back into itself, when, waking, he could dream of ice—happiest then and in his one-sided conversations with Nicholas, when his visions were made words. They multiplied, and he was near as he could come to crossing the cruel, tormented seas and arriving again in the world of his youth.

Another league brought him within view of Crookback Farm.

Of the farms in the neighborhood Crookback's was the largest freehold and the best situated. Here the earth was fertile and well watered, adorned by occasional copses and by the farmhouse, a double-jettied timbered structure of clay and wattle with a massive stone chimney at one end and a high pitched roof of thatch. It was a house one of the minor gentry of the shire might have coveted. Besides the house, Crookback Farm consisted of two hay barns and a large shed for cattle, a kitchen garden, a horse pasture, and a broad expanse of ground where in the appropriate season John Crookback raised wheat, barley, and rye.

The absence of signs life at the farmstead did not surprise Adam; it was the Sabbath, and he knew that Crookback and his wife and small children would already have walked the six miles to church and would hardly return before midafternoon—and perhaps not then should they decide to spend the day with one of the married daughters in Chelmsford.

He was about to call out as was his habit despite Nicholas's infirmity, when he felt a strange and sudden tightening in his chest. He paused about a dozen yards from the house and watched.

Adam saw no movement, detected no sound, human or animal.

He called out Nicholas's name. In all the stillness, his own voice startled him. No reply came forth. He approached the door and found that it stood ajar. Then he saw the dog.

John Crookback's huge mastiff lay on his side in the moist

dirt just beneath the low-silled window. The dog's head and neck were matted with blood.

Adam's heart began to race. He was sorely tempted to back away from the house. John Crookback had loved his dog beyond reason; Adam knew he would not have left his corpse unburied. And he did not like the looks of the dog's wound. Then he heard a whimper from within the house.

He pushed the door open and went in. The lower floor of the house consisted of one large chamber used as both kitchen and parlor, and two smaller, one a bedchamber for Nicholas and the other for the younger children. Crookback and his wife slept in a larger room upstairs. In the parlor everywhere there was blood, blood on the floor and on the walls, but there were no signs of the body or bodies from which this grim torrent had come.

Adam heard the whimper come again. He backed slowly toward the door, his eyes fixed on the wall. Then he heard the sound again, like no human sound but no animal's either.

Had it not been for the sound his eyes would have deceived him into thinking the little mound in the corner was nothing more than bedclothes carelessly strewn upon the rushes, but the movement confirmed what the voice suggested.

Adam said, uselessly, "Nicholas, It is I, Adam."

He did not bother to repeat himself; his own sounds were no more effectual than silence. He approached the huddled figure of the youth, bent down, and raised him up.

Standing, heaving with sobs, John Crookback's eldest son looked at Adam with a stricken expression, his eyes barely visible through the matted yellow hair that he wore long upon his shoulders since he could not abide to have it cut and his father was willing to humor him.

"Where's your father? Your mother?" Adam asked.

The expression of the boy did not change. It was not clear to Adam that he was even recognized. There was something terrible in Nicholas's face. The house had been visited by death. Why had Nicholas been spared? And where were the brutalized bodies of which the blood gave evidence?

13

Adam used signs, gestures that he had invented himself to communicate with his friend. He made the circling motion with his hand to indicate his surroundings, and then put on a puzzled, anxious face. Nicholas sighed heavily. Tears streamed down his cheeks, ordinarily as rosy as a girl's but now pale as milk. He would not stop shaking, and his chest, which was shallow for one of his height, heaved like a bellows.

Nicholas led Adam out of the house into the yard and from there around the rear of the house toward the barn, the door of which stood open. On the dead branch of a nearby tree, two ravens sat watching. John Crookback kept a pair of milk cows, but the creatures were not grazing in the pasture as they were wont. The earth was damp here, and Adam saw footprints and the marks of something dragged. How many of them had there been, Adam wondered, and why was he so sure they had gone but were not far away?

Adam thought Nicholas was taking him to the barn itself, but it was not so. He followed the boy around to the rear of the barn, where there was a well with a stone wall. Nicholas pointed.

Adam went toward the well and looked down into it. There was blood upon the stones, blood upon the black rock that lined the shaft.

The well was deep. Adam had once heard Crookback give it a good, round cursing, had heard him say the water was sweet but it must be painfully fetched since the well itself went all the way to hell.

Adam could see no glint of water reflecting the sky above, and from the depths came no sound to give hope that anything yet lived below.

Adam Nemo raised the alarm at the church, interrupting the service to the general disapproval of the congregation, who looked forgiving only when they grasped from all his stammering and wild gestures the burden of his report. He had brought

Nicholas in tow, not willing to leave him behind at the farm, and the truth was that Nicholas had shown no desire to remain alone there.

Two dozen men and six or seven of the hardier women, together with two dogs, followed him on foot and horseback the six miles to the farm. Among these was Master Stowe, the parson, Jeroboam, and Matthew Stock, the clothier of Chelmsford. Stock's wife came too.

"Damn you, Adam," said Jeroboam. "If this is but an idle tale you tell, you shall answer for it." He railed at Adam as the company progressed along the road, until Master Stowe told Jeroboam to be still. Matthew Stock said there was time enough for raillery when the story proved a fable, and Adam was relieved to see no disbelief in his face. Matthew Stock was much respected in the town and had often spoken kindly to Adam when he had come into the clothier's shop.

Chapter 2

It took the better part of an hour to bring the bodies up out of John Crookback's well. The stonemason, William Dees, because he had the strongest arms among them, had been prevailed upon to clamber down a rope. Afterwards, he brought each body up upon his shoulders, cursing and blubbering all the while that he had come from the depths of hell, so awful it was and foul below, until Master Stowe, who stood with the others observing these grim proceedings, reproached him for his profanity.

Dees said he could not help himself if he wept and cursed. "They have all been stabbed and drowned dead, like kittens in a bag. Who would do such a thing, for Christ's sake?"

Matthew Stock asked himself the same question. He had never seen the like, nor heard either, except perhaps in soldiers' tales of war. Nor had the slowly growing company of townsfolk who had come to the farm throughout the afternoon to observe these horrors for themselves.

Nicholas Crookback sat on the ground against the barn, his

head resting on his knees. He was as pale as a corpse himself but dry-eyed, which thing caused some comment among the townspeople, who thought he should be overflowing with tears since it was his mother and his father and his sister and brother who lay lifeless. No one could remember anything like it—a murder that was more than the bitter fruit of a tavern brawl—and the memory of a dozen or more of the onlookers went back fifty years.

Matthew Stock had taken charge of the proceedings because Simon Hunt, who was constable of Chelmsford for that year of our Lord, had been sick abed for a month. As one of Chelmsford's most prosperous tradesmen, Matthew was considered by his neighbors a suitable substitute for the ailing Hunt, whose usual, simple duties of arresting drunks and collecting taxes were not thought to exceed his competence. Murder was another matter altogether.

A short, plumpish man with a square, honest face, Matthew was amiable but shrewd, qualities he shared with Joan Stock, his wife of fifteen years. Matthew did business in the High Street, where he and Joan lived with their daughter Elizabeth above the shop. Joan ran her house with the same managerial competence that her husband did his shop, which was furnished with the finest cloth England produced and at the fairest prices. Matthew had an apprentice named Peter Bench, a cook named Alice, and occasionally one of several young girls from the town as maids, although Joan was generally too fastidious in her housewifery to endure another female's hand at those labors. The couple exuded an air of prosperity and were generally thought destined, in God's good time, to occupy an even higher rung on the social ladder.

Matthew had ordered the bodies laid out in a row upon blankets brought from the farmhouse. It was now late afternoon, and everyone was still dressed for church. Master Stowe's sermon that morning had dealt with the Resurrection, and Matthew supposed that not a few of those present would be contemplating the corpses in that glorious light. Would these pitiful dead, being good Christians, not rise at the first blast of the trump? And when they did, would they not name and denounce their murderer, crying out for vengeance to the God of Justice?

In the meantime, their vindication was in mortal hands.

Matthew assumed these supervisory duties with characteristic unassertiveness. He did not believe himself to be a leader among men, and he was not deceived in his belief. He was mild of temper and soft-spoken, and it was his custom to negotiate rather than dictate. Conducting an inquiry into these deaths was not a task he would have chosen for himself, but the parson had made it clear that the burden fell upon his shoulders and on no other's.

"Hunt is grievous sick," Master Stowe said, pulling Matthew aside as soon as the bodies had been discovered. The parson made a sad countenance as though he were already practicing for Hunt's funeral. "He may not live, Matthew. Nor is Tobias Whitworth of sufficient mettle to handle this. It must be you, or these horrid crimes will go unavenged, to the disgrace of the town. Should not such an event bring the curse of God upon us all?" The parson quoted chapter and verse and stared at Matthew with sad and accusing eyes.

With his own simpler theology, Matthew was not sure that he agreed with the parson's premise. He could not hold that God would punish a town because it could not discover the cause of such heinous murders, but his own strong sense of justice found the idea that such malefactors should go free a thing not to be suffered without a zealous effort being made to ensure the contrary.

"I will do what must be done," he said. "According to my ability."

The clothier and the parson discussed whether the bodies were to be borne into the town to be examined by the coroner or whether the coroner should be brought out to the farmstead, and when either should happen. They agreed that leaving the dead exposed to public view was a shameful thing. Malefactors were so treated as a public example, their bodies left to rot in the sun, but there was no purpose in so dishonoring a yeoman farmer and his family, who had done no wrong

18

to any man or woman. The parson was insistent on that point.

Matthew agreed the bodies should be taken to town. The coroner could examine them there, what examining needed to be done. The cause of the deaths was plain to the eye, he said: all four had been repeatedly stabbed, Crookback most brutally. But his wife and the two children also bore wounds, although it was not clear whether they had died of them or by drowning. "They shall in any case be buried in the churchyard—they shall be borne hence sooner or later, better sooner than later."

Since Crookback had no wagon suitable for such conveyance, Matthew sent the blacksmith back into Chelmsford to bring his. "Ask Peter Bench to give you a sable cloth large enough to cover the bodies. Don't stint as to the quality."

Then Matthew spent the better part of an hour persuading the onlookers to go home, finally threatening them with the power of the law if they did not. Aside from the indignity of the spectacle, the crowd had trampled all over the ground, destroying such evidence as there might have been. Heightened curiosity had driven many into the barn and into the farmhouse itself, where they observed the bloody rushes and walls, commented on the quality of the furnishings, and examined with finger and eye the most private possessions of the deceased—and carried off God only knew what valuables for their small pains.

Joan Stock, without any more authority than her own stern gaze of disapproval, had taken up her station there. To discourage thievery, she said, willing to call a thing what it was and being no mincer of words. Some of them in the house were total strangers who had heard rumors of the deaths. When Matthew came in and asked them all to leave forthwith, they wanted to know why Joan was permitted to remain. Was the clothier's wife better than they that she should be so privileged? Didn't the whole town have a natural interest in these crimes?

"It is an interest that will be better served if you leave," Matthew said. "Go, if only out of respect for the dead."

After that, the townsfolk began to disperse.

19

"Matthew, this is a dreadful thing," Joan said. "The murders are bad enough, but that these folk should show so little respect for the dead, or for the law."

"They will be setting up stalls and charging admission next," Matthew said.

"Since Simon Hunt is sick, what is to be done? Who is to look into this?" she asked.

"Your husband," he said.

She took this in, then looked at him very directly.

"Godspeed you then, husband. But I would wish it upon some other shoulders than yours. Why, where would you begin to unravel this business?"

He was sorry she asked this question before he had any answer. He wanted to begin with Nicholas Crookback, but knew because of the youth's infirmity that questioning him would be futile. Then he thought of Adam Nemo.

Matthew knew the servant only slightly; thus he had no opinion as to his character, whether he was honest or otherwise. Adam had come into Matthew's shop at times, sent by the steward, or Master Burton on those rare occasions when the latter was in residence at Burton Court, to buy cloth for household furnishings. Matthew had also seen Adam at church, but had only spoken to him a few times over the years. He reckoned the strange little fellow to be older than himself, but who could really tell?

He asked Joan if she would continue her vigil in the house and she said she would. "I have no fear of blood," she said. "Being that it is innocent blood."

He found Adam and Nicholas sitting side by side, their shoulders almost touching. Matthew squatted beside them and looked back toward the bodies, trying to decide what to say to Master Burton's servant and thinking that Adam was a strange sort indeed with his narrow eyes no more than slits and his round face the color of tanned leather.

"When you came to the farm, did you see anyone about?"

"I did not," said Adam, speaking in a voice so low that Matthew had to ask him to repeat the answer.

"Or observe anything strange there?"

"The house showed no life at all. And John Crookback's dog lay slain."

Matthew remembered the dog, alive and as it now was, the corpse in itself a pathetic little portrait of brutality. At least he would not need to uncover the motive for that crime: the dog had been in life a fierce howler and protector of his master. One wanting to usher John Crookback into the world to come would have had to reckon with the dog first.

"There was a deal of blood on the walls," Adam continued, staring ahead of him as if seeing the entire scene again as he spoke. "I found Nicholas in the corner. He was crouched down and whimpering. I did not know what to think of it, but was sore afraid."

Nicholas's eyes were shut and he seemed asleep. Matthew observed for the first time that there was dried blood on the youth's hands, which were curled around his knees; there were little blotches of blood on the sleeves of his jerkin and some on his chest. The thought struck Matthew that Nicholas might have put his parents and siblings down the well. Stabbed and drowned them himself. It was a disgusting thing to think, and he inwardly shuddered at so repellent a notion. Would a son murder his own parents and his innocent brother and sister? It was beyond Matthew's imagining, and yet he knew he must consider everything. Then he remembered with what effort William Dees had lifted the body of John Crookback and wondered if Nicholas would have had the main strength to do the same. He wished now that the crowd had not so badly trampled the yard. Perhaps there had been marks showing whether the bodies had been dragged. He supposed that given the bloody interior of the house, it must be assumed the victims had been killed—slaughtered—there.

"Nicholas said—made no sign to you of what happened. Or who was here?"

"He made no sign but wept piteously and cried little cries, like an animal caught in a trap," Adam said.

"Did you see any strange footprints or marks in the earth?"

"I saw the marks of many boots, and of something dragged. I saw no man about, and no animals that were yet alive. The cows were in the milk barn still."

While Matthew had questioned Nicholas, the parson and two men who had remained at the farm at Matthew's request drifted over to where he squatted and stood listening. One of the men was Jacob Darnley, also a farmer. A tall, rawboned man with a bristly red beard, Darnley stared at Nicholas and said, in a hushed voice, "I warrant the loony did it, killed his own family. Mark you now, there's blood on his shirt, and blood on the other's jerkin."

Darnley had nodded in Adam's direction and then turned abruptly to Matthew. "Ask him what he was doing here on a Sabbath morning when he should be in church. Marry, I warrant he saw more than he tells and did more than he has confessed to."

Sensing trouble, Matthew rose to his feet and faced the farmer with a stern look he hoped would serve to remind the man that investigating the murder was his business. "That may be, but let's not leap before we look, Jacob."

"Well," said Darnley, glaring at Adam from under heavy brows. "I doubt we shall have to leap far for to know who John Crookback must thank for this mischief. I warned him to send the boy off to London where there are a plenty of his kind. Of what use it is to keep a son who cannot speak or hear or work but must sit all day, doing naught but enticing a gentleman's servant to be his companion in idleness."

"I shall ask questions, not you," Matthew said.

"All well and good," answered Darnley, his face reddening. "I am a simple farmer, yet John Crookback was my neighbor, and if there is a murderer at large I have a right to look to my own safety as well. I have a wife. I have children. Is my own life not a thing of value? Will we sleep o' nights with this matter unsettled?"

Matthew's attention was drawn from this question by an anguished wail from nearby. He looked across the yard to see what it was and saw Crookback's two older daughters and their husbands. Someone had fetched them from town, the daughters having been too skeptical of Adam's report to have come from the church earlier. But the word of more reliable witnesses had convinced them, along with their husbands, and they were over where the bodies of John and Susanna Crookback and the two young children were laid out upon the ground in a row. Their lamentations struck Matthew to the heart, more than the sight of the corpses had done. At least the dead were beyond pain; the sight of the daughters bent over their parents and siblings' bodies was almost too much for him to bear.

After a decent interval during which he watched the bereaved women, Matthew walked over to join them. He knew them slightly, the two husbands better than the wives because both men had businesses in the town. The elder sister was Mildred Carew, a frail, stooped-shouldered woman in a plain russet gown bulging with a young Carew shortly to come. Her husband was Miles Carew, a chandler, who was even thinner than his wife, so that the local jest was that were they both to die they could happily share a coffin and have ample room left over. The younger daughter, Agnes Profytt, had favored her father. She had sharp features and close-set black eyes. Not much above twenty, she had large breasts that occasioned much comment among the men in town and not a little discussion among the women. Her husband was Hugh Profytt, a tailor—stout, ruddy-faced, convivial, known as a pleasant fellow who had married without proper caution a woman likely to rule his roost.

Matthew removed his hat and nodded to the sisters and their husbands. He could hardly find words of condolence, for how could mere words suffice? But it was not merely condolence he sought to offer but an apology. Already he felt in charge of matters, felt that he was to blame that there was no answer yet forthcoming as to who stood so fearless of God's wrath that he could commit the atrocity.

"I am told my brother Nicholas is yet alive," Agnes said. Behind her her husband looked on blankly while Mildred sobbed and leaned against her own husband. "How is it that he was spared and not my brother and sister, who were as innocent as lambs? Yet they have been slaughtered, my father and step-mother as well, and Nicholas sits idly by, keeping mum as always."

"He could not do otherwise," Matthew said, and then felt foolish, for of course she knew.

Agnes frowned, as though her half brother's affliction was more a perverse willfulness than an incapacity.

Her husband said, "You must admit it looks strange, Master Stock. Why should Nicholas be spared and they not? Surely it was his sin that he was born dumb; why should grace touch him where it did not do so before?"

Matthew had no answer to this question. He was uncomfortable with theological disputes, and he felt he was being drawn into one now. These weightier matters of God's justice and man's fate he was content to leave to the parson. As far as Matthew was concerned, if Nicholas had been spared it was his good fortune. "Perhaps he hid and the murderer did not find him."

"Do you really think one man could have done this—killed them all, I mean?"

This comment came from the tearful Agnes, who had gone into the house earlier and now reported that her father's silver plate, of which there were five good pieces of considerable value, was gone. "It is a common housebreaking," she said. "They have taken it all." She looked at Matthew fiercely, almost accusingly. "Four souls are dead. Too many for one man to kill himself. There must needs have been more than one murderer. Two by my reckoning."

Matthew could not help asking what her reckoning was. She seemed so sure. Has she some evidence to offer?

"Why, Master Stock, one to distract my father while the other thrust the knife into his heart," Agnes reasoned. "My father was a strong man. He would not simply lie down before the threat of a knife. He must have been taken from behind. And if there had been but one who attacked him, surely my

24

stepmother mother and the children would have run for their lives."

Matthew allowed that this reasoning had some merit yet he was loath to endorse it too strongly. He could see Agnes was heading somewhere with her theorizing. Agnes's next comment confirmed his suspicion.

"This is a profitable farmstead, Master Stock," Agnes said. "Which Nicholas our half brother now can call his own. No more must he take his parents' strictures. If you understand my meaning."

Her meaning was clear enough, Matthew thought. Nicholas as only surviving male heir would inherit; the law was plain on the matter. That meant to Agnes's mind that Nicholas had a reason to murder—greed, resentment, or who knew what combination of the two.

"We have been told that you will look into these murders," Agnes said, "and would know what course you intend to take."

"I am considering my course," Matthew said.

"Marry, I should think it plain enough," Agnes declared, "In light of what I have said. If you find a flaw in my reasoning, tell me what it is, Master Stock. The finger of suspicion points to our half brother who sits yonder, does it not? And since he is too simple to have done this by himself, he must have had a confederate."

Adam, Matthew thought. Agnes was nothing if not predictable. Already he could see how she would have the tale written: Nicholas in conspiracy with Adam, two "different" creatures, each in his way. Matthew had to admit it would be a plausible tale, yet he was hardly ready to act on it. And he was not about to turn his duty over to Agnes, who undoubtedly had her own ax to grind.

"I shall satisfy you of my course of action in time," Matthew said firmly. "You and your sister being next of kin shall be the first to know."

"We *know* already," Mildred said, looking aside at her sis-

25

ter, whose steady, hostile gaze confirmed that on this point the two women were in accord.

"Remember, Master Stock, we are not without influence in the town," Agnes said. "Crookbacks lie as thick in the churchyard as Stocks. Is that not so sister?"

"It is so," Mildred said, her jaw set as firmly as her sister's was.

The conversation had now grown tense and Matthew was almost relieved when the parson came up to say that Sir Thomas Mildmay, the magistrate, had ordered the bodies of the dead brought into the town. "Sir Thomas will have them shown," the parson said, shaking his head doubtfully. "He wants them laid out in the Sessions House for all to see."

"Why should he want that?" Matthew asked. "It seems every man and his brother have already seen the bodies, and an ugly sight they are. Besides, it's unseemly. Even the dead deserve some privacy. The Crookbacks were no criminals that their bodies be on show. How will the crowd keep out?"

"I asked him the same question," the parson said, "and was told that you were to see to it that order was maintained."

"Until Simon Hunt is able. He's constable."

"Simon died this past hour," the parson said sadly. "There is no constable in Chelmsford now. Sir Thomas says you must serve until another is elected."

Matthew felt the leaden weight of this charge. He would have gladly excused himself from it, but he could think of no effectual reason he should not do what was bidden. He had sought responsibility among his neighbors, dreamed of being alderman. None of his forbears had enjoyed such distinction, although they too had been honest men and true. There was no response of which he was capable but to say yea and do his best.

He looked at the sky. The light was failing; the air was still and cold. The house and barns of John Crookback were groping toward the night, distilling into shadows.

William Dees had returned from town with Matthew's wagon and shrouds for the dead, and Matthew called the dead man's sons-in-law to help him lift the bodies into the wagon. When this was accomplished, he heard Joan's voice behind him.

"What's to be done with Nicholas?"

He had almost forgotten about the surviving Crookback son. It was clear Nicholas could not remain at the farmhouse; no soul was sturdy enough for such an ordeal. Did the ghosts of the murdered not haunt the scene of the crime? Would the wretched lad not hear his parents' howls for vengeance when Matthew could almost hear them himself?

"And Adam?" she said, when he did not respond at once to her question.

"Adam? Why he shall return to Burton Court."

"His master's steward will not have it so," Joan said. "I heard it from this same steward, Jeroboam. The servants are terrified. They say some foreigner did the murders. Others think it is Adam Nemo who did it. They know Adam kept company with Nicholas and that Nicholas alone of his family at home has survived.

"They cannot remain here. It's unthinkable," Matthew said.

"We shall have them home with us, then," Joan said, as though her word settled the matter.

"Are you not afraid?" he said.

"No," she said, and a look of weariness passed over her face. "Only that the house goes to wrack and ruin in our long absence. Come, Matthew. This is the saddest Sabbath of all my life. The bodies of these poor dead ones go before us. Your wagon will bear a leaden burden. Let us follow after. Our lives will be changed now. You have made a hard bed for yourself and we twain must lie down in this darkness until the truth give us light."

Chapter 3

ה

It was a strange and solemn procession into town, along a road not the worst in England but not the best either and in any case one that only fools and madmen traveled at night. Joan and Matthew were with Dees in the creaking wagon while Crookback's grieving daughters and sons-in-law followed on horseback. Adam and Nicholas and about a dozen other men whom the cold and gathering darkness had not driven earlier to home and hearth completed the company. Some on horses, some on foot, but all silent and respectful of the lumbering wagon's mortal burden.

After a long winter, the road was in poor condition, full of ruts and holes, and the little company traveled slowly. A mist covered the sky; there was neither moon nor stars. A witness to this procession, standing by the roadside and cold sober, would have crossed himself thrice over and evoked a dozen saints, no matter how skeptical about the old religion.

When they arrived in the High Street it was clear that rumor's thousand tongues had done their work. Everyone was out of his house despite the cold, standing along the street, in doorways, or upon the corners, or half tumbling out of upstairs windows, watching the procession with lantern or torch in hand and in grim silence, as though the Crookbacks had been gentry and not yeoman farmers. The soot from the wood-fires within rained slowly down on them all like a pall. Men removed their hats as the wagon passed and spoke in hushed whispers. Matthew was aware of fingers pointing, not at him or Joan but at Nicholas, and could see that Adam was also suspect—because of his association with Nicholas.

The Sessions House stood at the market cross in the center of Chelmsford, where the High Street divided into roads north and west. Supported on eight columns, it was a solid wooden structure. So crowded was the street that William Dees was at pains to get the wagon through, and Matthew had to order the crowd to make way, which it did quietly but with obvious reluctance. No one seemed to want to miss anything, although there was little to see. The corpses were shrouded; the bodies of the children were so small they might have been bags of corn and have passed unnoticed completely if the horrid facts had not already become common knowledge.

Then, as Matthew and William Dees were preparing to remove the dead, the shouting began: appeals that the shrouds be removed so the bodies might be seen; prayers to heaven for the souls; expressions of horror; cries for justice, for vengeance. Shrieks as piercing as needles came from John Crookback's daughters, whom the assembled neighbors had stirred from their melancholy and advanced to a new position of public prominence.

The crowd seemed as fascinated by the reaction of Mildred and Agnes to the deaths as they were by the mystery of Nicholas Crookback's survival. The shouts became a growing din, which Matthew did his best to ignore. He motioned to Dees to help him lift John Crookback's body from the wagon. He was determined not to remove the shroud. The crowd pushed forward. Someone shoved Matthew from behind. He felt hands seize his shoulders, yet he struggled on determinedly, his teeth clenched and his heart racing, concerned about Joan but not willing to surrender his authority over the bodies.

Matthew let the stonemason bear the weight of John Crookback's body, the dead farmer having been a tall and broad-shouldered man, and turned to see if Joan was safe. She was by the wagon, pinned in by a group of men, some of whom were among the rougher sort of the town, haunters of alehouses and brothels, former soldiers or runaway apprentices. Although they probably did not know the Crookbacks, their voices were raised as loud as any in their demands that the bodies be disclosed. It was their right to see, they shouted, a public matter, not private business. Matthew heard curses and threats and felt the anger being directed against him, as though in the absence of an agreed upon murderer he must serve as the focal point of the town's rage and confusion.

So violent was the press and loud the cries that Matthew feared that presently the crowd would seize the bodies and satisfy their curiosity, but at that point there was a general quieting of voices as the beat of horses' hooves was heard on the cobbles.

Matthew had finished carrying John Crookback's little girl into the corn market when he turned to see whose arrival had subdued the crowd and saw that it was Sir Thomas Mildmay, chief knight of the district and lord of the manor.

Sir Thomas was a small, neat man who made himself seem larger by his erect bearing and by lifting his chin slightly when he spoke. He was accompanied by another gentleman Matthew did not recognize, and about six other horsemen, mostly grooms and other servants from Mildmay Hall. The commotion caused by their arrival had thoroughly distracted the crowd, who now fell respectfully silent as though nothing untoward had occurred prior to Mildmay's arrival.

Sir Thomas alone dismounted from the troop while the crowd opened up a path to the Sessions House. The lord of the manor marched immediately up to Matthew, looking quite angry. Matthew removed his hat and bowed from the waist.

"Where are the bodies?" the magistrate demanded. Matthew pointed the way, and the knight went in. He pulled back the covering of John Crookback's face; then did the same to Susanna's.

The crowd had inched forward and was now pressing to see what the magistrate saw. At the revealing of the dead woman, there were a few cries of anguish from those among the group who had known her well. Agnes's voice was raised above the din of the multitude: "Oh my dear father and sister and brother!"

"She's also been stabbed," Sir Thomas said, looking at the bloody bodice and pulling it down to have a look at the wounds in Susanna Crookback's breasts, which, laid out as she was, were as flat as a boy's.

No one protested the indecency of this exposure. Like her husband and children, Susanna Crookback in death had become public business, her rights to privacy gone with her living breath.

Sir Thomas did not look at the children, but turned to Matthew abruptly. "Where's the youth they call Nicholas, the one who was spared?"

Nicholas was standing by Joan near the wagon. Before Matthew could point him out, someone had thrust the boy forward and two other of the town's citizens had taken it upon themselves to bring the son of John Crookback to the magistrate, as though his guilt had already been determined and there was little left but to present him for execution.

Nicholas looked terrified, Matthew supposed as much at being hauled before the lord of the manor as by the crowd. When he came to where Sir Thomas was he all but fell upon his knees before the magistrate. Somewhere he had lost his hat, and his shock of unruly yellow hair flew every which way.

Sir Thomas said nothing but stared at Nicholas curiously. Nicholas trembled and would not look at the knight. He turned his head slightly; Matthew followed his gaze and saw Adam Nemo standing in the crowd.

"How is it with you, lad?" Sir Thomas asked.

"The boy does not speak," Matthew interjected, surprised

31

that Sir Thomas's informants had not told him that. But perhaps the knight only wanted to verify the boy's infirmity for himself.

Sir Thomas nodded. "Has it been so since birth?"

"It has."

"Is he simple as well?"

"He is, Your Honor," said Matthew.

"He is evil-brained," a shrill voice called from the crowd. It was Mildred's voice.

Sir Thomas turned to look at Mildred, who moved forward until she stood beside her brother.

"This is my father's son, by his second wife, Sir Thomas. He was ever loved by my father. Now see how my father is served. Stabbed and drowned, and my little brother and sister too, and Nicholas is spared."

She pointed to the body of her father as though expecting him to rise from the table on which he had been laid and join in the denunciation of his son and heir.

"He has their very blood upon his jerkin, as Sir Thomas may see," the second daughter, Agnes, said shrilly. "I warrant he and his minion"—she cast a baleful eye on Adam—"have done this deed in consort, whereupon the twain will thereafter set up housekeeping in the house of my father, their benefactor, and his long-suffering wife, may God send her peace."

Cries of "Shame!" and calls for justice came from all around at these words. Sir Thomas, who had listened patiently to Agnes's charges, turned to Matthew and for the first time addressed him by name. "Master Stock, what evidence is there beyond this poor woman's accusation and the bloody jerkin? I assume the boy was not himself wounded, and that the blood is indeed his mother's, or perhaps his father's or one of the children's."

"He cannot speak to say whose blood it is," Matthew said. "Neither to deny or affirm. In his case, silence does not give consent to these charges, since he is dumb."

"Irrefutable logic, Master Stock," Sir Thomas said. "There were no signs of brigands, no footprints or aught left after to signal the presence of strangers?"

32

"No, Your Honor. There was too great a multitude at the farm, tramping about, after the murder was discovered. There was silver plate taken, according to report. I know not what else of value, so that a housebreaking may have moved those who did this."

Sir Thomas's face darkened in disapproval. "It is ever thus. Tomorrow we shall return to the farm and search it thoroughly. John Crookback was reputed to be a man of means, although but a yeoman farmer. Let it be early, before dawn, and before the curious can collect there to look upon the scene or carry off evidence."

"Sir Thomas," Mildred said. "Our father's wealth was in his land; he had little else but the plate, which indeed is gone. Rumors to the contrary are but the false gossip of jealous neighbors."

"Well," Sir Thomas said, ignoring this latest outburst and keeping his eyes fixed on the subject of Mildred's accusations, "we shall see what we shall see. In the meantime, keep young Nicholas in close custody, Master Stock, if only to protect him against grieved relations and others who would usurp the queen's justice with a rash act."

"And these dead, what of them, Sir Thomas?" Matthew asked.

"Let Martin Day inspect with finger and eye to determine exactly the cause of death, the number of wounds and what kind, and aught else of import. Let every material fact be noted. This crime must draw much attention, and I would not be faulted for my own conduct in the matter. As for the bodies, let them be seen here tomorrow by anyone who wishes. Perhaps the sad spectacle will quicken the conscience of the malefactor or some other who can provide us knowledge of his identity."

Matthew said all these things would be carried out. Then Sir Thomas looked around and addressed the multitude. "Good people, now in the queen's name, go to your homes. Justice will be done in this sad business. You will have opportunity to see for yourselves what evil the devil can put in the hearts of men and, I trust, see too how God will avenge it."

The knight spoke in a clear, high voice that carried over the crowd. There was a mumble of discontent at this, especially from the winebibbers of the taverns, and several voices asked how the town was to be protected and whether the alarm should be raised in neighboring towns or the watch called out. Matthew feared for a moment that even Sir Thomas's command was not enough to bring order to the assembly.

"Do not be afraid," Sir Thomas said in a calm but authoritative voice. "My men will keep the peace in Chelmsford this night. Let no one go abroad from this hour on, save he thinks little of his life. Go to your homes and God bless you all. I declare tomorrow a day of mourning for the dead. There shall be no work at all, but as if a holy day."

This announcement seemed to pacify the crowd; it fell silent, and yet still no one moved to comply with the knight's command. Then Sir Thomas made a motion to the servants who had accompanied him, and they began to stir with their horses and cry out that Sir Thomas's commands must be obeyed, and the street cleared forthwith.

At this there was a general movement of the people toward their homes. But Matthew could see his fellow townsmen were disappointed. Despite the promise that the next day a viewing of the corpses would be permitted, nothing had been resolved, and he knew too that there would be a great fear among the people for their own safety.

Sir Thomas turned to Matthew. "Your neighbors have decided to be wise in this, Master Stock, and so must you. Look to the duties that have fallen upon you as a result of Simon Hunt's death. In the meantime I will cast about among my friends for someone with more experience in these matters to lead the investigation."

The unruly, noisy gathering of the people had reminded Adam of how it was when Frobisher had first brought him to England. How he had been paraded up and down and stared at, wondered at, and sometimes mocked, like a three-legged cow or bearded woman, even though then he had no understanding of the strange tongue of these stranger, pale people with their round light eyes like those of the blind. He had felt a widening fear as he followed the dead-laden wagon into town, comforted only in that his friend was at his side. Occasionally his hand brushed Nicholas's, but they exchanged no glances, as though the deaths were as much a cause of shame to them as of grief.

A double vision played in Adam's mind. He saw Nicholas's family as though they were alive. He saw the father, the tall Englishman who had brought him to Chelmsford. Crookback had always treated him kindly, had arranged for his service in Master Burton's great house and welcomed his visits to the farm. And the mother, less generous in her attentions, but not hostile or suspicious. And the two little ones—the angel children with the flaxen hair and ruddy complexions of their race. Was it possible that these spirits of the air were the leaden things that the wagon bore? He could not reconcile the two visions. He could not believe that he would not see Nicholas's family again, hale and hearty as before.

But for all his amazement at what had suddenly befallen, there was yet another emotion that seized him as he walked. This was fear. Fear for Nicholas, whom he already saw was under suspicion, had tightened in his breast and constricted his throat until he could hardly breathe. And there was fear for himself too—as he saw the hostile gazes aimed at him because he was, even after all these years, a stranger. It was as though he were not one of God's children but a creature somehow different, and his neighbors' hatred of this difference had been there all this time and had waited for just such an event to reveal itself.

Adam had hung back in the shadows, beyond the torchlight, especially after the great man came with his horses and the crowd had submitted to his authority and the suspicious, fearful eyes were fixed elsewhere. He wished the day might have been undone, that he could start again, arriving at the farm to find Nicholas and his family well. But he had seen the dead and knew such a wish was vain. This thing would not be undone by willing it so; not even the Englishman's God could undo events and make them whole again.

When the people were sent home, the clothier's wife had come up to him and said in a kind voice, "You must come to our house for the night. You and Nicholas."

When Adam questioned the need, the clothier's wife told him it should not be otherwise. "Jeroboam says you must not return to Burton Court. The household servants are beside themselves with dread. Jeroboam says the master's house will be locked up securely. Their fear is beyond reason, I know, but besides, my husband must ask you more questions. Tomorrow, not tonight. We're all tired unto death now, everyone. Come with me."

Adam looked at Nicholas, who was standing close to the clothier and the stonemason and looking back at him with the desperate expression of one adrift at sea and unable to make for land again. Adam's heart sank. He made no signal, but the clothier's wife caught the momentary exchange of glances with his friend.

She said, "Do not worry, Adam. My husband will bring Nicholas along later. I understand that you are friends. Friends must not be divided at a time like this. I'll find a place in my house for you both. These dark circumstances behoove us to put on mourning garments, yet you twain will be safer there than in your own beds."

He allowed himself to be led by the woman, moving down the street toward the clothier's house as though he were in a dream.

Joan had found beds for her two guests in an upstairs chamber tucked under the eaves. It was small but clean. Then she came downstairs to where Matthew sat in the kitchen, his elbows upon the trencher table that aside from the gaping hearth was the room's chief ornament. His head was so far bent over the table that she supposed for a moment that he was asleep or at prayer, neither of which, she thought, considering the circumstances, was unfitting.

"What's the matter, husband?" she asked, sitting at his side but realizing how silly the question was as soon as it had tripped off her tongue.

Matthew rubbed his forehead the way he did when he was perplexed. "The parson thinks I'm mad for bringing Nicholas to my own house for the night. He thinks even Adam should be placed in bonds and guard here or conveyed to Colchester Gaol."

"Does he?" Joan said, bridling at the report, for she often found fault with Master Stowe's sermons and thought him a timid little man at a loss to find a hat big enough to fit his head. "Does he think either dangerous? Have they been charged with a crime? Has either made a motion to flee? Certainly he can see what moves John Crookback's daughters to their accusing words. Their purpose is as plain as the noses on their faces: They have ever been ashamed of their brother because of his infirmity, and where there is such shame, resentment is its kin. Now, it takes no doctor of the laws to understand that Nicholas will inherit the farm where otherwise it might fall to them and their husbands."

Matthew looked up. "That's a serious charge, Joan. To think that greed would cause them to accuse their brother unjustly."

"It was seriously meant, husband," Joan said. "I know how these matters fall out. It is ever seen. Human goodness is no deep river but a shallow stream that will come near running dry when it crosses opportunity. Crookback Farm is good soil and plenty. Everyone says John Crookback had more wealth than he showed, that he lived simply to cover it up. Who knows what treasure is buried in his field or cemented in the chimney?"

"Idle tales, for my money," Matthew said.

She could see how tired he was, heartsick too. But she was determined to make her point. "Neither of the daughters is a saint. Few hearts are devoid of greed, when there's the smell of a rich inheritance. I know them both and know what I hear."

"Gossip. You women—"

"We women indeed!" Joan said rising to the bait. "If you men had ears to hear as well as mouths to command, you would learn a thing or two about this town you think you rule in your manly wisdom. There's more about you than meets the eye."

He looked at her and smiled thinly. "I see you will not be satisfied to let me go to bed before you've had your say, wife. So I will be patient."

"I mean only that there are few women in this town more hungry for the wealth of this world than are Mildred and Agnes. Both complain that their new husbands provide less than their wives deserve. Now, I do not deny their grief at the murder of their father and stepmother and their siblings. Who would not grieve at such a spectacle? But Crookback Farm inherited, say by the older, would enable them to build as grand a house as this town affords. Everyone knows that both Sir Thomas and Master Burton have coveted the land forever, since it lies between both their grounds. But John Crookback would not sell his patrimony, some said for sheer obstinacy."

"All these tales I have heard myself, spoken time out of mind in every alehouse in town," Matthew said. "Where's the special wisdom you women have garnered among yourselves? Tell me that."

"Don't belittle woman's wisdom, husband. It has saved many of your sex from the hangman's noose, as you well know." She leaned forward conspiratorially; her voice fell to a whisper, as though she really was afraid that her words would be overheard. "John Crookback's will—as I am informed by Agnes Profytt herself, and who would know better?—provides that his son Nicholas inherit, with the younger brother as guardian if Nicholas has not the capacity."

"But his brother was only a lad," Matthew said.

"John Crookback thought Nicholas would live to be a full man, and his younger likewise. Alice—"

"Alice?"

"Yes, our Alice tells me that John Crookback ever believed that Nicholas would be made right by some miracle. Since he believed it was God's hand that struck him deaf and dumb he trusted that his ears and mouth would be opened by a similar act."

Matthew remembered that Alice, the Stocks' cook, was a distant cousin of the Crookbacks. "And so the inheritance—"

"Is as Agnes proclaimed," Joan continued, "fallen to Nicholas, although Alice says that Agnes and Mildred had many times urged their father to change his will."

"But is Nicholas so cold of heart to kill his parents and brother and sister for land that would fall to him in the course of time in any case?"

Joan said she could not believe Nicholas could have any conception of what it meant to inherit the farm or to own it. "No," she said. "If I read faces aright, Nicholas is one in whom there is no guile. Were it otherwise, I would not endure his presence in the house. Not with daughter Elizabeth just upstairs."

Matthew agreed. He could see no fault in Nicholas—at least, none to warrant his arrest for murder. The boy seemed mild-mannered and shy. Very much like Adam, his older friend, who was every whit as strange in his own way. As for the scandalous accusations made by Agnes regarding vile practices, he thought that that must proceed from Agnes's overweening resentment of her father's favoritism. John Crookback doted upon his son, had long befriended Adam. There seemed nothing irregular there.

"Come, Joan. I must to bed," Matthew said with a broad yawn, so that the last word was unnaturally prolonged. "I relieve William Dees before cockcrow at the Sessions House. Sir Thomas would not have the bodies left unguarded for fear some mischief be done them."

"Why, what kind of mischief?" Joan asked, rising from the table and taking the candle in her hand.

"The Crookbacks have found in death that celebrity that

country living denied them in life. If news of this outrage does not spread to London by noon tomorrow I am no true man. Think what relics of the deceased would bring—a lock of hair, a shoe, shirt, or body part itself? Why, one of the children's bodies might be carried off. These deaths are no private matter but the town's business, perhaps even the queen's."

"Disgusting," she said.

"Nonetheless true."

"Will the stonemason be enough to guard the bodies?" she asked.

"Sufficient. His apprentice keeps him company. The two were playing at cards when I left them."

He took the candle from her hand and looked into her face, which by candlelight seemed drawn and sad. "Don't worry," he said. "All will be well. Simon Hunt picked an unfortunate time to go to his reward. He has left me with a larger task than ever he had in his constableship."

"Thanks be to God that Sir Thomas said he would bring some more experienced man to inquire into the murders," Joan remarked as they began to climb the stairs.

"So he did, but who knows when or if that man will come. And if he does, perhaps all will be resolved by then," Matthew said, rather hurt that his wife should think him incapable of solving the murders himself.

Agnes Profytt had asked her husband to see to the door of their house in the lower part of the High Street one more time, for she was half mad with fears, she said.

The request did not please her young husband, who had other matters on his mind. "I have twice done so within this very hour, wife, and I fain would come to bed to you, sweeting."

"Marry, I am sure you would, husband, and do me as my good sister has been done by her husband, yet will I rest more comfortable in your arms if our repose is not to be interrupted by a howling murderer. My half brother is at large, you know."

Her husband sighed heavily. The room darkened as he bore the candle away with him, and Agnes listened as his steps descended. Their bedchamber was much less spacious than the room she had shared with her sisters and brothers in her father's house before her marriage, and she spent much time wishing that it might be otherwise. She had consented to be Hugh Profytt's wife because although his means were modest he had bright prospects of increasing them. A woman whose diminutive stature belied the greatness of her ambition, Agnes wanted to live in town, not in the country; she would have preferred to live in London, a real city, and wear fine clothes and ape gentlewomen, although somehow she knew such dreams were beyond her reach.

"The house is safe," her husband said, returning. "Will it be tonight, sweetheart?"

"Will what be tonight, husband?"

"You know as well as I. You have denied me all this week with one excuse or another. Now your head aches you, now we must rise too early, now we retire too late."

She felt a stirring of hatred for him as he mimicked her complaints, all just cause of denial, according to her view. She raised her voice in outrage. "What, have you no feelings for me? My father, stepmother, sister, and brother have all died this day and you have so little respect for my grief that you would use my body?"

"As is my right," he said, growing heated himself.

"You have a right to be sensitive to my grief, you do, and little more," she returned with even greater vigor. "What, would you think any woman could be amorous when her family is slain—and by her father's own son? Where have you laid your brain that you cannot find it in your head?"

Hugh Profytt sat down on the bed. "I think you go too far, Agnes, in that charge. We have no proof that Nicholas—"

"Proof aplenty I have, sir husband, and pray you will have the wisdom to stand by me when I present it all on the morrow."

Her husband said nothing to this. He sighed heavily with

resignation, blew out the candle, and crawled into bed, keeping to his own side, as he thought she desired.

After a few minutes of silence, he heard her voice again, but now soft and wheedling. "If you do stand by me in this, husband, you will prove what I have sometimes doubted since we were wed."

"Which is what?" he asked suspiciously.

"Why, that your love is true and not mere pretense."

"My love is true; I am ever protesting it."

"But see how easy it is to prove. You need only confirm what I say to the coroner. So doing, you will stand true friend to me and to Justice herself, who must not be denied."

"I think it is you who must not be denied."

"Perhaps," she said. "Promise to stand by me."

"I promise."

He felt her hand slip between his legs, and a thrill of joy ran from his groin to his chest. She began to knead that manliest part of him as though she were milking one of her father's cows.

"A faithful husband must have his reward," she whispered in a voice that excited him because it did not sound like her voice at all, but like the voice of the wench in Moulsham to whom he had lost his virginity the year before he married John Crookback's daughter.

Chapter 4

ה

"When Nicholas Crookback and Master Burton's servant awake," Matthew said over the thin gruel that was all either of them desired for breakfast at this ungodly hour, "look well that they stay within doors. It's best no one but the family knows that they're here. And ask Elizabeth not to go abroad this day."

They were in the kitchen, huddled over a lamp. The house was as dark, as quiet as the town itself. Even the cock still slept.

"Elizabeth will want to see the goings-on at the Sessions House," Joan said.

"Let her remain ignorant," Matthew said. "And it would be well if you too were to stay home. These murders have drawn the dregs of the county away from their beer and whoring. There will be pockets picked, poultry snatched, and houses burgled while householders gawk and gossip, I trow. I tell you, Joan, more crime will ride upon the back of this sad event than Chelmsford has seen in a hundred years."

"Well," she said, "don't worry about me. I know my duties,

husband. I shall do what is expedient and will be no prisoner in my own house for all the murderers in the world."

"I say it for your safety. But be watchful, Joan. And remember what I said about our guests: while they are not formally accused of the murders, they may yet be. And while I lack good reason to put them under lock and key, yet I am answerable for them."

After Matthew left to relieve William Dees, Joan sat by the hearth enjoying the growing warmth until about the fifth hour, when Alice, the cook, came to begin her day at the Stocks.

Alice was a large fleshy woman in her early forties, with a cheerful round face and a sturdy body. She had worked for the clothier and his wife for several years. Because her husband Richard, who had been a soldier in the wars and had come back with fewer body parts than he departed with, could not work but only drank and talked with his friends at the taverns in town, Alice was the sole provider for him and their six children, who ranged in age from five to fourteen. Her eldest son, Tom, was a lanky, long-faced lad who on this morning had accompanied Alice because, she said upon her arrival, she feared going out of doors alone. She had been tempted to wait for the full light of day—indeed, she had been so afraid that she almost did not come at all.

Joan motioned to the table and Alice sat down, while Tom went to curl up by the kitchen fire, where he promptly fell asleep.

"My good husband is already abroad," Joan said pleasantly, not being one to lord it over her servants. "We have two guests in the house who must be fed, but can we not spare a quarter hour for a good talk? Now, tell me about this cousin of yours, John Crookback. Him I knew in part, but you the better."

Alice, relieved to sit after her journey from her own little house at the other end of town, began by explaining the complicated relationship between herself and the murdered farmer. As it turned out, Matthew had been misinformed: No Crookback blood flowed in Alice's veins. The connection was through Alice's husband, who was John Crookback's distant cousin.

Joan knew that much about Crookback. She remembered that he had been a sailor who had forsworn his nautical career and returned to Chelmsford to inherit the farm when his father had died. Everyone knew that, but it was an easy history to forget, for John Crookback had not been one of those mariners for whom his adventures were a constant source of anecdote, at least not in public, whatever his habit in his own family, and there were no relics of his seafaring years that Joan had seen at Crookback Farm.

Alice said, "Oh I think he was a good man. Or so my husband says that knew him when young, although not so well since then. John was a quiet man, as you know, as his father was. The Crookbacks ever kept to themselves. But when a sailor he had marvelous adventures, or so my husband says, sailing to remote parts; Cathay, I think, or perhaps America. Yet he talked never a word of it after but kept all to himself."

Joan wondered if Crookback could have been a pirate. Why would an honest seaman not be like other men, naturally boastful of his exploits? Reputation held him not so successful a farmer. His harvests were modest, and what wealth she reckoned he had was not so much in his farm's productivity as in the value of his freehold.

"Susanna was his second wife, you know," Alice went on, happy for an audience and obviously enjoying the fire, which was radiating a good deal of heat at last. "I don't know the name of the first. He married her in London, I understand, while he still went to sea. She bore him Mildred and Agnes, dying in childbirth of the latter. That was in London too."

"London," Joan murmured, bending forward not to miss a syllable of this rambling narrative.

"Then Abraham Crookback—that's John's father—died, leaving all to the son who had run off to sea as a boy. Susanna, of course, is one of our own. I think he married her straightway upon taking up his inheritance that the girls might have a mother.''

Joan had known Susanna, although the two women had never been close, and had known her mother, who had died the year before, and her grandparents, who had lived two houses away when Joan herself was a child. She had played with Susanna's brothers, rough boys, one of whom had been hanged. Chelmsford was a small town. Everyone knew everyone else and was kin to half the inhabitants of the churchyard, yet how long had it been since Joan had seen Susanna Crookback, except in church, which she undoubtedly would not have attended at all did the law not impose penalties on those who did not. Before the marriages of Mildred and Agnes, it was they who came to town on market day; after, Joan sometimes saw John Crookback there with his young children in tow. Never Susanna, however. She must have believed that the curse on her son was her own curse as well. A vision of a gaunt, middle-aged woman floated into Joan's mind, remained momentarily in conjunction with the visage of girlish innocence, and then wisped away like the spirit Susanna Crookback's soul now was.

"When it was discovered Nicholas was dumb,'' Alice said, "Susanna was ashamed and was little seen in the town. I suppose you know why?''

Joan did not.

"Well, she was swollen as a muskmelon before she was wed, whereby everyone knew she and John Crookback were thick and all. He was as lusty as a stallion and no better than any man should be, so there they were, you know, making the beast with two backs in his father's barn. Her father was very religious and there was a great to-do about it, all kept within doors because of the disgrace. Some say her father forced John to marry her, since she was carrying John's child and he would have no daughter of his mocked. The children of the first wife never got along well with those of the second, as is often the case.''

Alice began to tell of another Chelmsford family plagued

with such dissension, but Joan brought her back to the point. "What of Nicholas?"

"Well," Alice said, with a great breath, "he was ever a bone of contention. Although he was dumb, yet was he the favored of the father above all the others. I suppose John looked at the infant, so much the image of himself, and loved it beyond reason, as many men love their sons. Then when he found out the boy was wrong in the head, it was too late for him to feel otherwise. Of course, his daughters by the first wife greatly resented Nicholas and the way their father loved him. They thought they should be chief in his esteem, because they were the fruit of the first wife—and because Nicholas had been cursed for their father having lain with the boy's mother before they were wed. And they wanted no stepmother in the first place."

"Marry, if that were a just cause of cursing, half the town would be dumb—yes, and deaf too," Joan said. "I warrant there be some other bone that sticks in their craw."

Joan thought about the Crookback women, recalling their shrill, accusing voices, the rage that seemed more pronounced than grief. Into what devious and mortal paths could long-simmering resentment lead?

Murder? Perhaps. But to what purpose? If the will passed the freehold on to the eldest son, as Mildred had declared, what advantage was there to hasten the day of their father's death only that the detested half brother should enjoy his inheritance? And why should they have slain their stepmother and half brother and sister? It made no sense to her. The sisters were aggrieved, and undoubtedly greedy, too, but they were no fools that Joan could tell, nor monsters either.

"Everyone says that John Crookback had no enemies," Joan said.

"Well, there was never any love lost between John Crookback and Susanna's family, but her father is long gone, and her three brothers seemed to have made peace with their brother-in-law. Besides, none of them is so righteous that he could lift an accusing finger at John Crookback, who did justly by

Susanna after all, giving her the two younger children who were whole, in addition to him who is deaf and dumb.''

And what it came to at last as the cock crowed again and dawn began to pry through the kitchen windows was that Joan, for all the Crookback lore she had garnered from Alice, had no better idea than before as to who might have killed the mariner turned farmer, much less his innocent wife and children.

Matthew had a little talk with William Dees before relieving the stonemason of his duties. The two men hunkered down by the fire Dees built outside of the Sessions House, for he refused, he said, to spend the night with the dead bodies within, yea, even if they drew and quartered him for it. Dees seemed still shaken by the previous day's events. He said bringing those children up from the well was the heaviest burden he had ever borne and that he would remember the weight of it until the day he died. He said what a honest man John Crookback had been and ever his good friend, speaking in a hushed, reverential voice that Matthew had not heard from him before, for Dees was widely known as a surly, hot-tempered man with a foul mouth and little religion beyond what the law required of him.

"John Crookback was a good man, Stock," Dees said, seeming to forget that he had already declared this truth. "He didn't deserve that, nor his wife and children. It shakes my faith in the Almighty when I see such things. Believe me it does."

"The crime will not go unpunished," Matthew said.

"The town thinks Nicholas killed them, you know."

Matthew nodded.

"Perhaps with the help of that little foreigner, Master Burton's servant, him with the squinty eyes and sooty flesh and speaks with a thick tongue like a Dutchman."

"The town wants justice in an instant," Matthew said. "That's understandable, but I won't act until my mind is settled."

"Don't wait too long," Dees said. "There's a great fear in

Chelmsford—and anger. Now it's pointed at Nicholas and Adam, but you'll be to blame if you move too slowly. Several of our neighbors, who I will not name, broke Sir Thomas's curfew to visit me here. They wanted to see the bodies for themselves. I said they would not, for Sir Thomas commanded otherwise. They're hot for vengeance."

"They'd like to suppose it was one of John Crookback's own that did it," Matthew said. "That keeps the danger within another man's door. A passing stranger or band of brigands could strike anywhere."

"That may be," said Dees, rising with that pained look of one who has sat in one position for a long time and whose bones protest any change. "Their reasons will make no difference if their wants aren't satisfied. I am of the same mind. My house will be as close as a keep until this matter is settled. My poor wife is beside herself with terror. She will not let the children leave the house. Yet there is none that's truly safe, what must we do?"

Matthew sought words to alleviate the stonemason's fear but could find none. Of course there was danger. The deaths were not the work of God but of man. They bore the imprint of man's violence, of his inborn savagery and pitilessness. How else could one construe the murder of the children and the poor woman who was John Crookback's wife?

Matthew was almost grateful that Dees did not insist on an answer to his question. The stonemason stood silently looking up into the night sky whose film of clouds concealed the stars. He shook his head at the great mystery he had invoked and saluted Matthew with a little wave of his hand.

Matthew bid Dees good night, or what was left of it. He could already see the signs of morning, a pale contrast to the intense dark of the sky above. He stared into the fire and for the rest of his watch he thought about what Dees had said.

By eight o'clock Matthew's watch had concluded and again a great crowd had gathered around the Sessions House. He was relieved by three servants sent by Sir Thomas Mildmay, who also brought with them a letter of instruction, written, they assured him, in the magistrate's own hand.

Joan approached, carrying a basket. "I've brought you another breakfast, husband," she said. "And news."

Matthew lifted the cloth covering the basket, saw the carefully sliced cheese, the loaf, the pewter pot of honey, and a small package containing, he hoped, some sugary delicacy. The long morning's inactivity had left him famished, his earlier breakfast having been such paltry fare.

"What news?" he asked.

"Information about the Crookbacks that I never knew before," Joan said in a low voice.

"I have to go to the farmstead with Sir Thomas and his men. He wants the place searched top to bottom for what he calls evidence, before the coroner's jury meet in the afternoon. Every board unpried."

"I know," she said, taking his arm with one hand while holding the basket with the other.

"How do you know?" he asked, surprised. "I found this out only now with this letter."

"Sir Thomas's men came by the shop before coming here to you. They were confused about their own instructions, thinking you had been relieved of your watch earlier. I told them where you were and one of them told me you would be accompanying them and their master to Crookback Farm to search it. I suggested I accompany them, to which thing they made no objection. One of the men even said he thought it fitting, since a woman was among the dead and there would be a woman's things to finger through, which he was loath to do for decency's sake. Another said the more the better, for it was unpleasant work. He was glad to have it over with as quickly as might be."

"I don't know, Joan. I would rest easier if you were indoors."

"But look at your townsmen," she promptly answered. "All are here in the street. You assure them on the one hand that there is no present danger and at the same time keep your own wife under lock and key? Why, what hypocrisy is here, husband? Have the courage of your own convictions. If they see me walk about free of fear, then this will encourage them to do likewise. But if I lock up the house, who then will listen to your wise counsel?"

Matthew considered this, decided he had no effective rebuttal to her argument, and said, "Then bring yourself and your basket, for if Sir Thomas will have it so, then I will not deny myself your company. The morning will pass the quicker and merrier, despite what lies ahead."

Given the relatively short distance to the farm, Matthew suggested they walk, and the two were ready to start out when a handsome young man in Sir Thomas Mildmay's livery came riding up behind them. In his hand he held the reins of a second horse, already fitted out for a rider. "Here, Master Stock. My master bids you come straightway to meet him at the farmstead and has provided this horse for your conveyance."

Matthew looked at Joan, prepared to console her in her disappointment, but her face hardly reflected any. "This, husband, is the very man who bid me join you at the farm, saying a woman's presence would help much."

The handsome servant smiled pleasantly and said his name was Hubert Selby. Joan looked up at the horse he led, a goodly mare with a broad back and a long-suffering expression. She handed the basket to Hubert, then looked at Matthew.

"Well, Matthew, don't just stand there in a muddle. Sir Thomas has bid us come with dispatch. Already the morning leans toward noon. Help me mount. Unless I know nothing of horses, this beast is a gentle creature who will bear us both and with a good will, at least as far as the farmstead."

As it turned out, the mare Joan had praised for her gentleness was somewhat more spirited than she supposed, and while the ride to the farm was quick, it was also harrowing. Joan was more than a little relieved when they arrived.

51

She was amazed to see the great number of men who had congregated before the farmhouse. There was Sir Thomas Mildmay, of course, who was speaking to them all as she and Matthew arrived; at least a dozen men in livery; the gentlemen who had accompanied Sir Thomas the night before; and two of the six aldermen of the town, Stephen Marks, butcher, and Allan Ingram, another clothier. There was also a group of men who stood at a little distance from the others with shovels and picks. The men were not dressed in livery but in ordinary clothes, shabby and patched; they wore battered hats or none at all, and Joan could tell they were not farmers but simply poor men with no other business who had been pressed into duty. These were men who frequented the taverns of the town while good men worked, and Joan surmised they had been sought to do digging, but digging for what? Did Sir Thomas think there were graves or treasure to be uncovered?

As she and Matthew approached, Sir Thomas did not stop speaking but beckoned Matthew to come forward. Joan was relieved to see that her own presence among all the Chelmsford worthies was not taken by the magistrate as an offense. As they had ridden toward the farm it had occurred to her that the generosity of Hubert Selby's invitation might not necessarily have had the approval of his master.

Sir Thomas was speaking in a high clear voice as though he were giving a speech or sermon rather than just talking to a group of no more than several dozen men. He said his intent was to leave no piece of evidence undiscovered, for the whole country would look on these proceedings and he should be held answerable for his conduct. "Let no man say Thomas Mildmay failed in his duty, or that Chelmsford behaved in an unseemly fashion in accusing innocent persons in order to have an unpleasant matter done. Let us act prudently and with dispatch, and sweep nothing beneath the carpet."

Then Sir Thomas began instructing different groups of men in what they were to do. He said that his servants should search the outbuildings and the pasture, walking two by two, and that he and the aldermen of the town should take the

52

house itself. He nodded toward the laborers and said they should stand by until they were ordered to do otherwise and that his servant Faulkborne, a huge, brutish-looking man, would have command over them.

Another of Sir Thomas's servants, a man older than the others who seemed in more authority, asked what Sir Thomas wanted them to seek in the barns and pastures.

"Why, look for whatever seems unusual—say, a bloody knife, or a torn cloth, or whatever else might help us learn what happened here. And take care that in your search you do not trample or disturb what might be of use in this effort."

Sir Thomas dismissed the men to these duties, but told Matthew to remain with him. Joan watched from a little distance, uncertain what she was to do. Sir Thomas gave some orders to Hubert that sent him scurrying back to the horses. Then Sir Thomas cast an eye in Joan's direction; he motioned her forward.

"You are right welcome here, Mistress Stock," the magistrate said in a not unkind voice. "Hubert tells me you have come to offer your help in this sad business. Well, the idea is a good one, for we shall examine every piece of furniture and clothing in the house, including the dead wife's. A woman's presence may be useful under such circumstances."

Joan acknowledged this invitation with a little curtsy and looked at Matthew, who seemed happy to have his wife so honored by these attentions. But she still wondered about the diggers. Just what was it Sir Thomas expected to excavate? She did hope there would be no more corpses to bedevil her imagination with their ghastly countenances.

Then Sir Thomas told Matthew and Joan to inspect the upstairs, while he and the other townsmen would search the down. "Cover every inch, open every drawer, stir up the rushes to see that nothing is hidden beneath, and if there be false doors or the like, take note. This farmhouse is old and may contain secrets as yet undiscovered."

Relieved that she had not been appointed to the parlor with its bloodstained walls and other evidence of violence, Joan followed Matthew up a narrow stair to the upper floor of the house. Here she found a single large room that by its furnishings she knew had been the Crookbacks' bedchamber. At one end stood a canopied four-poster bed, a tall cabinet, a dressing table, and two chairs with curved backs.

It was not what Joan would have called a pleasant room. Its low, dark-beamed ceiling must have been annoying to John Crookback, who had been a very tall man; the small windows admitted too little light, and with no fire in the hearth below it was even more frigid than the out-of-doors, which at least had the benefit of what sunshine there was. But Joan was struck by the quality of the furnishings. Few farmers, no matter how prosperous, could afford so handsome a bed, one that might have served in a gentleman's house, if not in the master's chamber then at least in one afforded his most desired guests. The two chairs were also well crafted, with ornate designs on their backs and cushions of down and embroidered cloth seats of excellent workmanship.

She turned to look at Matthew, who was taking all this in too, and said, "Well, husband, where shall we begin?"

It took Adam Nemo a few minutes that morning to realize where he was. The bed was soft and comfortable; it had the faint smell of female flesh, a scent like decayed roses. A strange bed then, not his familiar straw-stuffed pallet at Burton Court but a mattress filled with soft goose down. Nor did the familiar sounds of Burton Court at break of day meet his ears. He stretched out his hand and felt flesh—an arm, delicately boned and downy. It was Nicholas then. The soft murmurs of his friend's sleep and the familiar feel of Nicholas's body assured him that wherever he was, he was not alone.

In the gloom of the attic, Adam could just make out Nicholas's face against the other bolster. The boy's eyes were shut, and with his yellow hair in a tangle about his face he slept the sleep of a man devoid of grief or guilt, who neither tosses nor turns nor wakes in fits as the images of his loss or his wickedness dance in his brain.

But Adam slowly remembered what his profound sleep had obscured, and with the memory came the dull ache of fear. He sat upright, wiping the sleep from his eyes. From somewhere below him he heard a young girl singing. It was a childish song, adorned with rhyme and a derisive lilt, and for a moment his heart almost stopped, for it seemed to him to be little Magdalen Crookback, Nicholas's sister, come alive again.

But then he remembered where he was, and that this must be Elizabeth Stock he heard, the clothier's daughter, whose small, dark features and curious expression—which seemed to ask, who, Father, is this strange man brought home and treated as a guest in the house?—he had briefly glimpsed the night before.

Magdalen had been a beauty, even at her young age; a radiant laughing angel, even when she mocked him, as she often did, because he was her brother's friend. Adam remembered how she had once come across him and Nicholas in the smaller barn at noonday, warm and secure. Finding them there, arms around each other's shoulders, she had stood looking puzzled; then a slow, mischievous grin spread across her face. She threatened to tell her father where they were.

"Wherefore should he care, little mistress?" Adam called after her. "He knows I am here."

His question caused her to stop in her tracks. Turning, she said, "Will you give me a ride on your shoulders if I keep my peace?"

"You may do as you like," he had said, then, "but I will give you a ride if that is your wish."

He had lifted her up on his shoulders and could feel her strong smooth legs around his neck, pressing into the sides of his face until he had to bid her cease.

"Forbear, I am no beast of burden," he protested, wincing with discomfort and humiliation.

Above him he heard her laugh derisively and sing new words to a taunting song she was wont to sing about the farm:

> *"Nicholas is cursed and cannot utter.*
> *Adam is his minion, more than brother."*

There were more words to the song, suggesting that there was something untoward about his friendship with Nicholas, and he remembered thinking that she must have practiced it, for it had come so quickly to her lips. Had she shaped it in her nimble brain or was it the work of one of her older half sisters, who always regarded him with such hostility?

Now that mocking voice was stilled; those sea eyes were shut. He would no longer be mocked by her, but he knew the farmer's older daughters lived to be his enemies. Had he not seen the malice in their faces, heard their filthy slanders, felt the heavy weight of suspicion upon him? John Crookback, were he alive, might have spoken on his behalf, said what a good and decent friend he was to the cursed son who had no friends otherwise. Who would defend him now? Not Nicholas, who could not speak even for himself. Never since he had been brought to England had Adam felt so strongly the bitterness of his exile, the alien feel of English soil.

Henry Sawyer, who was indeed born Henry Marsh of Colchester yet he used the name Sawyer as often as not, was five towns toward London when the news of the Crookback murders caught up with him while he was asking charity of the patrons of the Maidenhead, a shabby roadside tavern and brothel not too select in its guests.

The deliverer of this news was a man he knew and on any other occasion would have shunned, the earnest Jeroboam of Burton Court.

As Jeroboam explained it to the curious crowd at the Maidenhead, he was bound posthaste to London to acquaint his master with the appalling events of the week. His deep thirst and desire to be the center of attention along the way made it convenient for him to stop at regular intervals to relate the news, which he had done with such fidelity that by the time he arrived at the tavern he was thoroughly besotted and did not recognize Henry Sawyer as the notorious beggar and suspected thief of Chelmsford.

From the garrulous and inebriated steward, Sawyer also learned that suspected of the crime was the eldest son of the deceased farmer and his *friend*, a word Jeroboam pronounced with ill-disguised derision. That *friendship*, Jeroboam said, just in case any in his audience of swillers, whoremongers, and other riffraff missed the point, was "something more than was decent in God's eyes."

"Do you catch my meaning?" Jeroboam asked, casting a worldly-wise eye in Henry's direction.

"Oh, I do, indeed I do," said Sawyer, with the sad resignation of one who truly understood into what depths of depravity the world had fallen. "And the 'friend' the other man who is accused—now, good sir, I would fain know who he might be."

"Why one of my master's own servants by the name of Adam Nemo, a sort I have never trusted, for who can trust one with so filthy a visage and the eyes of snake? When the murderers were discovered, I sent word to where he was that he should not return to Burton Court. I took it upon myself to send him off, trusting that my master would approve most readily. Why, there are some honest wenches in the house, and of those who are not honest, they hardly deserve to be butchered for their wantonness. Two of the dead were female," Jeroboam said in the hushed tone of one conveying a terrible secret, apparently forgetting that he had communicated this information to Sawyer and others several times during the previous quarter hour.

Sawyer let out a little scornful laugh. "By God's precious blood, I think I know the very man! Short is he, small-built like a boy, with a face round like a rotten black Essex cheese? Hair coarse like horsehair, and he speaks with a bedeviled tongue, like a foreigner?"

"The very man," Jeroboam drawled, resting his head on the counter and seeming to prepare himself for sleep. "If you know aught of his crime, you would be well to tell it to Sir Thomas, who is magistrate there. I have no doubt that even as we speak the man is in bonds, he and the son, Nicholas. Sir

Thomas has sent to London for a learned friend experienced in the detection of crimes."

"Well, then," Sawyer said to himself after a few moments of reflection, "I think my fate bids me spin like a top, for where I was bound for London I see my fortune now awaits me in the place where I began."

"Have you information to impart then?" asked Jeroboam, suddenly alert with curiosity.

"Information? Well, we shall see," said Sawyer with a broad grin. "I warrant you, sir, if I have no information about me at this moment, yet I will have aplenty by the time I return to Chelmsford. Say, good sir, the way is long and the day as cold as a witch's teat. Could you for justice's sake spare me the cost of a good horse? I will have the wherewithal to pay you later twice over, or I am not Henry Sawyer himself."

Chapter 5

Fingering another woman's things was not to Joan's liking, be the woman dead or alive, friend or foe, and it was only her sense of duty that gave her the stomach for this impropriety, although it seemed to her that Matthew's engagement in the same enterprise with John Crookback's belongings somehow lessened her own offense.

The relics of Susanna Crookback's mortality were found in the cabinet, which opened, exuded the smell of sweet pomander and rotting apples. A carpenter wise in the needs of women had built it with two sides, one with shelves, the other open for the hanging of garments. Here Joan found two gowns of good broadcloth, well woven, both in the drab colors and with the plain stitchery Susanna favored, several petticoats, a kirtle, a wool cloak, and other garments suitable for the life of a woman living on a farm. Joan removed each item and, laying it on the bed, inspected every inch of cloth and every fold, uncertain just what Mildmay thought she might find but determined not to be faulted for having overlooked anything.

Bloody spots, perhaps. Yet did the cocky little magistrate so full of his authority suppose massacre had been so regular a feature of the Crookbacks' life that all their garments should be blood-spattered? The gowns were well worn, and one mended in the sleeves. Joan chose the best of them to bury Susanna in, which would be done after her neighbors had had their fill of the gory spectacle at the Sessions House.

On the shelves opposite the gowns Joan found divers pieces of linen, bone laces, shoes, both a good pair and a poor, a open box of ribbons, thread, laces, needles, a painted bobbin, thimbles, and buttons. On the upper shelf was a little coffer. Joan removed it and took it to the bed, where she opened it and laid out the contents. Now her heart quickened with guilt and anticipation, for surely these were Susanna Crookback's most intimate possessions.

Joan was further moved by how small a store was here to represent the sum existence of a woman who could not have been much younger than she. There was a gold chain, several pairs of earrings, an ivory whistle that might have belonged to one of Susanna's children, two neatly folded damask handkerchiefs of intricate design, a little hand mirror with a silver handle, and a leather purse. She untied the purse strings and poured the contents out on the bed. There were twenty shillings in white money, three gold pieces, and a silver ring with a jewel of some kind mounted in it.

"Come see, Matthew," she said, drawing him away from his work. "If what gossip says is true that the Crookbacks were rich beyond seeming, then surely the wife shared little of it. Her possessions are less than what one would have expected of a prosperous farmer's wife."

"And yet it is sufficient to prove, I think, that theft was no motive for these murders," Matthew answered, surveying the store of goods before him. "What housebreaker with the sense of a goose would risk his neck to invade a goodman's house and not pillage cabinets and chests? What's here?" He sifted through the coins. "A paltry sum in all, but here's a treasure, a portugee—the great crusado. A rarity indeed."

"Now where might she have got that?" Joan asked, looking at the inscription, which was in some language she could not read. As a hearty youth thirsty for adventure, John Crookback had sailed the tumultuous seas; perhaps he had given the coin to his wife for a keepsake. She looked at the coin's face and the curious lettering, Latin or Portuguese, she could not tell. Then she placed the coins in the purse again.

While Joan had been exploring the cabinet, Matthew had been plumbing the depths of the large chest that stood at the foot of the bed. The chest was unlocked and contained John Crookback's clothes and nothing more. Matthew removed each shirt, jerkin, and stocking, examining each with the professional eye of one whose livelihood redeemed nakedness from its shame. He crawled beneath the bed and found another, smaller chest. This piece was locked. "We may have something here," he said.

Matthew fell to work with his knife, inserting the tip of the blade into the lock and twisting it slowly. Joan watched. It was an old lock, Matthew remarked over his shoulder, nothing that would have deterred a dedicated housebreaker.

The chest sprung open and Matthew gave a grunt of satisfaction as he looked at the contents, for here were papers and several leather bags. One of the bags contained silver spoons, a round goblet, and a dagger with a jeweled handle in a fine-tooled leather sheath. The other bag's contents were more curious: Matthew drew out a crude necklace made of the teeth of some beast, "Perhaps a bear," he supposed aloud. There were several medallions made of yellowed skin, with curious drawings thereon as a child might have made.

There were also papers in the chest, two documents rolled and ribboned. One of these was a legal document of some kind; the other a letter. Matthew opened the first.

"Well, now here is John Crookback's will and testament, if I do not misread it, written in plain English and by himself. As we had heard, it gives the farm to his son, Nicholas. Enjoins him to see that his mother does not want. Small sums, personal items to Crookback's other children. Money, but not much. Dated just this year, and declares him to be of sound mind and body and the will written in his own hand. Sir Thomas will want to see this."

Matthew unfolded the letter carefully; it was addressed to someone named Ralph Hawking. The handwriting was tiny and difficult to read in the dim interior of the chamber.

"This is a letter from a Master Giovanni Baptiste Agnello, goldsmith of London." Matthew said. "This Agnello asserts that he has set up a furnace and proved therein a certain black stone given him to be gold worth forty pounds sterling to the ton. I suppose it is an assayer's report or some such thing. It is written to one Ralph Hawking, of the Cathay Company. The letter is dated January 15th, 1577."

"Why then it's almost twenty years old. I can see why John Crookback should have kept his will in this chest, but why a letter from one man to another? And what is the Cathay Company? And what did John Crookback have to do with it?"

"If it is—or was—a group of merchant venturers, then Crookback may have been employed by them," Matthew suggested, reading the letter over to himself again. "Forty pounds of gold to the ton, indeed. Now that is black stone to be devoutly wished for, for such a sum would buy a generous parcel of land."

"I have never heard of such a treasure," Joan said.

"Nor I. Well, we shall give both deed and Master Agnello's letter to Sir Thomas to see what he will make of them."

As Matthew said this, the gentleman himself came into the room.

"We have found nothing in kitchen or parlor that points to who might have done this," Sir Thomas said, clearly disappointed. "We are no wiser than before, although nothing below has been left unexamined. I see you two have not been idle."

"We have not, Your Honor, and have found naught but this modest treasure you see before you, John Crookback's will, and this letter from a London goldsmith to one named Hawking."

Sir Thomas took the letter from Matthew's hand. "The Cathay Company . . . gold. Why should an Essex farmer have this letter? Where was it you found it?"

"Why in this chest, sir, bound together with the dead man's will."

Sir Thomas took a few minutes to look over the will. "Everything to his son Nicholas, despite his infirmity. Well, there's no law that says a man can't leave his property to an idiot, I suppose. Many a father has. So there's no riddle there."

Turning his attention to Master Agnello's letter again, he made a shrewd face. "This is a certificate of value. Goldsmiths are ever issuing them. Someone brings something to a certain goldsmith to determine its worth. The goldsmith weighs it, subjects it to fire, water, or other substances to test its properties and to determine whether it be a true gem or false. This verifies that a certain black stone contains gold. The letter is old, I see; the men may well be dead by now. And what of this stone?"

For a few minutes Matthew watched while the magistrate continued to study the letter. "This black stone reminds me of something I heard once," Sir Thomas said, "but it is unlikely this has anything to do with these murders. Perhaps it is a letter Crookback found; admiring the penmanship, he kept it. Or perhaps he knew this goldsmith or this Ralph Hawking and kept the letter for friendship's sake."

"It is strange, I think," said Joan, "that he should keep it bound up with his will, as though it were of an equal if not greater value."

"Well, I shall turn it over to Master Fuller."

"Master Fuller?" Matthew asked.

"The gentleman I spoke of before. He's a learned man from Cambridge, a clever man and moral philosopher of some distinction. I have asked him to come to conduct the inquiry. What shreds of evidence we gather here and the testimonies of good people who knew the deceased family will all come under his scrutiny."

"But the coroner's jury sits this very day," Joan said.

"I have sent my secretary, Peter Simmons, posthaste to London, where Master Fuller now is," Sir Thomas said. "If it is convenient for him, we should expect to see him in Chelmsford by the end of the week. I have no doubt this case will prick his passion for a knotty enigma and give him matter for his learned lectures at the university."

"He won't be here for the coroner's jury, then?" Joan asked.

"Your husband must speak for us there," Sir Thomas said. "I pray God this charge does not overburden you, Master Stock."

"It does not, sir, only intrigues, if the truth be known. But I must add my voice to my wife's about Master Agnello's letter. I can't believe it is a little thing if John Crookback guarded it with such care. The man had no books in the house, hardly any papers. That he could read we know, for he wrote his will in his own hand. So he must have thought Agnello's letter important for its matter."

"Well," said Sir Thomas, "if the man had gold, I wonder that he made no mention of it in his will. The will says nothing about black stones or gold, only such silver plate as his daughter Agnes reported stolen. I had heard rumors that John Crookback had treasure buried on his property and that was why he held on to it with such tenacity."

Joan said she had heard that story, but could not say whether it was truth or fable.

"My man Harris heard it in a Moulsham tavern about two years past. I didn't know whether to credit it or no. The story is told of many a farmer who keeps to himself, as Crookback did. Crookback had been a mariner; there was always the chance he had had brought some booty home." Sir Thomas looked at the articles upon the bed. "Well, here's a mystery. If the housebreaker made off with the plate in the kitchen, why should he not have come upstairs to have this linen or yonder coin? Surely there's enough here to be troubled with."

Joan pointed out the purse she'd found in Susanna's cabinet, and Matthew said a little casket in the bottom of the farmer's clothes chest contained thirty-three pounds and some odd pence in English, French, and Spanish coins.

Sir Thomas said, "The question remains: why steal the plate but not the purses?"

"Perhaps he—or they," Matthew said, remembering Agnes's assertion that there must have been more than one intruder, "were frightened off before they could mount the stairs. Perhaps they were in the house when Adam Nemo came to the farm."

"Well, trust me, when Master Fuller comes he will solve this puzzle handily, or I don't know my man," Sir Thomas said gruffly, putting the will and letter beneath his arm. "Come. Let us go downstairs now and see what if anything my men have found in the pasture and barns."

Joan watched while the diggers continued to dig, with much talk among them about treasures real and imagined, but when after several hours nothing was uncovered but some animal bones and an old hiltless Roman sword, Sir Thomas said that the men had dug enough and that he was not about to oversee the digging up of the whole farmstead, no matter what Crookback had buried there. He said he believed what there was to discover in the pasture had been discovered and declared that there was no treasure and that the digging should stop and the ale that had been brought from the town evenly distributed among the workers. This announcement seemed to ease the disappointment of those assembled as they lay down their tools and began to move toward where the horses had been paddocked.

"Sir Thomas told me of what he hoped to find in the pasture," Matthew said while he and Joan were riding back to Chelmsford about an hour later. "One of his servants had heard rumors of treasure buried on the farm. Of course, we had all heard that old tale."

"No uncommon story," Joan said. "What farm or freehold but has not the same legend? Wishful thinking on the part of envious neighbors, I trow. We are a nation of treasuremongers who dream of finding what honest work should produce."

Joan said that for her part the treasure she sought was

truth—the truth about why the housebreaker had fled without his reward, why the murderer's violence had cut so broad a swath, cutting down two innocent children along with the parents, and what the black stone and gold and Agnello and Hawking had to do with a sailor turned farmer.

Matthew could provide no answers to these questions. Apparently he was as mystified as she. The journey to town passed with little talk between them, and Joan was left to her own speculations, which were not a few.

Agnello's letter made no more sense to her than the curious housebreaker who stole plate but not purses, who killed dogs as well as innocent children as if he were more concerned with revenge than simple larceny. Now here was a clue in her own mind: The brutality of the deaths argued that they were done with deliberation and contempt for the victims. Why stuff the bodies down the well? Why not just leave them where they were slain, in the house or in the yard? What did the murderer care? Unless, of course, he intended that they not be found. But they would be found, sooner or later. The bloody walls of the parlor would tell the tale. And why had not Nicholas been killed with the rest of his family?

The town now came into view and Sir Thomas, who rode well ahead of his servants, spurred his horse forward with the admonition that they hurry. Joan remembered that the coroner's jury would assemble at one o'clock and that the inquest would commence an hour after. She would not want to miss that event. Matthew's position as acting constable would guarantee her a goodly view of the proceedings.

Matthew kicked the mare's side so as not to fall behind, and Joan grasped her husband's waist all the harder.

Shortly after breakfast that morning Agnes Profytt went to visit her sister, Mildred. This worthy woman and her husband lived in a modest house at the end of the High Street, just where the fields and orchards began. When Agnes arrived, she was pleased to learn Mildred's husband was out-of-doors. "He'll not work today more than any other man in the town," Mildred said, with a heavy sigh of resignation. "He's at the Sessions House, hoping to see something."

Agnes asked how her sister was and appraised Mildred's rotund belly with a little envy, for although her new husband was turning out to be a disappointment to her, she did want a child, if only that she might not lack aught that her sister took delight in. She listened to Mildred's complaints for a few minutes, nodding from time to time in a reassuring way but already thinking ahead to how she would broach the subject that was the real purpose of her visit.

"Well, now, sister," Agnes said, finding a break in her sister's chatter at last. She glanced around the single chamber of the cottage, noting the humbleness of the furnishings. "Seeing that you will soon present me with niece or nephew and enlarge your own family too, have you thought about this child's lamentable future?"

Mildred's lantern jaw dropped at this remark, and she asked at once to what lamentable future her sister referred.

Agnes made a sympathetic face. "Dear Mildred, let me speak plain, as I am wont. Is it not well known that your husband is a poor provider? His prospects are hardly better than his present condition. Why, the town has sufficient tailors to serve this half of England."

As Mildred began to protest this statement, Agnes raised an admonitory hand. Mildred permitted her to continue. "Look at this place. A pig might call it home. Is it fit for a daughter of John Crookback? Were we not used to better conditions in our girlhood? Had we not reason to expect better things? I say we are both abused by these men we are yoked to and must look out for ourselves if we are not to slide into a condition below our desert."

Mildred looked at her sister without speaking, as though she were still trying to decide whether Agnes had come to insult her, to offer consolation, or to propose some ready road to the wealth denied them.

"Our father's death has enriched our brother," Agnes said. "It is not right, sister. It is not just."

Mildred moved in her chair with obvious discomfort. Agnes

thought she saw the baby kick and smiled despite herself. If her words stirred the unborn child to action, was not this an undeniable affirmation of the truth she told?

"I grant it is not right that our half brother should be enriched at our expense," Mildred said, resting her chin on her hand. "But what is to be done? Father's will is clear. He made no bones about it: Nicholas, for all his infirmities of mind, inherits Crookback Farm. Crookback's daughters are left with his good wishes and plate, which has been stolen. That's the whole of it. The laws of England will not help us."

"The laws of England may go hang, for all I care," said Agnes, with a venemous scowl that startled her sister. Agnes lowered her voice. "I know what's fair, and Nicholas's having what should be ours is not. Especially when it is so likely that he killed our father, and his mother and brother and sister too."

"Oh I hesitate to think it is so," said Mildred.

"You joined me in accusing him yesterday," Agnes said.

"But after prayer and sleep thought the better of it," Mildred said, resting her hand on her belly and assuming a beatific expression of contented motherhood.

"Think, sister. All evidence is for it," Agnes said. "The murderer slayed all, save for Nicholas. Why? Because he knew Nicholas could not speak? Yet who knows not that he can point and nod and yea, grunt if he must. Our half brother is not that devoid of sense that if he saw the murderer he would not signal it. Yet he keeps mum, answers no questions but with a shrug. Looks glassy-eyed, like the idiot he is. Now by God's blessed son, he has the farm for himself, to rule as he sees fit, or to sell it to Sir Thomas or Master Burton, who have long coveted the land. We are left with a few baubles."

"You care more for our inheritance than for Father," Mildred said, looking over her sister's shoulder as though the parent alluded to was standing there regarding them.

"Not so, sister!" Agnes said. "You misconstrue my meaning. But how must our parent feel in heaven where he surely is to know that his beloved daughters who survive must now be deprived by the one who brought him to his untimely end?"

Agnes leaned back and fell silent to let her sister consider this new line of reasoning. She was pleased to see that the seed she was planting seemed already to have sprouted.

"What will you say today at the inquiry?" Mildred asked.

"I shall tell the truth," Agnes said firmly. "No more nor less. I shall point out the plain facts—as I have done already to Matthew Stock and Sir Thomas. Let the coroner's jury hear my reasoning. I shall also describe certain troubles between our half brother and sister and Nicholas."

"What troubles? I knew of no troubles," Mildred said, shifting uneasily in the seat again.

"I speak of more than squabbles," Agnes said darkly.

"You mean Magdalen's taunting him, which she did, in truth, and Benjamin's sometimes joining in? But certainly that was mere child's play. I remember no—"

"Sister, such taunting is the beginning of more serious mischief," Agnes said, leaning forward to press her point. "Think of it, and comprehend of what you speak. These evidences are not without their meaning. Would you have Nicholas inherit? Say yea or no."

"Not if I could prevent it," Mildred said.

"Then listen to my own words and support me as a sister should. In heaven our father will be pleased, justice done, and our estates enlarged. It's as simple as that."

Agnes ignored the doubtful look on her sister's face. She had always despised her older sister for her timidity, and she prayed to God Mildred would not ruin things now.

William Dees came home after his night's watch in no mood for company. Fear and grief had swallowed him up and spewed him out. He wanted neither to talk nor think. He found his wife in a sour mood too, complaining again about her ailments, which were, according to her, more than any man could count. A pale woman in her forties and thin as a rail, she asked him if he wanted aught to eat and he said no. She asked him if he would tell her what passed on his watch, how the poor dead Crookbacks appeared, and who was suspected of the crimes. He said he would not tell. He wanted only to sleep, he said.

"You might as well do so," his wife said, "for I have heard you may not work today. It's a holiday, by order of the magistrate."

The petulance in his wife's voice irritated Dees. He walked around her without another word and went into the little bedchamber they shared, and sitting down heavily on the bed, he began to remove his boots. In the parlor his children were engaged in a loud dispute, their shrill voices causing his head to ache.

"Keep your children quiet, will you? I have not slept all the night."

His wife came to stand in the doorway, and folding her arms over her bony chest, she regarded her husband with a scowl. He looked at her and thought that she did indeed look ill. Her complexion was the texture and color of oatmeal. There was no meat on her body, and lately she had begun to smell bad. He imagined she would die soon and then he would be left with the children, for whom he had no strong affection but looked upon as creatures foisted on him by a trick of nature, a punishment for venery. He should need a new wife to care for that brood, besides which his wife had not served him as a wife should for many a month, with her aches and pains and whining about them at all hours; sometimes he was so rank with lust he could hardly stand it and would happily have taken up with some whore but for the cost and a dread of the French pox, which was all over the town, according to rumor.

He leaned back on the bed and thought about eligible women, thinking it a sad thing that Agnes Profytt had married before he was widowed, for she was a ripe wench with a lickerish eye and skin like velvet, and for all the sharpness of her tongue, Dees supposed himself man enough to tame her. And now, Dees thought, Agnes should share in Crookback Farm, one male heir being dead and the other likely to meet the same fate when the law took its probable course.

From the attic window of the clothier's house Adam Nemo looked down into the street, but cautiously, so as to not be seen. The clothier's wife had told him he was to remain indoors, he and Nicholas, until they were wanted, which she said they would surely be later at the coroner's inquiry. She had explained it all carefully when the pleasant-faced cook of the family had brought the two men their breakfast of cheese, bread, and good strong ale. The clothier's wife had said nothing about remaining hidden, although Adam somehow knew concealment was wise. He could hear excited voices in the street, which was full again, as full as it had been the night before. All of the shops were closed by Sir Thomas Mildmay's order, yet Adam had never before seen so many strangers in the town.

Nicholas sat not on the bed but at its foot, his head resting on his arms. From time to time he wept softly while Adam stroked his head and hummed, as he had not thought of doing in a very long time, a song he did not remember the words to, only the melody. About midmorning, Nicholas no longer wept, neither did he move, but stared at the wall opposite him as though there were visions passing before his eyes.

Adam leaned toward his friend and touched his shoulder. Nicholas turned to look at him. Adam held up four fingers and then made a vigorous slashing motion with his fist, the imaginary knife. He pointed to his eye, and made an expression of puzzlement.

A look of painful comprehension momentarily crossed Nicholas's face, and then he cast his eyes down again, and Adam knew Nicholas had not seen the murders. He had been spared that, at least. Only the aftermath had he witnessed, horrible enough.

Adam Nemo turned away and remembered . . .

The larger of the Englishmen brought him down as he tried to escape, a giant golden-bearded man whose

71

eyes flashed angrily and who beat upon him and perhaps would have killed him with his blows had their chief not called him off. The chief was Martin Frobisher, Adam later learned, when the garbled sounds coming from the alien mouths became words with meanings. He had never learned the brutal man's name. He knew none of their names save Frobisher's and Crookback's, because he had to do with them later, and could remember none of their faces except Frobisher's and Crookback's and, yes, the brutal man's. Nor could he remember any of the faces of his own people, although sometimes he beat upon his own head in wordless fury to bring them back.

Chapter 6

The press of bodies around the Sessions House, more like the clamor of market day than a grave legal proceeding, was so considerable that it was only by the blast of a trumpet that enough decorum was obtained for the coroner's inquest to commence. And even then there was a long delay while Sir Thomas and the coroner, Edmund Vernon, a youngish gentleman with nervous eyes, fresh in his office, debated whether fourteen jurors would be sufficient, as Sir Thomas argued, or eighteen were required, as Vernon maintained. This issue was finally resolved in compromise, that the jury should split the difference between the two positions and sixteen jurors be chosen.

Another hour passed while a jury was selected, a process made more difficult by Sir Thomas's anxiety that all jurymen should be free of prejudice against the deceased family, and the legion of clamoring volunteers who offered themselves for the duty and had periodically to be silenced by threats from both Vernon and Sir Thomas. Thereafter, another hour passed while the two gentlemen discussed who should give evidence and whether Nicholas Crookback, being deaf and dumb and mentally unsound as a consequence, was a competent witness.

On that point it was decided that competent or no, he should be made to appear, and Adam Nemo, and William Dees as well, because he had brought the bodies up from the well, and likewise the deceased's daughter, Agnes Profytt, who had made a special request to speak, for she said she had evidence to give and would not be denied, if she must go door to door otherwise.

Matthew observed while all this was going on, then went to his house to fetch Nicholas and Adam Nemo and returned with them.

By the time this was done Vernon suggested that the hour was so late the inquest might as well be held over until the next day. To this Sir Thomas objected strenuously, saying that the townsfolk had already enjoyed one holiday over the murders and that two in a row would induce such idleness that there would be no working for the remainder of the week.

"We shall have to meet past dark, then," said Vernon, with a shake of his head. There followed a lengthy discussion between the two men as to whether it was lawful to hold a coroner's inquest in the nighttime, with Vernon noting that he could find no precedent for it, and Sir Thomas insisting that an inquest might be held at any hour so long as there was honor to the queen and good order in the proceedings. Finally, Sir Thomas prevailed over Vernon's objections.

"Then let there be torches," Sir Thomas said, with a look of disapproval at Vernon, whom everyone saw he disliked. "I have no reason to believe that your deliberations will be as protracted as was the impaneling of these worthy men."

The jury of sixteen men were all from Chelmsford and Moulsham. Matthew Stock knew every one, and his wife, his children, his dog. Honest men, good Christians, men of business for the most part but a few farmers too. Were some matter of his being judged he would not have minded such a jury. And yet he wondered if their deliberations would be quite as simple as Sir Thomas supposed. He worried what Agnes Profytt would say, how she might stir up the more that which seemed already stirred enough.

Matthew asked Joan, who had returned to the Sessions House with him, to bring him his supper and something for Nicholas and Adam, for he said he thought it too risky to move the two up and down the street again, not with the town full of strangers and everyone curious about Nicholas and Master Burton's servant and struggling to catch sight of them.

"You shall have no decent meal in a basket, husband. Can you not leave them in another's charge?"

"Whose?" he asked, looking at her helplessly. "Besides, I dare not leave again. Not with this multitude abroad."

At six o'clock Sir Thomas returned with his men, bearing so many torches that one might have thought it daylight in the market cross. The whole town seemed to be on fire, and this extraordinary illumination in streets that were customarily dark after sundown seemed to increase the general excitement. The people, anxious that they should not lose their places, had hardly moved. There was a great deal of jostling, boisterous laughter, visiting with friends, and hawking of food, for the tavernkeepers and other tradesmen, seizing the opportunity, had sold meat pies, bread, and other dainties at high prices, despite Sir Thomas's declaration that the day should be a holiday. It seemed to Matthew that every brothel and alehouse in Chelmsford and Moulsham had emptied itself into the street.

It was as raucous and unruly an assembly as he had ever seen in his town, and the spectacle amazed and terrified him. He was a small, unprepossessing man whose recently delegated charge was little recognized beyond the town precincts, and yet here he found himself an image of authority whom others now depended upon to maintain order. What was he to do if riot erupted? Call out the watch? The citizenry of which it was composed would no doubt be participants in the rioting.

His only resource was the large number of armed servants

Sir Thomas had brought in from the manor, and their presence did little to lessen the confusion and danger presented by so many crowded into the market cross. Besides which, they were under Sir Thomas's command, not Matthew's. Yet during the intervening hour no less than five of his fellow townspeople came to him claiming that they had been victims of pickpurses, and he personally broke up two fistfights between apprentices, aided a woman who had fainted from the press of bodies, chastized a drunken apprentice for pissing on the cobbles, and was called upon to resolve a dispute about a broken window and silence one barking dog so annoying to those around him that there were cries on all sides for his master to shut the creature up or see him hanged on the very spot. The master, a large ugly man somewhat resembling his beast, threatened to cudgel the first citizen that so much as sullied the dog's fur, but Matthew knew the man from the cloth trade and, after an earnest entreaty, prevailed upon the man to take the noisy animal home.

Sir Thomas ordered that another blast be sounded on the trumpet, and then a second and third, and was about, he said, to proclaim the assembly a public riot when the noise abated, and a hush of anticipation settled over the crowd. The magistrate looked at Vernon, who seemed to have been very upset by the disorder, and told him to commence the inquest.

The jury was now called forth and provided with benches to sit upon, as were the gentlemen present. A long trencher table and chairs had been brought from nearby houses and set up for the coroner, Vernon, and his clerk, whose name was Ruggles, and for Sir Thomas. Chairs were also provided for a few of Sir Thomas's friends, who had come to see the excitement, who Matthew had heard had actually paid for their seats. Matthew and one alderman and the sixteen jurymen, being of less social importance, were provided only stools, which were arranged at a right angle to the table where the coroner, Ruggles the clerk, and Sir Thomas sat. The chairs for the gentlemen observers were set up opposite, so a great U was created, in the middle of which the bodies of the dead were laid out, covered now with cerecloth.

Directly in front of the coroner's table a speaker's stand had been set up for the witnesses. Even with this arrangement, it was difficult for the audience to see or hear, the ceiling being so low and the pillars obstructing the view on three of the sides. There were a number of complaints about this, but it was so clear that nothing could be done, most of the crowd seemed content just to be within earshot and those beyond merely to be present at an event that was sure to be spoken of for years to come.

The jury having taken their oaths before, Vernon now announced what everyone knew, that the purpose of the assembly was to inquire into the deaths of John Crookback, yeoman, his wife, and their two children. He got the name of the boy wrong and was corrected by a number of the jurymen who had known the Crookbacks well enough to be intimate with these details. Then Vernon asked Martin Day, who was a physician, to stand before the jury and explain the cause of death.

Day, a hearty man in his sixties with a thick, barrel-shaped body and gray hair that he wore down his back, was one of the few persons in the county with any claim to medical training beyond home remedies—he was a frequent witness at coroner's inquests, and his ability to identify a cause of death amazed Matthew, who had been a juryman himself on more than one occasion.

"You have examined these bodies?" Vernon asked.

"I have, sir."

"And found?"

"The man, John Crookback, died from being stabbed with dagger or poniard, thrice in the chest and once in the throat. He lost a great deal of blood from these wounds."

"He did not drown, then, in the well?"

"He would have been dead before," said Day, looking from the coroner to the body in question, as though the response would reanimate the corpse to verify the physician's assessment.

"And the wife?"

"Stuck with a like instrument, in the shoulder, chest, arm, and belly. Which wounds might have proved fatal had she not

77

been drowned. She was a sickly woman, not hale like her husband.''

Day continued by describing the wounds of the two children, which Matthew could scarcely bear to hear and which provoked those in the assembly to cry "Shame!" and "God help us." The children, Day said, had died of drowning, although both had been stabbed repeatedly.

"You conclude, then," said Sir Thomas, "that these deaths were murder and not the result of self-inflicted wounds or of accident or misadventure?"

"They could have hardly been other than murder," Day said, "No man could stab himself in such a manner. He would have fainted before the second or third thrust. Besides, there are the circumstances of their disposition—I mean the fact they were found at the bottom of the well. For Crookback to stab himself, his wife, and his children and then throw himself and two children into the well would be a feat beyond Will Kempe's skill."

A sprinkling of nervous laughter followed upon mention of this famous clown's name, although Day had made it in utter seriousness, and then the coroner told Day he was excused. The coroner's clerk removed the cloths from the bodies and the jury was instructed to inspect the wounds for themselves, which they did with a good deal of eagerness; there was as well much craning of necks to have a view among the gentry present.

Matthew turned his attention at this time to the jurymen as they inspected the bodies. He noticed that they appeared more curious than horrified due, no doubt, to the fact that there must be few among them who had not seen worse spectacles: rotting heads stuck upon pikes, decaying corpses still dangling from the hangman's tree, an occasional horror left in a ditch to bloat and molder because no one would take responsibility for its decent burial. He knew it was not a gentle age in which he lived, and England not a gentle country, although he would not have traded it for any other he knew of in Christendom. They were fellow citizens of the victims filing past, and did it not make a difference when the horror had been visited on one's own neighbor? Did that not bring the specter of untimely death much closer and a cold grip of fear to every heart?

Matthew watched the faces of the jury for signs of these emotions, and for something else too—guilt. For he was persuaded by Joan's reasoning that the crime against John Crookback and his family had not been incidental to housebreaking and larceny; no, the theft of the silver plate had been a ruse to hide the real provocation. Crookback had known his enemy. The murderer was no passing stranger, but someone of the town—maybe even one of the jurymen themselves.

So Matthew scrutinized faces, half ashamed of his own suspicion, his ability to transform friend and neighbor into suspects in so vile and unspeakable a violation of God's sanctions. But he saw nothing beyond what he might have expected. Were his friends, say Tom Deal the scrivener or Jack Terrill the goldsmith, guilty of much more than a morbid curiosity stronger than compassion, or of a strong stomach for the gruesome? Could the actual murderer have looked upon his victims' bodies and not cried out in spiritual torment, his very soul wrenched by conviction of his damnation? What were the strictures of the queen's law compared to the indictment and judgment of God? Could one of the jurymen have been the author of this horror? Would heaven have permitted such cruel irony?

The last juror had seen the body and there was general concurrence with Day's opinion that the Crookbacks were dead, had been stabbed, and three of them drowned as well. Sir Thomas asked specifically if any of them supposed the deaths to have been caused by any other hand than a murderer's, and no one spoke up in disagreement with the consensus.

Then Sir Thomas called Nicholas Crookback to come forward.

For Nicholas, no stool had been provided. He had been sitting on the floor of the Sessions House directly behind Matthew, so still and motionless that Matthew would not have noticed his presence had the boy not occupied so central a position in the case. At the name, Matthew rose and turned, making a motion for Nicholas to rise and follow.

During the jury's inspection of the bodies the audience had grown noisier, as whispers swelled to a steady murmuring, but upon Nicholas's taking his position, the crowd fell into a great stillness. Being newly appointed and not native of Chelmsford, Vernon had not known the Crookbacks, and although Matthew and Sir Thomas had acquainted him with Nicholas Crookback's infirmity, Vernon treated him as though he were fully capable of both speech and hearing, asking him to state his name, his place of residence, and his relationship to the deceased persons, none of which questions Nicholas seemed to comprehend at all.

"He cannot speak or hear, sir," Matthew said.

"Can he be made to understand with signs, then?"

Matthew admitted he did not know. "He has a friend who is here, Master Vernon. His name is Adam Nemo, a servant of Master Burton of Burton Court. Perhaps he can make this boy understand your questions."

There were no circumstances in which a legal proceeding would have been to Adam Nemo anything but confusion and threat. He hated hissing, barking, bellowing crowds now as he had hated them twenty years before, when out of the professed goodness of his heart, John Crookback—it had been almost as many years since Adam had inquired into the motives of the mariner turned farmer—had borne him away to the relative peace and blessed obscurity of the Essex countryside, covering his escape with the ingenious fiction that Adam was as dead as his namesake. Then Crookback had seen to his placement in the great house at Burton Court, so that his fellow servants could forget, if they ever knew, from what foreign clime he had come and how alien to his blood was the verdant island of Britain. No, for this atmosphere of legal wrangling, of rancor and punishment Adam had no stomach. He crouched down low behind the clothier's stool, wishing himself to be dead and buried rather than to have to suffer before the public these proceedings, the significance of which he was not sure he understood, and which were as vexing to anticipate as were snarling dogs and body lice.

"Go, Adam, speak the truth. Be not afraid," Matthew Stock whispered, pointing to where he was to stand by Nicholas at the thing that looked like a preacher's pulpit.

Adam made no reply to this counsel but only nodded and went to take his place. He lifted his jaw and focused his eyes on the clothier and then on the stern countenance of the coroner, who regarded him with the mixture of curiosity and distaste to which Adam Nemo had grown inured during his years among the English.

"Tell us your name, fellow," Vernon said.

"I am called Adam Nemo."

"Say it again, that the jurymen can hear it."

"Adam Nemo, if it please Your Honor."

"And your vocation?"

"A household servant to Master Arthur Burton of Burton Court."

"You must speak up, man. Don't whisper."

"Yes, my lord."

"I am not a lord."

"Yes, sir."

"How many years have you been in Arthur Burton's service?"

"Near twenty, if it please Your Honor."

"You speak with an accent. From whence come you?"

As the coroner asked his questions, his clerk wrote down Adam's answers. Which were easy to give, Adam thought, except for the answer to the last question. Where indeed was he from? His native place had a name he had almost forgotten, a name in his own birth tongue. He thought of the name. Now it sounded like grunting even to him, and he knew that to utter it would only create bewilderment and perhaps render him guiltier in the eyes of this hostile company.

"I am from an island. An island in the northern seas. Sir Martin Frobisher brought me from there, many years ago."

An island, yes, and larger than this one, he suspected. An island of neverending white in which the seasons brought no glorious progress of changing scene and temperature but perpetual snow and forlorn view. Adam realized that on speaking this he had answered truthfully—for the first time in years. His heart almost stopped beating at the realization of this fact, but he was relieved to find that his confession seemed to have no particular significance to coroner or his jury.

So he had exposed himself, but no harm done. His courage rallied a little, yet he was still unnerved at being the center of so much attention.

The coroner asked Adam if he could communicate with Nicholas by signs.

"Sometimes, sir."

"Only sometimes?"

Adam caught the incredulity in the question.

"Well, let us put your skill to the test," Vernon said. "Ask this young man if he was present when his parents and brother and sister were slain."

It was the question Adam had asked of Nicholas himself but he thought it wise to comply. He made therefore the same gestures, repeating them until he could tell from the expression in Nicholas's eyes that he understood.

Nicholas nodded affirmatively; a murmur passed through the crowd.

"Ask the witness whether he saw the man or men who murdered his parents, brother, and sister," Vernon said, intensifying his voice like a lesser actor conscious that for one brief moment he is center stage.

This question Adam found more difficult to express in gestures. He tried different motions with his hands and movements of his head and eyes and got a nod or two from Nicholas as response, but he was unsure as to whether Nicholas's answer corresponded to his own question or to some other.

"If he saw, and the murderer is in this place," Sir Thomas

interrupted impatiently, "can he point him out? Can you tell him to point out the murderer with his finger?"

"I cannot be satisfied, Your Honor, that he understands the question put to him," Adam said turning to face the magistrate.

"Well then, sirrah, make him understand," Sir Thomas snapped. "You two are friends, and you do speak to each other in this curious way."

Which thing was true, Adam knew, but how could he describe communication that even he only partly understood? The truth was that the two of them shared feelings rather than thoughts, things that could not have been put into words had Nicholas Crookback been the most eloquent orator in England. Information such as the coroner sought was not feeling; it was comprised of ideas, of words. Adam's friendship with Nicholas had not involved a transfer of information. Their own distinctive language, if that was what it was, had no vocabulary for such an exchange.

"Try again, Adam Nemo," Sir Thomas said, before Vernon, his little eyes flashing angrily, pointed out to the lord of the manor that he, Vernon, and not Mildmay—be he knight of the manor or no—was in charge of the inquest.

"Well, then, proceed with dispatch," Sir Thomas shot back. "This matter need not take all the night."

Adam saw Sir Thomas lean over to make some comment to his friends among the gentry, who all seemed to be amused by the conflict between him and the coroner and firmly on the side of the magistrate.

Adam, confused by this dispute between two men he considered to be in the same camp, made another effort. He used his fingers to signal the number of the dead and then, putting his hand over his brow as though shielding his eyes from the sun, asked Nicholas if he had seen him who had killed them.

Nicholas responded with a shake of his head.

At that instant a shrill female voice Adam recognized as Agnes Profytt's burst from the crowd: "Well may you deny you saw the murderer, Nicholas Crookback. You may not be gifted with speech and yet you are no fool, for who can see himself? So, rightly you proclaim by your dropped head that you saw no one."

Vernon responded sharply to this outburst, telling Agnes to be silent until her turn came.

"I cannot endure his lies, Your Honor," Agnes said. "It is wrong, and this honorable court aids and abets his mischief."

"This is not a court, Mistress Profytt," Vernon said in placating tones, "but an inquest. Our purpose is not to determine guilt but to establish by what means these unfortunates died. I pray you be patient until we have heard all the evidence."

This request seemed to have its intended purpose. Adam saw Agnes Profytt standing near the front of those who had been asked to testify. She folded her arms in a gesture of acceptance, but her little black eyes flashed defiantly. Leaning to the side, she whispered something in the ear of her sister.

Adam made one more attempt to make Nicholas understand, but it was futile. Nicholas simply stared back, apparently confused by his stepsister's anger and uncertain of what role he played in these events. Adam dropped his hands to his side in a gesture of defeat.

"It appears we shall have no evidence given by this man," said Vernon to Sir Thomas. "Let us move on, then, and not waste further time. You may sit down," he said to Nicholas, sighing heavily.

Adam took Nicholas by the arm and began to lead him away. "No," said Vernon. "You remain, Adam Nemo."

Adam stayed where he was and looked at the coroner and then at the faces of the jurymen, almost all of whom he had seen before, but not one of whom he counted as a friend. These were for the most part the honest burghers of the town, who regarded themselves a cut above a household servant. Their faces now were stern and disapproving, and he was suddenly conscious again of how different he must appear to them, how outlandish must seem his origins and, to their way of thinking, his feelings. Perhaps they held him to blame for the fact that Nicholas could not be made to understand questions that must have been perfectly obvious to any soul with half a brain, for he knew that not everyone in town regarded Nicholas as being feebleminded as well as deaf and dumb. Or, perhaps like Agnes Profytt, they suspected him of being Nicholas's accomplice.

"Tell us what you found when you came to Crookback Farm yesterday morning? What hour of the day was it?"

"It was morning, sir, about ten or eleven of the clock."

"How could you know that with such precision?"

"The servants at the Court do go to church at that hour—"

"But not you?" Vernon asked sharply. "You do not go to church as the law requires?"

"I go, sir, but not yesterday."

"Wherefore not?"

"Jeroboam, who commands us in the master's absence, said I was to stay with the maids sir, who were sick abed and unable to go to church. He wanted some man to be there."

"And how was it then that you left your duty as watchman at Burton Court to walk three miles to the farm? Is this how you obey Jeroboam's commands?"

Adam was about to say that the maids weren't sick, but only feigning so that they might stay home and make merry, but he thought the better of it. They would be called to testify then, and not wishing to be fined they would surely deny his words and make him out to be a liar. He decided it would be better were he merely regarded as disobedient.

"Will you answer the question, Adam Nemo?"

"With Jeroboam gone and the maids sick there was none to stay me, sir."

"I see," said Vernon. "Well, I suppose it is too much to expect of servants these days that they obey without someone to watch them at each moment. Proceed, then; tell us then what you found at the farm."

"I found the house all quiet—"

"Speak up, man! The jury must hear."

"I found the house silent, Your Honor, the dog was dead in

85

the yard. There was blood splattered on the wall of the parlor. And Nicholas was huddled in a corner, as pale as death and quivering. He took me to the well.''

"How is it he knew where the bodies were?''

Adam started to answer, but Mildmay interrupted. "This strange fellow is no more capable of knowing what Nicholas Crookback knew or did not than the wretched boy is to tell it.''

"With all due respect, Sir Thomas," Vernon answered. "We shall not know he does not know until he is asked.''

Sir Thomas let out a loud sigh of exasperation.

Adam looked from coroner to magistrate, unsure as to whom to respond to. Deciding it should be the coroner, he said, "He may not have seen the bodies put there, sir, but he knew where they were. I looked down the well and saw no water reflected, as ordinarily I could.''

"You saw no bodies, then, yourself?''

"Not until later, when William Dees fetched them forth on his back.''

"Then how did you know there was a murder done if you saw no bodies and Nicholas Crookback lacked wit to tell you?''

At this question there was a murmur of voices among those assembled, even the jurymen, who had been as quiet as if in church until this point.

Adam's mouth went dry; he heard his voice tremble, although he tried to control it. Matthew Stock had told him to speak the plain truth, which truth he had told. Then why was that not enough? Why, did his truth sound like dissembling, even to himself?

"I saw the blood on the walls of the parlor and on Nicholas. There was too the dog that was much loved of John Crookback. When Nicholas led me to the well, I looked down and could not see the water. There was something there, like a shadow. I knew not what it was. I could always see my own reflection in the surface of the water below, as in a glass, but there was nothing there to be seen.''

"Whereupon you came straightway to the church, where you should have been before, and broadcast news of murder, although you claim to have seen no proof thereof."

"If I may speak, Sir Thomas," Adam heard Matthew Stock say behind him. "Adam Nemo never said there was murder done at the farm, only that something terrible had happened there and that we should come. Those of us who followed after him knew only that and nothing more until we ourselves discovered the dead where they had been cast."

"I would still fain know how he even knew that in the absence of visible evidence."

"He saw the blood," Matthew Stock said.

"Let Adam Nemo answer!" the coroner said.

"I did see the blood, Master Vernon," Adam said. "It was all upon the walls of the parlor, and fresh. I could tell by Nicholas's face that violence had been done. When he took me to the well and I could not see my image back again, I knew what it was he showed me, although I could not see it with my eyes."

"You simply *knew*, then?"

"I knew what it was that was there, although I could not see it," Adam said again.

Vernon leaned over to whisper something to his clerk, and there was silence for a pace.

"Did you ever quarrel with John Crookback?"

"Never, sir. He liked me well."

"He made no objection to your friendship with his son, or to the fact that you, a servant of another, spent time idly at the farm."

"He seemed most grateful that his son had a friend."

"And what of the rest of the family—Susanna and the children? Did they approve or disapprove?"

"They were never my enemies, nor I theirs."

Vernon whispered more words to his clerk, then he told Adam he could return to his place and he asked William Dees to come forward.

"State your name, fellow," the coroner said when the stonemason stood before him.

"William Dees of Chelmsford, stonemason."

Vernon asked Dees if he was any relation to Arthur Dees of Colchester; William said he was not.

"I understand it was you who climbed down into the well to bring the bodies up."

"I did, sir,"

"At whose behest?"

"At Master Stock's and the parson's, who said I should do it because I was strongest amongst them."

"Did they say what you were to find below?"

The stonemason paused; then he said, "Now that you ask, they did not, only that I was to go down and see what was in the well. Master Stock said there was something there and we needed to see what it was. We all suspected murder, you see, sir, because of the blood, sir. And so nobody was surprised that there were bodies at the bottom of the well, because murder is what we thought had happened."

"And what did you find?"

"Where, Your Honor?"

"In the well. What, are you simpleminded then that you balk at my questions?"

"May his soul rest in peace, it was John Crookback, sir. I brought him up first upon my back, and a heavy load he was. Then his wife thereafter, and last the poor innocent babes, who were hardly a load at all."

"So you were the first to see the bodies, that is, to know indeed that they were there."

"God bless me, I was, Your Honor."

Vernon nodded, said that it was an act of Christian charity that the stonemason had done for the dead, and that Dees was excused.

Vernon next called Agnes Profytt to come forth, which she did, her head thrown back proudly and her high pointed breasts before her like banners. There was first a great stirring of persons standing in front of her, none of whom seemed eager to grant her room to advance.

"You are the dead man's daughter, I understand?" Vernon asked when Agnes was where Adam had stood before.

"I am, sir," Agnes said, and looked accusingly at Nicholas with her little black eyes, which Adam thought were like an animal's, quick and shrewd and dangerous.

"The hour is late. Tell us, therefore, what you have to tell us."

"I will speak briefly," Agnes said, lifting her chin but still focusing her attention on her half brother, who was not looking at her but at the ground with what seemed a kind of shamefastness. "Adam Nemo has not spoken truly. My half brother and my father and stepmother had many difficulties, and with my siblings, God rest them in heaven, Nicholas had the more. Why should there not have been trouble, given how different he is from the rest of us? He bore a curse of God from the day he was born, for that he cannot hear or speak must surely mean some odious thing. Nevertheless, I leave that to the learned to say."

"What do you mean, Mistress Profytt, by 'trouble'?" Vernon asked. "What manner of trouble was this? Dissension of the ordinary kind, perhaps, such as parents often have with their children?"

Agnes drew her eyes from Nicholas and turned her head to face Sir Thomas. "I know not what is ordinary in other households, but I know what I saw as child and virgin in my father's house. Who are better witnesses than I or my dear sister, who will agree to every word I speak? My father and his son by his second wife were ever at odds, and on this I will swear before this assembly and before God."

With this, Agnes gave a little snort of triumph, folded her arms before her, and flashed her black eyes as she had done before.

"Are you saying, then, Mistress Profytt, that Nicholas Crookback murdered his father, your stepmother, and your siblings?"

A great quiet fell upon the crowd awaiting Agnes's answer. She did not respond at once but seemed to hold her breath, looking upward to the ceiling as though she were transfixed by some vision. Then she said, "I say no more, Master Vernon, than I have said. Yet I think it passing strange that of my family, Nicholas alone survives and will tell no tale, not even make a dumb show, of which I know right well he is fully capable. Why does he not make a sign if he is innocent? And if the blood is not upon his hands, why does he not point the finger at him who did this?"

Agnes herself pointed to where the bodies lay. There was a loud murmur of voices, indicating to Adam that many in the assembly were in agreement with her.

Agnes withdrew and her sister Mildred was now called forth. Vernon asked her the same questions he had put to Agnes, and as Agnes had said she would, Mildred confirmed her sister's account of how there had been trouble between father and son but was equally vague as to what this trouble was. Then Vernon called Matthew to come forth, which the clothier did.

"Master Stock, you were present yesterday at Crookback Farm and today when it was searched for evidence. Were any weapons found, bloodstained perhaps, that might have accounted for the wounds upon the bodies?"

"None was found," Matthew Stock said.

"Or any other evidence indicating murder or the agent thereof?"

"None but what has been offered here—the bodies themselves, their disposition, and the theft of some plate, suggesting perhaps that the murderer was a housebreaker."

"What plate was stolen?"

"Five silver plates, two goblets also of silver, and several pieces of good pewter."

"In which case," Vernon said. "I think we have heard sufficient. Master Stock, have you anything else to say?"

"Not at this time, Master Vernon."

"Then let this honorable jury confer among themselves as to what their verdict is and let those here keep good order and silence in the meantime."

*   *   *

90

The jury did not move from their places but whispered among themselves. Adam watched their faces, looked for some sign of where their sympathies might lie, and saw how frequently those same faces were turned toward himself and toward Nicholas. He had been informed by the clothier on their way to the Sessions House that the inquest was to be no trial for murder, only a means of determining cause of death. But Adam felt it was otherwise.

He reckoned it must be near midnight as the coroner had warned, but no one made a move in the assembly to go home to bed. All eyes seemed fixed upon the jury, where discussion continued. Finally, Miles Pynchon, a stout greengrocer who had been appointed foreman, signaled to the coroner that the jury's deliberations were concluded. The silence that fell now made the earlier quiet seem a din in contrast as everyone strained to hear what would be said.

"What say you, Miles Pynchon? What verdict does the jury give? And pray you speak it so that my clerk may not require you to repeat it."

"As to the matter of cause, sir," Miles Pynchon replied in a loud clear voice, "we say that John and Susanna Crookback, and the issue of the aforementioned, Magdalen and Benjamin, died of wounds received and by blade and by drowning even as Master Day declared, and that all was murder rather than misadventure."

"And as to the agent thereof?"

Pynchon cleared his throat, seemed to gulp some air, and said, "On this point we cannot agree, sir. With some of our number being of one opinion and some of another, saying that evidence permits no accusation, although some of our number think it does."

"Well, then," Vernon said, addressing himself to his clerk. "If such be the case, then the record must show that the verdict was murder by a person or persons unknown."

Adam Nemo heard this decision with great relief and he could not help smiling. He looked to where Nicholas was, but of course Nicholas had heard nothing and wore the same expression of fear and bewilderment as before.

Chapter 7

On the cusp of midnight, Vernon concluded the inquest, but the crowd remained about the Sessions House as though there were some ceremony yet to be performed or further announcement to be made. They remained even after Sir Thomas had admonished the people to go home and he and his friends and his servants had ridden off on all the fine horses that had turned the market cross into a paddock and left the cobbles smeared with their excrement.

Fearful of the crowd's temper, Matthew had taken Nicholas and Adam home, left them in Joan's care, and then returned to the Sessions House where he found the lingering assembly had fixed its attention on Agnes Profytt and her sister, who were holding forth with their version of the murders. Others with lamps and candles filed by the bodies of the dead, which remained in their places in the Sessions House and, according to Master Vernon's instructions, were not to be removed until the next day, although the insidious odor of decay was already blending with the smells of woodsmoke, human sweat, animal ordure, and hysteria.

Matthew noticed too the pervading air of disquiet, the sense that nothing had been settled that had not been well-allowed before. An empty ceremony, a fruitless spectacle, he thought with disgust. Who, after all, had supposed the deaths of the Crookbacks to be anything but murder? And Matthew had taken Nicholas Crookback and Adam Nemo back home with him because he feared for their safety and, as Joan had observed afterwards, where else could either go? Nicholas could hardly return to the place of his new inheritance. What Christian soul, be he witty or witless, could abide a place where memory would be more fearsome than howling ghosts of the unavenged dead?

And the strange little man called Adam Nemo, whose eyes were like slits and whose face was as brown as wrinkled leather, was now without employment, having been cast out of Burton Court peremptorily despite twenty years of faithful service. Neither man could sleep on the cobbles, and no charges had been preferred against them. Besides, Joan could see how high feeling in the town was running. She was mightily afraid of the number of strangers who had filled the New Inn and every other and left the alehouses so dry, it was currently observed, that nothing remained to drink but old ditch water and horse piss. Everywhere in the darkened town there was talk of the murders, and the jurymen, who were thought to have been privy to some testimony unheard by the general assembly—and may have been indeed, for how could those perched on the very rooftops or in the outward darkness of the street be able to hear more than a few words?—were now beseiged with questions from their curious neighbors as to what was said by official and witness.

Matthew listened a while and having heard as much as he cared, and seeing that the dispersal of the people must depend finally on their own sheer weariness of talk and of standing in the cold, returned again to his house.

"You were wise to bolt the door," he said when she let him in, explaining to him that the whole house was in bed and she had been upstairs and had not heard his knocking. But Matthew knew that was not quite true. Joan had beforehand conducted Nicholas and Adam to their little attic chamber, but daughter Elizabeth, shamelessly bright-eyed and in her afore-bed dishevelment the very image of her mother when a young girl, was sitting at the kitchen table with a bowl of chicken broth between her forearms. Matthew was too hungry himself and the savory brew too redolent of home and peace for him to question the propriety of a young girl hardly more than a child being up at such an hour. Joan served him, and the three of them sat down and what else, pray, was there to talk of but the murders?

Joan said, "I think this should be the longest day of my life."

"And of mine, Mother," Elizabeth said, her voice full of excitement. "For I have seen in it things which I never thought to have seen in this life, and heard too."

"You have seen too much, daughter," Matthew Stock grumbled between spoonfuls. "Did I not tell you to stay at home? Had I known you were in the midst of that multitude I would not have been pleased."

"You said the same to Mother, but she went to the market cross," Elizabeth pointed out. She smiled mischievously and kept her eyes fixed on the table.

"The child will learn nothing of life if she is locked in when the whole town is in the street," Joan observed. She spoke with calmness, as she always did when she contradicted Matthew's will. "If it is murder you worry about, husband, were the two of us not safer in the midst of our neighbors than hiding away in this house where an intruder might enter at his pleasure and slit our throats, having satisfied his lust upon our bodies afore?"

Matthew winced at this vision of criminal invasion and shook his head. He was cursed with a headstrong wife who would not readily submit to husbandly rule. Why should it surprise him if the child of her body should have the same willful nature? He despaired of finding a husband for Elizabeth, who with her rough good humor and independent nature seemed as unsuited to the yoke of matrimony as a dog to a doublet. What man in his right mind would marry her? Should she not become an old maid and tend neighbors' children, cluck like a hen, gossiping in the chimney corner, and grow sour in her solitude?

He dropped the dangerous subject of their lack of compliance and raised one more agreeable.

"Tomorrow I shall resume my old duties and be once more only husband, father, clothier, neighbor."

"But not a ferreter of things mysterious?" Joan said, looking up. Elizabeth continued with her broth but seemed disappointed.

"Sir Thomas told me that his friend from London comes by midday to take charge. It is all arranged. He is Simeon Fuller, a man very learned in the law and acquainted with crimes and malefactors of every sort. Sir Thomas says Fuller will set all in good order."

"Well may he say that," Joan observed, collecting the bowls, all of which were empty. She went to the cupboard, addressing him over her shoulder. "Although I trow it is easier said than done, this business of finding out who did what, and why."

"Sir Thomas thinks it will not be difficult for Fuller."

"Let time disclose whether it will be difficult or easy," Joan said. "In either case, I doubt he will do better than you would do in the same situation. Take the things you found in John Crookback's chest. I mean the curious letter from the London goldsmith to—what was his name?"

"Yet how little he made of it," Matthew said.

"Then that speaks ill of him. I know it is important."

"How do you know?" he asked, and by her expression knew he had asked foolishly. Joan simply *knew* things—not by reason but by some womanly intuition that sometimes frightened him with its uncanny power. Was it of heaven or the devil, this knowledge of what was beyond the normal senses? He prayed to God he had married no witch!

"When this matter is settled and the truth is known, you will see, husband, that what I have said is true as the Gospels. John Crookback did not use that chest to keep useless trash, but for those keepsakes precious to him for whatever reason. Mark my words. And you, Elizabeth," she said, suddenly turning to her daughter, who was slumped in her chair, sleepy-eyed at last. "You must to bed, and better dreams than the sights you have seen this day, with bodies dead and rotting in the market cross and no conversation save such as concerns murder and housebreaking. Fine views these to entertain a young girl's head."

Joan had to stir Elizabeth from her half sleep, and then, kissing her on the forehead and blessing her twice over, she pointed her toward the door and the stairs beyond.

Elizabeth gave a little wave of her hand and said, "good night, dear mother and dear father too," and Matthew felt a surge of paternal emotion as he watched his daughter go off, taking one of the candles with her, for she was a light in his life, despite his frequent complaints to Joan that he had fathered a child no man could tame.

As for Matthew, he was too wrought up to go to bed but thought he might stay up all the night, so busy was his brain. He was grateful Joan seemed similarly cursed, for he needed someone to talk to, and who better than she?

"So to what conclusion did Sir Thomas come concerning the inquest?" Joan asked before he could speak himself. "He looked unhappy with Master Vernon's conduct thereof. More than once I thought he looked disappointed that nothing more was resolved."

"He expected no indictment," Matthew said. "He told me so himself. He told me Vernon thinks Nicholas Crookback killed his family, probably with the help of Adam. But Sir Thomas is of another mind. He thinks such a solution is too simple and that the town wants the matter settled and prefers speed to truth, just to put to rest its own fears."

"And what think you?"

"I think he's right," Matthew said after a moment's hesitation in which he considered his next words. "Adam Nemo has the look of an honest man, though not of English blood. I would far rather trust him than some Italian or Frenchmen."

Joan agreed. Whatever race Adam Nemo claimed as his own it could hardly be so untrustworthy as the Italian or French.

"And as for Nicholas Crookback, I would as soon suspect

myself of the crime as him. When I look in his face I see nothing more sinister than grief and confusion. If he knew who killed his family he would find a way to communicate it. He's not as simpleminded as our neighbors think. I see intelligence in his eyes."

Joan agreed. Then they talked of what they had seen in the crowd. Matthew told her of his feeble efforts to keep order, of the dog that would not be stilled and the apprentices who broke windows. He bemoaned the shamelessness of leaving the Crookback dead exposed to public view. "And pray what was accomplished thereby but stir the grief and fears of the town and reap profit for our local merchants of drink and the innkeepers and brothels? Had the Crookbacks been malefactors, the exposure of their bodies would have served some redeeming example of vice to be shunned. But to treat innocent souls in such a manner outrages decency."

"The funeral is tomorrow in the afternoon. They will be buried in the churchyard," Joan responded, suppressing a yawn. "I must go to bed now, husband. My eyes burn from the candle and from weariness. I cannot stay up more. Come. Enough of this talk of the dead. Come to bed."

Husband and wife had set their course in that very direction when a pounding came upon the door, the sound of muffled voices was heard, and the clatter of cobbles thrown against the house. Joan looked at Matthew with alarm.

"Some trouble, I warrant," he said, nudging her toward the stairs and commanding her in a voice that brooked no denial that she should take immediate refuge above.

Matthew didn't know what trouble it was, but he thought it must be roisterers from one of the alehouses, or some honest townsmen with some grievance. He hated the thought of going back out into the cold, and as he made his way through the shop he imagined how he might appease the complainers and still stay withindoors. Promise them a pot of beer when next they met, or a patch for their doublets. The pounding sounded the note of urgency, but the casting of cobbles bespoke anger.

Despite his injunction that she go to bed, Joan had followed him as he went with his candle through the dark shop to the door. When he drew near he could see through the nearly opaque glass of the mullioned windows the flickering light of torches. He told Joan to stay back from the door. The pounding came again, and now loud voices commanding him to open. Some of the voices he recognized, but their tone had naught of friendship in it.

He gave Joan the candle, unbolted the door, and opened it. Outside were about twenty or so men and a few women. Matthew recognized Agnes Profytt and her husband, and several members of the coroner's jury. William Dees was also there and seemed to be the leader.

"What is it?" Matthew asked, afraid he knew the answer.

"We would know if you have Nicholas Crookback within."

"And Master Burton's servant, Adam Nemo," added Hugh Profytt.

A rumble of voices from the other men affirmed that this was undeniably the purpose of their visit.

"What if I do?" Matthew answered, trying to keep his voice steady. "What business is that of yours, William Dees, or of yours, Hugh Profytt?"

This response seemed not to be what either of the men addressed expected, for an awkward pause followed, during which Matthew and the men stood looking at each other as though both sides expected the other to speak next. Agnes plucked on her husband's sleeve and whispered something in his ear. The pair seemed confused by Matthew's opposition.

"I have taken them in for the night, seeing that neither has a place to go," he said, his confidence growing a little.

"Well, we like not that," said Hugh Profytt.

"What don't you like?"

"That you have taken them within your doors."

"They are my doors," Matthew said. "May I not invite within whomever I choose?

"I suppose you may," said Hugh, looking at his companions uncertainly, "yet still we like it not."

"What he's trying to say, Matthew," William Dees said as he

came forward, "is that we do not think it fitting that one suspected of murder be treated as a guest in an honest man's house."

Matthew waited until the murmurs of assent to this principle died down before responding.

"No warrant issued from the coroner's inquest," Matthew said. "I am not aware that either Nicholas Crookback or Master Burton's servant is suspected of anything, much less murder. If you have more evidence than was presented earlier this night, I suggest you take it to Sir Thomas and let him have a look at it. If he finds it material, he can let me know of it and I will turn my guests, as you call them, over to him or to any other officer."

"We have such evidence," declared Agnes Profytt in a shrill voice. Agnes's husband turned, and the men closest to the door allowed a person whom Matthew had not recognized before to advance. The man was shabbily dressed and he walked with a limp. Matthew recognized him and nodded.

"This is Sawyer," Hugh Profytt said. "He has come all the way from London to bring us evidence."

"What manner of evidence?"

Sawyer was now pushed forward and urged to speak. It was clear from the man's bleary eye and unsteady gate that wherever he had come from earlier that day, he had spent the more recent hours in some alehouse.

"I saw your Adam Nemo, as he is called, on the morning of these murders," Sawyer said, his voice thick and husky. "He was in a foul mood when I met him."

"Where did you meet him?" Matthew asked.

"Why, even as he was walking toward Crookback Farm. As I hope for heaven, he had the look of a murderer about him, and he was swearing out mighty oaths of vengeance upon John Crookback for what he did."

"Mighty oaths—against John Crookback?"

"The very man," said Sawyer.

"What did he claim the farmer had done?"

"Cheated him," Sawyer said after a moment's pause while he gulped air.

"Cheated him of what?"

"He did not say, but he threatened the honest man."

"Threatened him in what manner?"

"Why, with death!" Sawyer said, and everyone with him also looked more stirred up than before. "He said old Crook-back, whom he called a very knave, would be mightily sorry for what he'd done and would do it to no man again, nay, not in this life or in hell either, where this servant swore his victim would surely go."

"What more proof do you need, Matthew?" asked William Dees. "Will you not deliver to us these miscreants? Then let us all go to Sir Thomas and see justice done."

"This is but one man's testimony," Matthew protested, looking at the witness with contempt. Did he not know Sawyer's kind—idle, drunken sots making capital of another man's misfortune? If he had ever heard a flimsy and malicious slander it was this.

"And you swear that you heard Adam Nemo utter these words? Will you then describe Adam Nemo to me?"

Sawyer looked surprised by the question, snorted, and said, "He is a small man—by your leave, smaller than yourself—with a round brown face like a prune and eyes that are no more than slits in his head. He speaks with a heavy tongue. Sometimes you are at pains to understand his meaning."

Matthew had asked Sawyer about Adam Nemo's appearance expecting that his failure to describe him with any accuracy would reveal his story to be the self-serving slander Matthew knew in his heart it was, but Sawyer had given a decent description of Master Burton's strange servant. Perhaps Sawyer had been in Chelmsford earlier than he had said. Perhaps he had seen Adam at the inquest, or had heard him described by others. Matthew concluded that his question had been for naught. Sawyer's answer proved nothing.

"I'll tell you something else," Sawyer said, smiling grimly. "The little fellow had a big knife. I saw it at his belt. A man could do a lot of damage with a blade that length and breadth, I said to myself when I saw it. And I was afraid. It's an awful thing for a man to threaten death to an entire family."

"I thought you said he was only threatening John Crook-back?"

"Well," Sawyer said, not losing his grim smile, "I meant all of them—the wife and the girl and the boy too. He also said he had a friend at the farm, someone who would aid him in the endeavor. To see his right maintained, or so he said, but would not say what right he meant."

"Is this not evidence, Master Stock?" Agnes said. "Shall we not present it to Sir Thomas, and this Adam Nemo and Nicholas be taken?"

From all sides there were grumbles of assent to this proposition. Matthew thought it better to make peace with his neighbors than try to impugn their witness.

"I promise to convey all of what you have said to the magistrate in the morning. You have my word. Now, neighbors, I pray you, go to your beds in peace and let the law take its course."

"We are content that the law take its course, so long as the law does its duty," Dees said, looking around him for support and getting it promptly in yeas on every side. "But we must have these twain you keep within as guests if you will not carry them forthwith to the magistrate."

"Who has been asleep this hour or more," Matthew said. "Will you have me wake him when there is nothing he could do anyway until the morning? I know not which of us then would displease him and his lady the more, you or I. The men you speak of are in my custody and as secure here as they would be in Colchester Gaol. If indeed this man speaks truly and Adam Nemo uttered threats against John Crookback and his family, and if he truly claimed to have Nicholas Crookback as an ally in this business, then Sir Thomas will take all into consideration, and justice will be done."

"You say 'truly,' as though you doubted this good man's testimony," Agnes said, "or dispute our words. Are the testimonies of your friends not good enough for you, Matthew Stock? Is your heart so prideful that you give no heed to what honest men declare?"

Matthew wished that Agnes Profytt's voice was less shrill.

101

Certainly these accusations carried along the entire street and would be repeated among his more immediate neighbors, who, if lights in windows were any indication, had been awakened from their sleep by this uproar and would remember— and report to those not privileged to have heard it firsthand— every syllable of this conversation, embellishing the same to little credit to himself. Matthew did not feel himself above such as were assembled before him, but he well knew that this was a common and often devastating accusation to level against one who with good intentions undertook civic responsibility. Tomorrow the accusations would be all over the town, how Matthew Stock was declared to think himself better than he was because he stood in the place of the constable who was dead.

"How I am called to serve by those above me has naught to do with my belief or disbelief in this man's testimony," Matthew said, raising his own voice and glaring at Sawyer, who stood as silent as though he were asleep with his eyes open. "This man has had much to drink this night, as have many of you. Drink clouds our reason, as is well known. It makes us easily angered, and we act before we think. You shall more prevail upon Sir Thomas in the light of day, and with clearer heads and tongues less thick with drink, than in your present state."

"You will not give over these men to us, then?" Dees said.

"I will not," Matthew said firmly. "And I have given you good and sufficient reasons why I will not. Now go to your homes and beds. Keep the peace, or risk the law's displeasure on that account."

Dees's eyes blazed. He advanced a step, and Matthew's heart leapt into his throat at the prospect of this assault, but Agnes Profytt held the stonemason back. "Nay, William Dees. Let good Master Stock keep his guests for the present. As for presenting this evidence to Sir Thomas, we will hold him to his word. And we will even accompany him to Sir Thomas's manor house, bringing Sawyer with us."

"I give my word I will go with you in the morning," Matthew said. He told them again to go home, and this time some of them complied. Dees, Agnes, and her husband were the last to leave, taking Sawyer with them.

Matthew closed the door, bolted it, and looked at Joan, whose face in the candlelight was pale and glistening. In the excitement, he had almost forgotten she was there, listening behind the door. She was shaking; he could feel it as she embraced him.

"What is it, wife?"

"I was afraid, that's what it is."

"They are our neighbors. It is they who are afraid, and confused too—and a little drunk."

"Neighbors!" she snorted. "Hotheads, knaves, and troublemakers you mean, and that Agnes Profytt! There's a rotten branch of an infirm tree if there ever was one. Her poor husband!"

He laughed. "She is something to be reckoned with." Matthew did not tell her how relieved he was that they were gone and how frightened he himself had been, especially when William Dees, with his powerful shoulders and arms, had advanced toward him. He was too ashamed to admit the gratitude he felt toward Agnes Profytt for having dissuaded the stonemason.

"You don't think Sawyer is telling the truth?" Joan said as they made their way upstairs.

"I think he has found a way to secure free drinks at the alehouse and make himself a name in all the ballads to be spawned from this crime. But he may do great damage to our friends before he has done."

Our friends. He marveled at his own choice of words. At what point in these inquiries had Nicholas and Adam become that in his mind, rather than merely persons involved somehow in a murder? Was it simply because they had slept under his roof? Why was he so sure his own instincts were superior to those of William Dees, or even Agnes Profytt? As obnoxious as she was, yet she might be right. Perhaps he was harboring murderers.

He looked at Joan. She seemed as persuaded as he that this so-called evidence, the word of a notorious beggar and probable thief, was fabricated for ulterior motives. The pride he took in his temporary office had not blinded him to the risk of keeping the two men within his own house, had it?

"Will you take him to Sir Thomas in the morning?" Joan asked.

"I said I would, and so I must," Matthew said, sadly, wishing there had been another way to pacify the neighbors Joan had cursed as hotheads and knaves and thinking that it would be better were Nicholas and Adam Nemo in Colchester gaol, for had it been the case, both they and the Stocks would be more secure.

Nicholas Crookback was drowned in the deepest of sleeps, that kingdom where just men go when the day is ended and reason surrenders to the powers of the night; what the English called "a little death" and what Adam Nemo's own people called something quite different. Adam could see his friend, even in the candleless dark of the attic. But as late as it was, the clothier's house still creaked with movement somewhere below, and he imagined Matthew Stock and wife in their kitchen conversing in that companionable way he had observed before. They were different from other English he had known, especially John Crookback and his wife, who had often fallen into prolonged silences. The marriage of the Stocks was more like the friendship he enjoyed with Nicholas, an easy and sweet companionship, a refuge in times of trouble, as now, even when one of the friends slept.

Adam himself struggled against sleep, for he knew what he would dream. And then, almost with relief, he knew there would be no dream, for he could not possibly sleep—at least not yet. He heard the hail of cobbles, the pounding at the door and the sound of men's voices raised in angry protest, and he remembered something that he had forgotten for a long time, and the pain of it helped him to understand why.

Some of the sailors had taken him to a place where
there was a great group of men, all crowded into a
low-ceilinged, filthy chamber, drinking and singing
and wrangling. They had gathered round him,
prodding his body with staffs and knives and pulling
their eyes back toward their ears to mimick the shape
of his own. Then there had been a fight between one
of the sailors and two of the other men, and a great
noise of shouting and pushing. Confused and fearful
for his life, he had dashed from the tavern, as he now
knew it to be. He was running down a cobbled street
with the brows of houses tipping over him and ribald
laughter mixed with shouts of rage at his back. It was
an unknown language, but he knew the tone of
violence; weaponless and friendless and unsure of
where safety lay, he ran, his heart racing, his legs
weak from the long voyage he had spent with irons
on his ankles. Yet sheer terror gave him speed, and he
outran them, hiding in an alley amid boxes and
barrels and full, like the city that seemed to have no
end, of strange and to his nose putrid odors and the
unpleasantly warm damp of the English spring.

Hiding there until his stomach was so empty that
he would have gladly gnawed upon the staves of the
barrels in his hidingplace. Hiding there until he heard
a familiar voice, its naked sound not threatening but
calming, reassuring, and since he was without
strength and supposed the worst was death—and
better that than perpetual exile—he came forth at the
sound of the familiar voice and saw that it was his
particular Englishmen, the tall, golden-haired men
from the ship.

He prepared himself for death by their swords, but
death did not come. Nor did they bind his arms or
place the heavy irons on his legs but covered him in a
cloak so long it dragged upon the cobbles and took
him off to a chamber in a house, where the men
talked for a long time.

Adam lived there in that room, sleeping on a pallet
at the foot of the larger bed in which both men slept

*and eating the fish they cooked over the hearth and
learning to enjoy the thing the men called bread. For
how long? There had been no way for him to reckon
time. Long enough for him to realize that even
without bonds and manacles he remained a prisoner
uncertain of his offense and less certain still of his
future. Long enough for the strange sounds emitted
from the mouths of the men to begin to take on the
shapes of words. He thought the two men must be
brothers, so much alike they seemed; tall,
broad-shouldered, fair-haired men with strange,
light-colored eyes such as among his own people one
saw only in the faces of the blind.*

This time he could understand the angry voices, and he knew
those at the clothier's door had come for him and for Nicholas.
Adam listened. He heard the accusations, recognized the voice
of Sawyer, and understood the implication of his words. He
shook Nicholas.

"Up, friend," he said. He pointed to Nicholas's shoes, on
the floor by the bed.

Adam knew Nicholas could not hear the voices, but the boy
could recognize alarm when he saw it. Adam helped Nicholas
on with his shoes and then put on his own. He listened again,
and through the thin panes he could hear Agnes Profytt's
shrill, hysterical treble, then the stonemason's booming
threats, and finally the clothier's reassuring voice endeavoring
to appease the crowd. Adam wished the clothier well, but he
could not depend on him. Adam was like a man who falls in
the darkness and is consoled only that he has knowledge of
the hole into which he has fallen.

Motioning to Nicholas to follow, he made another gesture
urging him to move with the greatest stealth, and the two descended the stairs and made their way through the kitchen
while the clothier and his wife were at the door of the shop,
inquiring into the cause of the tumult without.

Chapter 8

ה

Matthew woke Joan to tell her their guests had vanished without a word of thanks or explanation. Their bed was empty, their clothing gone. The blanket of lamb's wool she had made with her own hands the Christmas before had disappeared. Matthew presumed they had taken it with them, and because he knew Joan had made the blanket with loving care, embroidering it with roses and leaves so real you could almost smell their sweetness, he was more sorry for its loss than for the flight of his charges.

He had awakened before her, troubled by dreams of dangerous encounters with vicious dogs and their truculent masters. Had climbed to the attic on some premonition that something was amiss.

"Where?" She asked, sleep still heavy upon her.

"Just gone," he said. "They're not in the house, or about it. I have looked in the barn and outbuildings and walked the length of the High Street. They've fled, god only knows where. They may have gone hours ago."

She wondered aloud if the two men might have heard the unruly company at the door and been afraid. Why should she have thought anyone could have slept through that, the impertinent pounding, the hail of cobbles, the accusations and threats? Was not Agnes Profytt's peremptory treble alone sufficient to wake the dead?

"If they heard," Matthew said. "I cannot blame them for fleeing. The evidence mounts against them. I would have been obliged to fulfill my promise, to convey them to the magistrate along with Sawyer as a witness."

"But Nicholas has no ears to hear."

"No, but Adam may be more proficient in making his young friend understand than we have supposed, and than he was able to demonstrate at the inquest. In any case, it is I who am in the maw of difficulty now, for when our earnest neighbors have learned I have allowed our guests to escape they will say I had a hand in it, warned them of the coming danger, and perhaps even know of their present whereabouts."

"Oh, I doubt they would do that," Joan said, climbing out of the big four-poster bed. She went to her wardrobe, opened the door, and began searching among her clothes, of which as a successful clothier's wife she had a goodly store. "Your honesty is well allowed. None will believe you had any hand in their disappearance."

"Honesty is only well allowed until it is impugned, as a pail is only held to be sound until it leaks."

He watched her while she unlaced her nightgown in the candlelight and laid it carefully on the bed. In the soft light of the taper, her bare body was plump and pleasing to his eye, round like the smooth contours of a lute. Fifteen years of marriage and Matthew was still fascinated by the sight of it, but he was too preoccupied now to be stirred to amorous thoughts. "Consider what Agnes Profytt will make of this," he continued. "What she will say to Sir Thomas, to whom she will go as soon as she learns that Nicholas and his friend have fled. Their flight will confirm their guilt. It will raise doubts about my wisdom in not putting the two into chains from the beginning. Where Agnes had only a handful of hotheads at her beck before, the whole town will now rise up to complain of me."

"Well," Joan said, plucking at the sleeves of the gown she had put on and taking the long taper to her mirror to see how her face showed at such an hour, "this burden was not chosen by you. You are not constable of the town, only a substitute. Why should you be blamed? You were given no charge. My house is no jail for miscreants. Never did Sir Thomas or Master Vernon say, 'Here are your prisoners, guard them well.' Marry, you were not even cautioned. The jurymen declared that there was no evidence to accuse any person. In sum, our guests were guests, not prisoners of this house. And cannot a guest come and go as he chooses? Then if you are blamed by Agnes Profytt or anyone else, the blame is theirs, not yours, and so be quit of your worry, husband."

"I shall be quit of my worry when this matter is settled," he said, "the murderers identified, apprehended, and hanged, as is proper. I doubt my quittance shall come before that."

The cock crowed; Matthew heard the church bells sound five of the clock. Despite Joan's encouragement, he could find little cause to hope that the disappearance of his two guests would not be taken badly—and by just about everyone concerned.

Matthew decided to make no voluntary report of the flight of the two men. Why should he, since as Joan had reasoned in her commonsensical way, he had not been charged with being their jailer? But he was hardly surprised when within an hour of his conversation with Joan in the bedchamber, he was visited by an even larger contingent of townspeople than had come on the previous night. This time, although Agnes Profytt and William Dees were notably present and a more sober Henry Sawyer, the leader of the group was Master Vernon.

"We have come for Nicholas Crookback and his companion," Vernon announced as soon as Matthew opened the door to clamorous demands that Nicholas and Adam be delivered up straightway.

"They are not here," Matthew said, searching the assembly for a friendly face. But he saw none. The townsmen seemed like strangers, all bundled up in their cloaks and heavy winter hats and many of them visibly shivering, with cold or excitement it was impossible to tell.

The crowd behind the coroner waited for no explanation but continued to give cries of anger and complaint, and the accusations flung at him were not that Matthew had negligently let his guests flee but that he was deliberately concealing them from lawful authority. Demands to search the clothier's house and even to burn the malefactors out if need be came from every direction, and sometimes from persons Matthew accounted as his good friends.

Matthew shut the door behind him and stepped out into the street so that he was practically nose to nose with Vernon. The clothier hoped his wife knew she was to prepare the house against the invasion of this unruly assembly.

It took several minutes for Vernon to quiet the crowd so that Matthew's protest that he was concealing no one could be heard. In the meantime, Matthew's more immediate neighbors in the High Street, having heard the commotion, streamed out of their houses to join the crowd, despite the bracing temperature and the difficulty of movement in the already crowded street.

"Don't believe him, Master Vernon!" cried Agnes, who stood right next to the doorpost. "We brought Henry Sawyer to him last night and Henry told him all that he had seen. Stock was fully aware of the guilt of these two men, on the word of a reliable witness. He even promised to accompany us to the manor house this morning. Let him not lie then and tell us he did not do so. A hundred persons in this company heard him."

Shouts of affirmation came from the crowd at Agnes's words, and Matthew heard still more demands that the house be searched. Now the prospect of violent entry was more immi-

110

nent. Matthew prayed that Sir Thomas would come with his servants and establish the order he was himself beyond establishing.

"I do not deny my promise," Matthew said loudly. "But the persons you seek left my house by night while I slept."

"Yea, you slept," Agnes cried, "as well you might, with murderers under your roof. Admit you told them of the evidence against them and admonished them to flee."

"I never did," Matthew shouted back, realizing as he did so that it was vain to debate the point with Agnes, who was determined to find him an accomplice in the escape of the suspects and whose shrill voice was immeasurably superior to his own when it came to being heard by the noisy crowd.

"Whether you knew or did not know of their flight," Vernon said in the magisterial tone he had used at the inquest, "you should have taken proper care of these men. While no warrant was issued against them and you were not obliged to serve it if there were, still you had been informed of this worthy man's testimony and should have expected that a warrant would be forthcoming as soon as I was apprised of this new matter. Thanks be to God that this good woman"—he nodded at Agnes—"brought me Henry Sawyer as a witness, which leaves little doubt of the malice of Adam Nemo and raises such questions concerning Nicholas Crookback's complicity in these murders as to make the imprisonment of both of them a logical certainty."

Matthew wanted to say—and would probably have done so had he the capacity to be heard above the uproar—that Henry Sawyer was at best a dubious witness of another man's perfidy, Sawyer having a reputation as an idle person whose practice was to exchange good stories for ale and beer, but he knew this was neither the time nor place. His chief concern was to prevent what was surely to be the ruinous invasion of his house, which he could hardly have stopped by impugning the character of a witness the crowd had decided was reliable. He turned from Agnes to Vernon, who despite the uproar still seemed to hold his place as spokesman for the assembly.

"My house and shop are but modest in size, good sirs," Matthew said. "Since I speak truly when I say the persons you seek are not within, I have no objection to your confirming my words with your own eyes. But I beseech you as a neighbor, do not do my house or family violence. If a multitude enters in, will the house hold them? Will they not in their zeal break windows and doors, endangering themselves as well as my house? My merchandise might be lost, or other damage done to possessions years in the getting. I pray you have respect too for my wife and daughter, who are also in the house and surely terrified by this civil unrest."

Matthew's words seemed to have a calming effect on the crowd, who became less noisy than before. Vernon seemed especially appeased by Matthew's request, although Matthew suspected that the use of the daunting phrase, "civil unrest," had done more than compassion had to curb the coroner's aggressiveness.

"Master Vernon, you are welcome to come in, you and say two or three other of these present who dispute my word."

Agnes Profytt at once offered herself as one of the inspection party, but Vernon chose William Dees and the parson, who had just come up from the church to see what all the hurly-burly was, to accompany him inside. Vernon told the others to surround the house to see that none escaped through windows or back door.

"There's none within to escape," Matthew said, trying to make his voice sound as calm as possible. "As I said, the persons you seek departed during the night, while I and the rest of the house slept. Nonetheless, enter as you please."

Vernon, Dees, and the parson now entered the main chamber of the first floor, which was Matthew's shop, looking rather shamefast, Matthew thought, as though they were unsure what to do now that they had got their own way. They glanced at the heavily laden tables on which Matthew's store of cloth was displayed, and the parson felt the material as if he were contemplating a purchase, while Vernon walked into the kitchen and peered up into the chimney as though he expected the two fugitives to be concealed there. William Dees stood awkwardly in the center of the room, his long arms dangling at his side like an ape's.

As the search party climbed the stairs, they encountered Joan on the landing. She was standing as straight as a post, her arms folded across her breast. Matthew could see that there was a dangerous look in her dark eyes.

"These men seek Adam and Nicholas," Matthew said. "I invited them in when they would not believe me when I told them the two had left earlier."

"What?" Joan said without softening her expression. "They would not believe you? Why not? Are you an infamous liar whose every second word must be questioned? God in heaven, if you are not offended by their mistrust, then, by your leave, let me express my own offense."

"We meant no offense, Mistress Stock," said the parson quickly in a conciliatory voice. "But we thought it best to be sure."

"Well, now," said Joan, looking at the parson, for whom she had no great liking, with something very like contempt. "I find it strange indeed that a man of faith cannot take on faith the word of one of his own congregation, who pays an honest tithe and hardly misses a Sabbath in his pew."

"We know your husband to be an honest man, Mistress Stock," said the parson, even more abashed than before.

"If we can take a quick look upstairs, we will be on our way again, and we promise to disturb no member of your household," Vernon said.

"Marry, good sirs, you won't find them that you seek upstairs or anywhere else in my house," Joan said. "There is only I and my daughter. We have searched the house ourselves and are more than satisfied that Adam and Nicholas have gone."

"Still, we would like to see for ourselves," Vernon said. "And we must not be denied. Your honest husband has wisely given us permission to search your house. Now we pray you, let us pass, in the queen's name."

Joan didn't move. She stood as she had stood before—if anything her expression darkened—and her full lips were pressed tightly shut. She glared at Vernon. "My honest husband may say what he wills, but this is my house you have entered and my own bedchamber you and these worthy persons with you are about to inspect. If an honest housewife tells you there is no man hiding beneath her bed, should she not be believed? Have you any reason to suspect I am telling anything but the truth? What say you, Master Parson?"

Matthew turned slightly to observe the parson's response. The man seemed completely unnerved. Matthew looked at Vernon questioningly.

Joan turned to the stonemason. "And what of you, William Dees? I know your wife and am certain she would not be content to have her own bedchamber searched in the manner you propose. Would you not defend her right to tell those interlopers where they might look instead, if they insist on invading an honest woman's home? I trow you would, given that I know you to be an honest man and a decent husband, as husbands go in this wicked world."

"I would defend her right, Mistress Stock," Dees conceded.

"I would know too by what proper authority this search is undertaken, Master Vernon," Joan said, turning her attention back to the coroner, who during this time had advanced no farther up the stairs. "Have you a warrant for the arrest of the persons you seek, or have you leave of the magistrate to search the house of an honest townsman, one in whom Sir Thomas has put much trust? What will he think when he learns that one appointed by him to find out the truth of these mysterious matters is treated no better than a common criminal? Will he not be offended?"

"We will only take a few minutes in our search, Mistress Stock," Vernon said with a glance behind him at the parson, who had already retreated somewhat down the stairs during this confrontation.

"It matters not how much time it takes, Master Vernon," Joan said firmly. "The rub is not time, but the event itself. This is my house. I have told you there is none here you seek. I do deny you permission to search it and ask you, if you honor the law, to secure permission to do so in a lawful way. What now would you think were you to return to your house only to find an unruly multitude demanding entrance on some pretext? Would you not be concerned for the safety of your family, for the integrity of your treasure, whatever it may be? By our blessed Lord, I think you would. Do as the Scriptures say, Master Vernon: Do the good you would that others do to you."

Having quoted sacred writ, Joan looked meaningfully at the parson. Then she fixed an icy stare on Vernon.

"I must insist, Mistress Stock," Vernon said.

"My good wife has said no, Master Vernon, and now I see the wisdom of her defiance. The law must be obeyed if we are to honor the queen, whose great name you invoked just now. But the law is the law, and the law of England is such that a man's home cannot be invaded without just cause. If Sir Thomas as magistrate commands me, then my doors shall be open to whomever he deems should enter. Otherwise, I must join my wife in insisting that you leave our house."

There was an awkward moment during which Matthew was unsure what his support of Joan's position might have wrought. His heart pounded, and he was damp beneath his shirt, but Joan showed no wavering from her resolve and he was determined not to surrender either. The parson and even Dees already looked as though they were ready to depart in peace, but Vernon still seemed unprepared to leave. He was a young gentleman, full of his new authority but also unsure of himself, and it was clear to Matthew that to be put to flight by a sturdy English housewife would shame him. On the other hand, Vernon had secured entrance to the house over Matthew's initial objection; perhaps, Matthew supposed, Vernon would reason that he had accomplished enough, had made his point. Matthew hoped this was the case, for he wanted no trouble with Vernon or his neighbors, or with his wife, now it came to that issue.

"Well," said Vernon, turning to glance at his companions, "I suppose we have seen enough. We will take your word,

Mistress Stock, that the men have gone, and we will report the fruits of our search to those who wait without."

Joan Stock did not alter her stare or stance during Vernon's short speech but stood as before, her arms across her chest as though the sanctity of her upstairs was as great a treasure to her as her personal virtue. Matthew suppressed a sigh of relief; his heart beat less quickly.

Vernon and the other two men descended the stairs. Matthew followed them out through the shop and closed the door behind them, but through the sturdy oak he could hear Vernon declaim that the house had been searched from top to bottom, omitting mention of the fact that to search the upper floors had not been a privilege accorded him. He then announced that he was going to the manor house to see Sir Thomas. He said that all who wished to accompany him might do so. From their window Matthew and Joan, who had come downstairs after Vernon's retreat, watched while almost the entire multitude moved off after the coroner.

"They are not willing to miss a thing, are they?" she said.

"Not a thing."

He turned to look at his wife and kissed her on the forehead, which was smooth and warm to his lips. "You were magnificent, Joan. You have more backbone than I, for I let Vernon in, and it was against my better judgment, too."

"And in doing so, saved our house from the rage of the town," Joan said. "You acted wisely, husband. Vernon is a coward, and a cockscomb. I know his kind. Like almost all men, he is a lion when he has a hundred at his back, but when only two or three remain he is as timorous as a mouse, and easily defeated if he meets stern resistance."

"But you showed a manly courage in keeping him downstairs."

"You mean I showed a womanly courage," she said, lifting her chin. "For I know not why men should garner a fighting spirit to themselves as though it were as peculiar to their sex as that bawdy part that dangles twixt their legs."

He laughed at this and granted that women could show as much strength of heart as men.

116

"And yet I was afraid, if truth be told," she said.

"Afraid?"

"Afraid he would see me shaking and think me afraid. Afraid for you and what his anger at you might cause. But I have no fear now."

"As well you should not," Matthew said. "If he complains to Sir Thomas he was forbade the search of our whole house, he will make public how he was put to flight by a housewife."

"A breed not to be taken lightly, husband."

"Curse me with the pox twice over if ever I do," he said, kissing her again.

Matthew followed his neighbors to the manor house, which lay only three miles off. It was hardly an hour's walk. But what an odd picture this excursion made. Several hundred men, women, and children and not a few dogs on a frigid morning, shuffling along the high road as though in flight from battle or plague.

It was clear that this was to be another day in which there would be no work done, despite the want of official permission. Yet this was no holiday crowd, full of merriment and mischief. Their faces were grim and determined, and growing raw from the heartless wind. Most of all, they were afraid. Matthew knew their minds. It might be warm enough indoors, but who wanted to be alone in his house with murderers at large? In company there was some measure of safety, even if the company was out-of-doors.

They had not traveled half the distance to the manor house when a group of horsemen approached, which group turned out to include the very man they sought, a handful of his servants, and another gentleman, who was dressed in a somber black cloak and a black, high-crowned hat pulled down over his ears, so that he made a fearful impression with his dark clothes and his solemn, jowly face, and eyes that seemed as cold as the wind.

Matthew, who brought up the rear of the townsmen, now made his way to the front, where Vernon was talking to Sir Thomas.

"Master Stock, there you are!" Sir Thomas said, motioning

him to approach nearer. Sir Thomas turned to the cloaked gentleman at his right. "This is he of whom I spoke to you," he told Matthew, "Master Simeon Fuller, down from the university."

The magistrate rattled off the black-robed, solemn personage's other distinctions, but Matthew made little sense of them and afterwards was unsure as to whether Fuller was a cleric or lawyer or physician, or perhaps all three. The important thing Matthew grasped was that he was given his official release as acting constable.

Matthew made the gentleman a polite bow, but Fuller acknowledged Matthew with only a quick, noncommittal glance before looking beyond him to the crowd that was now forming a circle around the magistrate and his companions.

"We have a witness, Sir Thomas," Vernon said, pushing Henry Sawyer to the forefront. "This man can testify that Adam Nemo swore to kill John Crookback, and we believe Nicholas Crookback was his accomplice in murdering his own kin."

Matthew watched while Sawyer told a tale very like the one he had told the night before, but greatly embellished, making Adam's dislike for John Crookback more forceful and malign. When Sawyer completed his narrative, several other persons, including William Dees, then came forward to assert that they also believed Adam Nemo hated John Crookback, although no one furnished any particulars as to why Adam should, nor did anyone seem to think that question was important. It seemed taken for granted rather that Adam, being a foreigner, should have enmity for John Crookback, who was as English as the soil beneath their feet.

When these testimonies were given, Sir Thomas turned to Fuller and asked him what he thought.

Fuller, who as yet had not spoken a word but sat his mount frigid with dignity, either, Matthew supposed, because of the cold or because he disliked where he was, said nothing for what seemed a long time. Nor did Sir Thomas hurry his response.

Finally he said, "I think these worthy persons have spoken honestly, but that we should not act without further inquiry. I would know more of the evidence against the individuals named, the motive for the crimes, what was to be gained or lost in committing the evil of Cain against his brother. Men do not kill other men without cause."

There was a murmur of disappointment at Fuller's words. The crowd seemed prepared to go off immediately in search of the accused. But Sir Thomas agreed that there should be more investigation before the hue and cry was raised, and in his own mind, although there was little in Simeon Fuller's intimidating appearance or rigid demeanor for Matthew to approve, he did think that the man's caution was fitting. What evidence, after all, had been presented against Nicholas and Adam but gossip and the dubious testimony of Agnes Profytt and the even less credible witness of a notorious idler like Henry Sawyer?

"Why, then they'll get away," Agnes Profytt cried.

Fuller turned to Sir Thomas as though to ask who this woman was, and Sir Thomas told him she was a daughter of the deceased family. Fuller made a sympathetic face and raised an admonitory hand. He spoke loudly. "Have no fear, good woman. Justice may be delayed so that it will be surer justice. When I am in full possession of the facts, I will act, believe me. Your wrongs will be made right."

Then Sir Thomas suggested that he and his party should proceed to Chelmsford as they had planned, and that such persons as might give any reason why there should have been hostility between Adam Nemo and John Crookback and his family might come forward. Fuller said he was most interested in anyone who might give a history of the victims, for he said that murder was often rooted in old sins and scandals. Upon which comment a number of voices were heard to say amen, and there was much nodding of heads in agreement with this sage observation.

*　*　*

119

An hour later Matthew returned home again, winded from the walk out and back and chilled to the bone, for the weather had turned the more fierce and even his own great cloak, gloves, and hat were insufficient to protect him. The skies above Chelmsford seemed heavy with snow, where before they were only a pewter gray, although all those with knowledge as to how to predict the weather had been saying for the month that snow would come that year and with a vengeance for the mild winters recently past.

He reported to Joan all that had happened on the road, warming himself by the kitchen hearth and with a great cup of hot caudle until he could feel sensation in his fingers and toes. Then he put all of his heavy clothing back on and went out.

Master Fuller of Cambridge had set up his headquarters in the manor court house on the north side of the Market cross, with Sir Thomas's servants posted by the stairs below to insure that the curious townspeople kept their place. All during the late morning and early afternoon a succession of witnesses went up and came down again to relate what they had been asked and answered, and then went home or stayed to wait for others who should testify. Matthew had not been invited to be privy to any of these interrogations and had to depend on what he overheard the witnesses say to others and what he received directly from Sir Thomas's servant, Hubert, whom he liked, and who had been appointed to bear food and drink to his master and his master's friend above and who brought back from these frequent excursions news as to who was saying what about whom.

It had seemed to Matthew from these reports that Fuller was hearing little more than idle gossip and speculation. Matthew knew that Agnes Profytt and her sister had been with the visitor at least an hour, and he was sure they delivered to him a great earful of accusations and complaints, some of which he felt certain were about his own conduct of the case prior to his release from that responsibility. And indeed, when the women came down they regarded him with undisguised disdain and Agnes whispered so a dozen around her could hear,

"That will show our little constable, he who thinks so much of himself."

The accusation stung and embarrassed him, but he said nothing in response. What was there to say?

He stayed around the manor court house with the hardier and more curious of his fellow townsmen until late in the afternoon, during which time the skies grew so dark and the north wind blew with such violence that he wondered if the end of the world had come.

But the worst was not the weather, but the company. Standing there in the most public place of the town, where under normal circumstances he would have been engaged in a dozen conversations in as many minutes, he found himself shunned by persons who ordinarily would have been pleased to converse with him, even in such an ill wind. What had he done but provide a roof and bed for two men who, under no official condemnation, chose to absent themselves without leave or thanks? That was no crime on their part, or on his.

He was about to go home himself when he saw Alice, the cook, approaching.

"Have you seen my husband, Master Stock? I believe he's here somewhere, for they came to your house inquiring if he was there."

"Who came?"

"Why, some of the magistrate's men, Master Stock. I told them for all I knew he was at home, but they said they had been there already and he was not to be found. Then try the alehouses I said, knowing that on such a day he would want to be indoors somewhere, and with a cup of warm wine in his hand."

"Did these servants of the magistrate say why your husband was wanted?"

"To tell them of John Crookback's history, which history he knows better than any living man since he is John Crookback's own cousin."

Now Matthew remembered this connection and was sorry he had not inquired directly of Alice's husband himself. At that moment the man himself appeared, descending the stairs from the upper room of the manor court house.

And then Matthew thought of the assayer's letter, that business about stones, and what Master Fuller, who was a learned lawyer—or doctor, or cleric—had said about a murdered man's history and how it contained the seeds of the violence against him. Crookback had been a mariner; perhaps his past had been an unsavory one, full of crimes and outrages that might all these years after have been avenged. Stranger things had happened. Men nursed grudges for years, biding their time until opportunity offered its forelock to the avenger, often as much to his damnation as his victim's.

Alice's husband waved to his wife. Fuller and Sir Thomas descended the stairs behind him. Sir Thomas hailed Matthew and beckoned him to approach, but it was Fuller who spoke, addressing Matthew as though he were an underling.

"Master Stock, I understand you are serving in the late constable's stead until another townsman can be elected."

Matthew said that he was, containing his disappointment that he should not be released as yet from his temporary calling.

"Then you must call out the watch and raise the hue and cry for Nicholas Crookback and the servant of Master Burton who is called Adam Nemo."

"You are persuaded then that there is sufficient evidence against them?" Matthew said.

"I was not before but am now. A motive has been uncovered," Fuller said with a note of triumph in his voice, "by which his murder of John Crookback comes within the bounds of reason. Sir Thomas has issued warrants for the arrest of both. They must be hunted down forthwith."

Matthew looked up at the sky. A light dusting of snow had begun to cover the ground and the light was fading fast. He was frozen stiff as it was, and the prospect of a search of the countryside in such weather was no more to his liking than the assignment to hunt down men he continued to believe were innocent.

* * *

Adam Nemo did not know where to run, only that he must.

Having traveled a dozen miles in darkness the night before, he and Nicholas had concealed themselves during the day in a thicket with only a thin blanket taken from the clothier's house to cover them. Exhausted, they had lain locked in a fast embrace for additional warmth, the boy's head on the man's chest, the man's hands clasped behind the boy's back. Nicholas had slept soundly, breathing with the easy rhythm of one whose sleep is undisturbed by evil dreams or a bad conscience.

But Adam had not slept. With the prospect of a pursuit his whole body was tense, and in his excited state, his memory quickened. His flight across the rocks and ice and capture by the Englishmen, who seemed as tall as the great white bears standing upon their hindlegs and as broad in shoulder and chest, returned to him. Again he saw the face of their leader, the man who later he learned was called Frobisher, and he remembered another man, his eventual benefactor, John Crookback, who had plucked him from harm's way when the London riffraff had threatened him and who had seemed to want nothing for his efforts. Only he had said, later when Adam could understand the tongue of this nation, that Adam be free. But free of what? Free for what purpose?

All these things he remembered, but his memories were disquieting, for he perceived some inconsistency in his memory, some as yet undiscovered gap. And he could not tell what it was or what it might have to do with the danger that faced him now.

Adam well knew the penalty for murder. In his twenty-year sojourn in an alien land he had seen the necks of more than one quaking prisoner stretched upon the gibbet for crimes great and small. In Colchester five years earlier he had watched a man hanged for stealing a mongrel dog not worth twenty shillings. Adam did not fear death for himself. His life had been long enough and painful. But he was determined

123

that Nicholas should not die, and his resolve to save his friend made him more determined to survive himself.

And thus Adam did not sleep for all his exhaustion, but kept a close watch on field and road while Nicholas slept his sleep of innocence.

He watched the skies too, for he had not forgotten how to read their messages. That wisdom was inbred in his nature, despite his recent years of living within doors as a household servant. He could sense rain or snow a day before it occurred, could smell it a hundred miles or so from where he was, or detect its ominous presence in the shape and color of clouds. And so he knew a storm was coming. No ordinary storm, but one of such severity that the brown earth would be covered with a deep snow—a snow so deep that it would be difficult for the warm-blooded English to move upon it. He would have the advantage then.

Some instinct told him to head north, not south or east where London was, the great city of refuge for the rural fugitive. Pursuers would expect to find him there, where his strangeness would be less-marked in a city in which there were many foreigners. But Adam had been to London. He would not see that city again.

Snow began to fall. He let Nicholas sleep until dark, and then man and boy set out into the very mouth of the tempest.

Chapter 9

ה

As to the hue and cry ordered by Master Fuller, the cooler head of Sir Thomas Mildmay prevailed, although not without some wrangling over strategy and complaints about the threatening weather. To the debate Matthew had added his own voice, and the magistrate agreed with Matthew that there would be no useful purpose in pursuing the two fugitives in the dark.

The spectators in front of the manor court house had all gone indoors; the market cross was empty. Drifts of snow were beginning to mount against the houses, and the blasts were so strong as to make their very foundations shake. It could not have been more than four of the clock by Matthew's reckoning, but the heavens were so dark and the snow so thick it might have been midnight. "We shall start first thing in the morning, snow or not," Sir Thomas said, to which resolution Fuller acquiesced, although not cheerfully, but then, Matthew thought, what was there to be cheerful about?

The storm was too severe for Sir Thomas to return to the

manor; he instructed his servants to make their beds in the manor court house, and because it was discovered that all the inns were full, Sir Thomas and Fuller accepted Matthew's invitation to come home with him. "My house is no manor house, sirs," Matthew told them, "yet it is clean and neat, and my good wife will set an ample table. There's a goodly fire even as we speak."

Sir Thomas accepted the invitation graciously, but Fuller made a sour comment about the irony of Matthew's having hunted and hunters as guests on successive nights. Which of course was true, and yet Matthew could do nothing about that. If it was irony the facts were called, then that's simply what it was. He did not have the will or wit to argue the point.

Hubert Selby, the servant whom Matthew liked, stayed with his master and put the horses of the two gentlemen in Matthew's barn. Joan was surprised by the unexpected appearance of houseguests but not, as far as Matthew could judge, put out by it. Supper had been prepared by Alice before, and the table was already laid in anticipation of Matthew's return. Joan assured them there was more than sufficient food for them all, the family and the two gentlemen and Sir Thomas's servant too.

During supper Sir Thomas laid out his plan.

"We shall need a company of good men, Stock, of which you shall be one, and we shall divide into two groups, for we do not know whether the twain have headed north, south, east, or west."

Matthew wondered how two groups of men could cover four directions, but Fuller explained, "They are unlikely to head to the east. Their faces would be to the marshes and the sea. They are unlikely to find hospitality among folk in that region, who are naturally suspicious of strangers but will be ever the more so of these twain. West offers no brighter prospect. They are most likely to follow the road—not travel upon it but in its general direction—heading for Norwich or for London, where it may be impossible to find them if they escape so far."

"I shall lead a company toward London," said Sir Thomas,

"sending a few men on before to warn the towns to be watchful of them and offering a reward for their capture. Master Fuller will lead a similar band to the north."

"And what would you have my husband do?" Joan said from the fire, where she was taking another turnip from the cauldron simmering there. Having sent Alice home earlier when it became clear that the storm would grow worse before it subsided, she had full management of the serving and had not taken a bite herself, so busy had she and Elizabeth been in serving the men.

"Your husband is most necessary to this enterprise," Sir Thomas replied, turning a little to see her. "We shall need at least thirty or more men of the town, and your husband is in the best position to call them to this duty. We shall have a *posse comitatus,* then. Yet they must be good, dependable men, not mere idlers looking for adventure and an excuse to brawl."

Matthew, who knew little Latin, did know the meaning of the phrase Sir Thomas had just used: *posse comitatus,* the power of the county, an ancient statute by which all men over the age of fifteen might be suddenly summoned to serve under arms to carry out the law. But he shuddered at the task, imagining himself going door to door before dawn the next morning, rousting out his neighbors that they should spend their day—and who knew how much longer—pursuing fugitives across the snowy waste. Sir Thomas had asked for strong, dependable men; would those whom Matthew chose to pull away from home and workplace blame him for the imposition rather than be honored by the selection, while those he spared felt no gratitude but supposed he thought them inferior? It was clear to Matthew that the execution of his duty would provide him with little joy, however it came out.

Despite the unhappy prospect of the morrow, Matthew did have the satisfaction of learning what it was that Alice's husband had conveyed to Fuller that had made the man so certain Adam Nemo had murdered John Crookback. As Joan and Elizabeth cleared the table, Fuller told the story.

"This man affirms of his cousin the local impression, that

John Crookback was a sailor in his youth, serving with Sir Martin Frobisher, who died this past year of wounds honorably received in combat with the Spaniard. Martin Frobisher sailed to discover the passage to far Cathay and its wealth but found instead a land of perpetual ice and snow, bringing back with him one of the savages of those parts. This savage, thought to have died, was in fact stolen away by John Crookback when he returned to Chelmsford to take up his inheritance. That savage is your Adam Nemo.''

"This is a story most amazing,'' Matthew said, sitting up straight on his stool. "We knew that Adam Nemo was a foreigner and hailed from the ends of the earth, and yet how does that affirm him a murderer?''

"Adam Nemo had cause to hate John Crookback,'' Fuller said. "It was he who captured him and took him from his native place, made him an exile who might have been a mighty prince among his own people.''

"And murdered the whole family for his hatred?'' Joan interjected, not caring how the heavy load of her skepticism might offend the learned gentleman.

"Adam Nemo is a savage, Mistress Stock,'' Fuller pronounced with a strange excitement in his voice. "Good English cooking, worsted hose, and Christian baptism will not change that fact. They are different from us, which difference goes beyond those features of face and form by which they are singular. Read the accounts of our voyagers among heathen peoples; learn how the savages massacre their enemies, sparing none, including children. Why, it curdles the blood. These depravities they visit upon their own brethren. If they can act with such cruelty toward their own, then why not toward those strangers against whom they have a long-seething thirst for vengeance?'' Fuller paused and shook his head sadly. "John Crookback might have expected this, dealing as he did with a savage.''

Fuller looked across the table at Elizabeth, who was sitting next to her mother and taking all this talk of savages and murders in with the greatest interest. Then he turned to Matthew again.

"You are sheltered here in this pleasant countryside, Master Stock. You have not traveled, I think."

Matthew admitted that he had not. He had hardly been beyond the bounds of his own county; that there was a larger world beyond, peopled by heathens such as Simeon Fuller was describing with such fervor, he accepted on faith. Joan's experience had been even more limited.

"Master Fuller's brother was killed by savages in Sir Frances Drake's expedition," Sir Thomas said reverentially. "He knows whereof he speaks."

"Still," Matthew said, "It seems strange that Adam Nemo should have waited twenty years to avenge himself. That is a long boil for any pot. Would he not have acted sooner, and have made a quicker escape? Why, he reported the deaths himself."

"A subterfuge, Master Stock," Fuller said, his elbows firmly planted on the table, his bald head glistening in the candle-light. "Savages may be devoid of true intelligence but that does not mean they are not cunning and devilish. Adam Nemo bided his time. A revenge delayed is no less sweet than one executed at the moment of offense. Indeed, it may be the sweeter by far, just as a wine grows the better with age."

"There were letters found in John Crookback's bedchamber," Matthew said. "Have you seen those?"

"I have perused them with great care," Fuller answered. "They serve to confirm what your cook's husband has told us as to John Crookback's service with Frobisher. The letter from the assayer, for example."

"The Italian?" Joan said, obviously as interested in this story as her daughter.

"The very same," Fuller said. "When Martin Frobisher returned from his voyage to discover the passage to Cathay, he brought home with him a large quantity of stones, as black as sea coal but heavy as metal. He knew himself not what they were, these black stones, but the chief of the investors, a certain Master Lock, believing devoutly that God had led Frobisher to gold, took a sample of this same stone all over London. Repeatedly he was told by wise men who know such things that the stone was worthless, was iron pyrites or marcasite. But he would not be satisfied until he found an assayer who would confirm its precious contents."

"Agnello," Joan murmured.

"Yes, Agnello. He claimed to have found a fine powder of gold. Since he was the only one to so confirm, even Lock was suspicious. He asked Agnello how it was that other worthy assayers had arrived at a different conclusion. Agnello said that sometimes nature needed a little coaxing."

"What did he mean by that?" Joan asked.

"I don't know what Lock supposed. Perhaps that Agnello had used some magical substance that in conjunction with the stone turned it into gold. Or perhaps he realized Agnello was simply jesting. With a man like Lock, as devoted to his money as to his idea of religion, it is difficult to tell."

"Who then was believed?" Matthew asked.

"The view of the majority prevailed, but not before rumor had it that Frobisher had brought home with him the wealth of Cathay and more. Some said he had found the very mines of Solomon, from which that ancient king derived the gold for the holy temple that bore his name. Others smelled a rat in all these claims. At last an investigation followed in which Frobisher and Lock were blamed for perpetrating a fraud. Frobisher survived the scandal, winning honor later."

"The great wonder is that the virtue of these stones should be credited in the face of so many worthy assayers proclaiming them to be without value," Matthew said. "Did not Frobisher suspect something was amiss?"

"Oh, he may have indeed suspected. Frobisher was hardheaded but no deceiver. Yet it is difficult even for an honest man to turn his back on a golden opportunity. He needed money, that was the long and short of it. As for the credulity of others, that is not such a wonder as you might suppose, Master Stock," Fuller said, resting his chin on the steepled tips of his long fingers. "While the experts in these matters cried fraud, the greater public were in an ecstasy of hope. They believed not the truth but what they wanted to believe, and who does not wish in his heart of hearts that the great El Dorado has been found, Solomon's mines delivered up, or some other dreamed of treasure trove opened to aquisitive hands? Such is the nature of mankind. Frobisher had to beat potential investors off. Everyone wanted a share in the prospective harvest. Frobisher was appointed high admiral of Cathay and the routes leading thereto. Lock himself was named governor of the Cathay Company. Special concessions were granted. They were to pay only half the custom dues for twenty years. It was a time of golden opportunity.''

Joan wanted to know when all this was. She said she had never heard of any of it, except of course, for Cathay. Who had not heard of that wondrous land and its riches?

"It was in the year 1577 and thereabouts," Fuller said, obviously pleased to have so appreciative an audience. "I remember it well. I was a young man. My own father wanted to invest, but my mother discouraged him, not because she did not believe in the stones but because she wanted the money saved for my sister's dowry.''

"What happened to the stones?" Joan asked.

"Well may you ask, Mistress Stock. They were taken to the Tower of London, placed under lock and key—as though they were part of the Crown Jewels. I do not know what has happened to them since. Surely they have been cast out by now as dross. Somewhere in England there are piles of this wretched stuff, and those who pass by are ignorant that it comes from a place more remote than their imaginations can conceive.''

"Perhaps someone has built a wall or chimney out of it, if it be good hard stone," said Elizabeth. Since the arrival of Sir Thomas and Fuller and especially since Sir Thomas's handsome young servant Hubert Selby had come indoors, she had seemed as demure as any maiden ever was around her social superiors and, as her doting father supposed, as winsome. Her mother cast her a severe glance as though to remind her that tolerance of her presence in this company did not include permission to intrude into the conversation of gentlemen.

"But the mistake was detected?" Matthew asked.

"Shortly thereafter, and believed to be a fraud perpetrated by Frobisher and Lock. There was an investigation and a great scandal. The investors were enraged, believing that they had been duped. They cared nothing for Frobisher's higher purposes. What was charting unknown seas or discovering unknown peoples to them who wanted only gold and silver and something better than ten or fifteen percent? They suspected Frobisher knew the stones were worthless and was merely trying to conceal the fact that he had found nothing on his journey but ice and savages and had brought back of any value only some sealskins. Later, Frobisher redeemed himself, showed he was as duped as any, but the venturers lost their shirts. It's a wonder he was not murdered by one of them."

"How did John Crookback obtain this letter, do you think?" Matthew asked.

"I don't know. But the fact that he had it in his possession confirms what your cook's husband has said. Other persons told me stories too. His daughters and this stonemason."

"William Dees?"

Fuller looked at Sir Thomas, who nodded back and said, "Yes, that is his name. He knew John Crookback from his boyhood, had heard all the tales of his exploits and had a vivid memory of them."

"Which he rarely spoke of to anyone else, then," Joan interjected.

Fuller's eyebrows rose at her comment. "Some men are secretive," he said. "Perhaps John Crookback was ashamed of his past. But the stonemason affirmed that Crookback had been one of Frobisher's crew, had brought back to Chelmsford the savage they called Adam Nemo, and had arranged to have him employed as servant to Master Burton."

"I wonder he did not keep him to work on his own farm," Matthew said. "Wouldn't that have made more sense?"

"Dees said Crookback's new wife didn't want him around. She was afraid of him, his strange looks and language—for he could hardly speak the queen's English then, Dees said—and gave her husband the choice of his savage or her. One can hardly blame the woman for that. That she was marrying a man with two children by another wife was already enough of a burden. Besides, she was already with child by John Crookback when she married him. So that meant a husband and three children, for a woman who was then, what? perhaps eighteen or nineteen. Not many years older than your daughter here."

Everyone looked at Elizabeth, who blushed furiously at this sudden attention and especially at the attention of Sir Thomas's young servant Hubert, who had been sitting in the chimney corner, his eyes fastened on Elizabeth, since he had come indoors.

"And was she to have this heathen lurking around the house?" Fuller went on. "She wondered what her family would think of it, and what the neighbors would think."

Joan said she supposed that would be quite a handful for any woman. Matthew agreed. The town had not been easy on Nicholas Crookback and his infirmity as it turned out later; would it not have been worse if John Crookback had kept Adam Nemo about his farm? Would not the decent Christians of Chelmsford have concluded that the pitiful condition of his son and heir was somehow the result of his keeping a heathen about to practice upon an innocent child God knows what witchcraft learned in remote parts where the devil reigned?

"It was all easier at Burton Manor," Sir Thomas said, picking up the thread of the narrative from Fuller, who used this as an opportunity to drink deep of the wine at table. "A gentleman's servants aren't quite so public, and his reputation is harder to impugn. According to Jeroboam, the steward at the manor, Adam Nemo, although a savage, learned quickly to speak English, conducted himself shrewdly, caused no trouble among the women of the house, and made himself as inconspicuous as possible. Doubtless he was anticipating vengeance all the while. Jeroboam never knew where he came from. Perhaps Master Burton did, but Jeroboam says his master fancied him, especially when Adam was a young man."

"Thus this Burton nourished a viper in his bosom," Fuller

said. "He was fortunate that it struck another before it could strike him. We shall find the viper and pluck out its fangs."

"But now we must to bed, Master Stock," Sir Thomas said, rising from the table. "The hour is late, and I want to be in pursuit of our quarry by dawn. You must rise the sooner to begin the hue and cry."

All at table had stood with Sir Thomas's rising, and Matthew assured Sir Thomas he would do as the magistrate bid and offered to show his guests to their beds, which involved a general shifting of sleeping arrangements, with Matthew and Joan's bed going to Sir Thomas, daughter Elizabeth's to Simeon Fuller. Sir Thomas's servant would sleep at the foot of his master's bed, while the clothier and his family would make beds for themselves in the attic, where Adam Nemo and Nicholas had lain before their escape. It was another irony not lost on Matthew Stock.

At the other end of Chelmsford was an alehouse of very bad reputation. There the host, Mattias Killigrew, was reaping the fruit of the recent human and natural disasters—to wit, the Crookback murders, which had brought a great number of visitors to the town, and the sudden storm, which had prevented the same visitors from leaving. The upper chamber of his establishment, ordinarily reserved for the use of himself, his wife, and their five children, he had rented out at an exorbitant sum to six men—or perhaps there were seven after all—gentlemen, by their clothing and airs, who had come all the way from London and were desperate to have a warm place to lodge for the night. They and a good twenty or thirty other men, most rough fellows and some unemployed, were crowded before a huge fire in the lower room, drinking up Killigrew's stock—the price of which he had reluctantly raised, or so he proclaimed—and listening to the accounts of Henry Sawyer and William Dees.

Sawyer had given a stirring description of the malicious statements of Adam Nemo, whom he now referred to as

"Frobisher's savage," although there was little evidence that many in the room had ever heard of Frobisher or his deeds. The edification of his audience as to the identity of Frobisher, and John Crookback's connection to him, had fallen to William Dees, who, having received an enormous amount of attention and not a few toasts and free drinks for the telling of his descent into the well to pull out the bodies of the Crookbacks, was now every bit as drunk as Sawyer. Every time Dees told the story the well got deeper, the sides more slippery and treacherous, the air below fouler and more unwholesome, the bodies more hideously disfigured.

"I would kill such a one, even when first I saw him," swore one listener to Sawyer's account after Sawyer had described the bloody wounds in the face and chest of little Magdalen Crookback and her brother Benjamin. Although John Crookback's wounds had been more terrible, descriptions of them had not aroused equal sympathy. "Such a vicious savage should not be allowed to walk God's earth," said another in the room.

A chorus of approving voices came from all sides at this assertion. Sawyer grinned, pressed his elbows down on the table, and ran his tongue around his lips to moisten them. He motioned to Killigrew to refill his glass. He had a prodigious dry mouth, he said, with all this talk and the heat of the fire, which indeed was intense.

"By Christ, hanging will be too good for them when they are caught," said Dees, including the farmer's son in the indictment. This statement was also well received, and some of the men said it was too bad that justice must wait upon the law when so many honest men and true were firmly convinced of the guilt of the fugitives. Why could action not be taken more quickly? Did no one have a stout rope?

"Will you sacrifice your life to this pestilent storm?" asked Dees of the scrawny little man who had suggested this action.

"With luck both the savage and the dummy will freeze stiff. God will not be mocked," said another man.

"It would be better were they caught and hanged," Killigrew inserted, not content to leave the issue to his patrons. "They then can serve as an example—first to savages coming to our shores, then to sons overly eager to inherit their father's lands." He looked about the room, taking in the faces of his guests, as though he expected more than one he saw to be either savage or patricide and perhaps both.

Killigrew's remark was punctuated by a frigid blast of air and snowflakes as the door opened and then was shut firmly by one so completely wrapped in a heavy cloak and his face so shadowed by his hat that he hardly seemed human at all. Killigrew gasped with surprise and a little fear, for during the past two hours no one had arrived to show that the storm permitted such journeying. Conversation among the other men had stopped during the stranger's arrival. All watched as the newcomer, cursing under his breath, unwrapped himself, revealing himself at last to be the coroner, Vernon. Master Vernon, his teeth chattering so vigorously that Killigrew could hardly understand the man and his face as white as the snow piling up without, asked Killigrew if there was room to be had, because his horse had fallen in the snow two miles from town and died there. He had had to walk the distance and was nearly frozen.

"Then you must have a hot caudle and a place by the fire forthwith, Master Vernon. My humble house, such as it is, is at your honorable disposal." Killigrew waved his hand around the room. The attention of the company was still fixed on the newcomer, and some had stood out of respect.

Killigrew ushered Vernon to one of the tables, motioning to its previous occupants to make room, and seated his distinguished guest. Already having estimated what Vernon's appearance might be worth in public recognition of his establishment, he went at once to pour a cup of the steaming liquid, bringing with him a plate of cheese and other dainties that he had hoped to use, after all others had gone to bed, to placate his wife for the dispossession of her house.

As the talk in the room resumed, Vernon slumped in the chair and seemed almost asleep, but Killigrew woke him with a companionable nudge, called him sir, and placed the plate and cup before him. He waited at hand like a household servant while Vernon sipped at the cup, pronounced it good, and then began stuffing pieces of the cheese into his mouth without complaint, although Killigrew, having sampled some earlier, thought it was aged almost beyond redemption.

While Vernon was restoring himself, the men in the room slowly gathered around the table at which he sat, as though expecting that upon finishing he would deliver to them as readily as Sawyer and the stonemason had done some further intelligence of the inquest or the gathering of evidence that had followed that day. But Vernon sat as stiff as a stone, as though the cold had reached so far down into his being as to freeze his heart. After a while, however, he seemed improved, and looking around him, he motioned Killigrew nearer and told him he had something to say to the entire room.

"Now give ear all of you," Killigrew bellowed, and he repeated this injunction until all that could be heard was the wind blowing the snow against the windowpanes and the crackle of the immense fire. "Master Vernon would have a word with us. Therefore give heed."

Vernon, who was not a tall man, stood slowly, leaning forward on the table to brace himself. "You men must know that a warrant has been given for the securing of two persons of this town, namely one Nicholas Crookback and him they call Adam Nemo. These men are now fugitives, and it behooves any man who knows where they might be to say so or himself face the strictures of the law."

As Vernon pronounced this, he raised his head slightly to have a better view of the room and then waited a few moments.

It was very quiet still, but no one volunteered information.

Vernon nodded and continued. "Tomorrow morning the hue and cry will be sounded. Any able-bodied man above the age of fifteen may be summoned to duty, and perhaps all of you. Sir Thomas Mildmay will lead a *posse comitatus.*"

"Shall we bring our pikes and staffs, Master Vernon?" asked William Dees.

Vernon turned to see who had spoken, recognized Dees,

and said that Sir Thomas would instruct them all on their duties.

No one said anything about the storm and whether that was to make some difference. Killigrew thought about this, surveying the assembly, most of whom seemed eager to be summoned and even more of whom seemed so far in their cups it was anyone's guess as to whether they understood what they might be getting themselves into.

Then Sawyer called out, "Master Vernon, is Master Stock to accompany the *posse?*"

"I think it likely," Vernon said.

"Well, then, finding the fugitives will be the harder."

Several of the men wanted to know why Stock's being along should hinder the expedition.

Sawyer laughed as though the question were a ridiculous one. "Why, don't you know Stock? He's your little clothier with the shrewish wife, he who thinks so much of himself because he's richer by the year while some of us who are no less honest grow the poorer for his advancement. The miscreants we seek were in his very house, eating and drinking and making merry, as the Scriptures say. Yet Stock let them go without even so much as securing permission from Master Vernon here or Sir Thomas. Now then, if Stock's to be with us, I say we have more than the raw elements against us."

At this comment several voices were raised in protest. One man said he had had dealings with Matthew Stock and that he was as honest as the day was long, whereupon Sawyer said that the days did not seem the length they used to be and there was an outburst of general laughter at this witticism.

After this, Killigrew ushered Vernon up the stairs, with Vernon limping along like an old soldier although he could not have been more than five and twenty. The rest of the men continued to talk, the discussion focusing on where the fugitives might have gone and how they should be treated when they were found and whether Matthew Stock was to be trusted or no.

Toward midnight, Killigrew gave a mighty yawn and announced that he was dog tired and that his store of liquor was exhausted. He said it was time for bed, ignored the few voices of protest, woke roughly those who had fallen asleep at the bar or at tables, and held the door open as most of his customers filed out to make their way home, wherever home was. Then he extinguished the lamps, and with candle in hand led the gentlemen who had rented lodgings up the stairs, praying they would not be disappointed at the furnishings, which even he acknowledged as being meager.

As he went upstairs he thought about the next day, wondering if he would be summoned. He thought of himself as hale and hearty for his age of fifty; on the other hand, he had no stomach for a march into the snowy wilderness. His body didn't take the cold as it used to. He remembered the joy with which his customers had heard that the hue and cry was to be raised and wondered again if the men understood what they were getting themselves into.

The snow was falling so thick and fast that Adam could hardly see where they went. Both the wind and the danger of being seen had made the carrying of a lantern inadvisable, even if they had had one. He kept one arm extended before him, groping in the whiteness like a blind man. With the other he held firmly to Nicholas, determined that they should not be parted.

He was sure of his direction, but not his destination. He was heading north, but what would they find there? His instincts told him only that the howling gale was more friendly to him than a roof over his head in Chelmsford.

Adam had never seen such a storm in England, an island of mild winters, more damp than frigid. But the unusually cold, blank landscape reminded him of his native island, and he remembered things he had not remembered in years.

He had been fishing with his brother, in the little leather boats the English so marveled at, the boats that enclosed a man around the waist, the boats that

made his people look half human, half boat. A storm
had come up over the island, blowing down viciously
off the ice until it nearly took his breath from him
and his extremities were almost past feeling. He
remembered his brother's warning. The sea had
become choppy, the wind whipping it into a foamy
chaos. Adam's boat was sturdily made. He had built it
himself, and its design and artful construction
coupled with Adam's experienced handling of it kept
him alive for a long time, a long time after his
brother whose name he could almost remember
disappeared in a great swollen mountain of water.

   Adam had brought himself and his craft to a haven
in the rock where a cliff protected him from the wind,
and the sea was calmer. He remembered sitting in the
crevice, not daring to get out of the boat, although
there was a shelf of rock at hand that would allow
him to do so. He had not wanted to think about his
brother; he had not wanted to accept the certainty
that his brother could not have survived so mighty a
wave. He understood the strength of the storm, but he
had let his brother die.

   He had let his brother die.

He led Nicholas by the hand, from time to time shouting
words of encouragement. He had not forgotten that Nicholas
was imprisoned in a world of silence, but he was enough of a
Christian to know that miracles sometime happened. If this
storm itself was prodigious in its fury, why could these untoward circumstances not unleash something long stifled in
Nicholas's body? And so he called out, but there was no answer, and sometimes the snow was so thick he could hardly
see his companion's face or its expression of wordless terror
and confusion.

Chapter 10

ה

It was inevitable that William Dees should be chosen to go with them; he was strong and dependable, he had voiced strong opinions, and Matthew could trust him to be of a mind to go, since John Crookback had been his friend. Besides, Dees would be able to bring word to others, saving Matthew the trouble of tramping all over town with the hue and cry.

The wind had died sometime during the night but the snow was falling still, and rooftops, cobbles, and fields beyond were robed in a ghastly whiteness that struck Matthew to the quick of his soul when he saw it in the foredawn moonlight. There would be no need for torch or lantern, for his way would be clear enough. Matthew had made himself warm with as much clothing as he could put on his back; leather-gloved and muffled in the heaviest wool, he left only enough of his face exposed to be able to see. He had drunk long and deeply of the hot caudle, hoping it would warm his belly and protect him, but he was hardly ready for the appalling cold when he stepped forth into the street.

Joan had wept when she wished him Godspeed at the threshold. She had a fearful look in her eyes that had made his courage almost fail. He went out the door into the softly falling snow with a heavy heart and a fervent promise on his lips that if he ever came home again he would do so resolved to be a better man, if it killed him to be so.

He had been right about Dees, who was already up and about when Matthew, having trudged all the way to the end of the town, had knocked at his door. Smoke poured forth from his chimney, and standing on the doorstep Matthew could hear the voices of Dees's wife and children within and he could smell something savory cooking for the family's breakfast.

Matthew had to say who he was, given that so little of him showed forth from his garb, and then told the stonemason outright what was needed. In no time at all Dees was ready to go, encased in a cloak heavier than Matthew's own and with a fur hat pulled down so as nearly to be one with his beard.

"Sir Thomas will provide us with horses," Matthew said.

"Well he might," Dees said. "It will make travel the easier in these drifts. It is the worst snow I can remember." Dees had no sword but did possess, he said, a crossbow and six arrows with forked arrowheads, a knife as sharp as a razor, and an arm as strong as any man's in Chelmsford. Matthew knew the claim was true. He had seen Dees shoot and knew that the stonemason had been suspected of poaching deer in the neighborhood. Matthew himself had brought no weapon beyond his knife. He had none in his house, not liking them very much and having no skill with bow, sword, or pistol. He supposed the fugitives would offer little resistance, and he himself was wary of weapons in inexperienced hands. Was it not as likely that one or another good honest townsman would shoot himself in the foot—or worse, shoot his neighbor—as that weapons would be needed to bring Nicholas and Adam to ground?

"Sir Thomas will also furnish some weapons, and of course the gentleman in the company will be armed." Matthew gave the names of six other men of the town and asked him to pass the word among them. "We will gather at the market cross. Sir Thomas would leave at dawn and wants all in readiness."

From William's house, Matthew proceeded to Abraham Pierce the grocer's and then on to the home of William Fytche, mercer. Fytche made the excuse of being sick abed, a condition his wife confirmed, although Matthew suspected the sickness was a pretense to avoid going out-of-doors. Fytche was ever complaining about the cold even in the milder weather of May or June.

On another occasion Matthew would have investigated the excuse with more care and had the mercer dragged from his fireside if need be; there was simply no time now.

Each of the men summoned was then asked to pass the word to three others, and by five o'clock more than thirty men were in the upper room of the manor court house, where a huge fire was roaring and the men all standing around talking about the murders and what direction the fugitives might have taken. Also present was a group of about the same number of men, demanding to know why they hadn't been included in the company.

"Sir Thomas wants a small number of men. More manageable, he says," Matthew explained to those not chosen, who blamed him for their having been excluded and grumbled that they could not see why they were not as good as the next man for such service.

Within the half hour Sir Thomas and Fuller arrived, and Master Vernon from the other end of town, where, he complained, he'd spent a horrid night at a filthy alehouse, on a mattress so full of vermin that he had not slept a wink. His complaint was greeted with a great burst of laughter from Sir Thomas. The knight said Vernon had chosen an odd time to fall from grace—the alehouse was hardly better than a brothel and everyone in town knew it. "Are you sure what was stirring was vermin, not some hot whore?" the magistrate asked with a derisive grin.

This question, to which those present responded with another great burst of laughter, sat very poorly with Vernon. He gave Sir Thomas an ill look and marched off to talk to Dees, who was shooting dice with the grocer. Matthew had watched the exchange between Vernon and Sir Thomas and thought it bode no good for the whole enterprise, promising as it did a continuation of the acrimony between the two men. Besides, how far could they travel in the snow, even on horseback? With snow still falling, there would be no tracks that would not have been covered within minutes of their making. Nicholas and Adam Nemo could hide in a hedge or thicket and the search party might pass by within a few feet and never see them. Further, there wasn't any real proof that the men had left town: No one had ordered the town searched.

It was growing light when the last few stragglers reported for duty. One of these was Matthew's apprentice Peter Bench, whom Matthew had chosen because he trusted Peter as much as he trusted any man and because Matthew doubted there would be any business the next few days, given the weather. What business there was, Joan and Elizabeth could handle well enough, since they knew cloth almost as well as he.

Peter was not terribly happy about his summons. A tall, quiet young man, he disliked violence or the prospect thereof and was of so inoffensive a disposition that Matthew was hard put to get him to set a mousetrap. But Matthew knew Peter would voice no complaint. Peter arrived in the company of Hugh Profytt and Miles Carew, the sons-in-law of Crookback. Matthew had chosen them not so much for their hardihood as to meet the predictable objection of Agnes Profytt that kinsmen of the deceased had been excluded from the hue and cry by some insidious design to frustrate her rightful revenge. But neither Hugh Profytt nor Miles Carew appeared vengeful in their demeanor. Hugh Profytt seemed no more pleased about the summons than was Peter Bench, but Miles Carew greeted everyone boisterously. He seemed excited at the prospect of the trek through the snow.

The magistrate now addressed the company and gave them their instructions. He said he would take charge of one half of the men and he put his friend Fuller over the other half, divid-

144

ing his servants, of whom there were about ten, between the two companies.

Sir Thomas assembled his forces with remarkable dispatch, as though he wanted to show Vernon how such matters might be expeditiously handled, and there seemed to Matthew to be neither rhyme nor reason to his choice. Matthew, along with Vernon, Peter Bench, the sons-in-law of the Crookbacks, and William Dees were placed under the command of Fuller, which appointment Matthew regretted because he would have much sooner been with the magistrate; he felt distinctly uncomfortable around Vernon and especially around the Crookback sons-in-law. Matthew was sure the two young men would report every detail of his behavior to Agnes Profytt and her supporters.

And then there was Sawyer, the beggar redeemed from poor clothes and public contempt by his new celebrity as a witness against the fugitives. Matthew had almost missed him in the growing crowd of excited men, where he now seemed to be regarded as a townsman. He had not been Matthew's choice. To Matthew his presence was no help in the present circumstances, and he felt a twinge of resentment at one who had wormed his way into public affection with a tissue of probable lies, one who was no better than a vagabond and likely thief that under other circumstances would have been driven from town as a danger to public safety. Vernon or Sir Thomas must have invited him, Matthew supposed, and indeed Matthew learned through a comment of the magistrate's servants that Sawyer was there through Sir Thomas's express command.

Sawyer was outfitted better than he deserved to be, in a good warm coat and boots that rose high on his calf and gloves of good leather. Other men, perhaps most in the troop, were more poorly garbed, although they had decent callings, honored the queen, and contributed to the good of the town. Not so with Sawyer, who had earned a patron. His expenses were being provided for; at the thought, Matthew felt another surge of disgust.

"My company will take the road to London and the regions

145

thereabout," Sir Thomas called out loudly. "Master Fuller's party will search to the north. Whoever finds the fugitives will send word to the other party. My own servants shall have their pistols, and each of the others shall have a horse and those who have not their own will have a sword or pistol provided them."

There was a good stir of excitement at this announcement, and the animated talk that had subsided at Sir Thomas's words now resumed, with several of the men complaining that they were not good riders and declaring that they hoped they might have gentle animals to bear them. Most voices, however, expressed the need for swords, for almost every one of the townsmen wanted one, although Matthew guessed that few knew little about using them other than which end to hold on to. None of the men had been soldiers that he knew of; almost all were peaceable men like himself. Matthew wondered if this was a *posse comitatus* setting forth or an army anticipating an opposing force of equal magnitude. Nearly forty armed men, evenly divided into two companies, was considerable strength to bring against a soft household servant and a mere boy who, for all Matthew knew, had no weapons at all and neither inclination nor skill to use them. Was there not something singularly unfair about a lion setting out to stalk a rabbit?

Yet Matthew kept these reservations to himself.

Fuller spoke up to say this was a very good plan that Sir Thomas had conceived and several of the magistrate's servants said by God it was a good plan, but Matthew remembered that Fuller had recommended it himself and he had grave doubts as to whether any plan could deal with the seemingly insurmountable problem of the snow. There would be no tracks to follow as long as the snow continued to fall, and one could see only a short distance. It all seemed a futile effort to him, who continued to doubt that Nicholas or Adam had anything to do with the murders. He imagined all the company lost in the white wilderness, foundering waist-deep in drifts, the horses having run off or broken their legs because of the ice.

146

It was an hour before the two companies were mounted and armed, during which time there was a great exchanging of horses and weapons among the townsmen, some of whom now demonstrated how unaccustomed they were to riding the beasts, struggling to mount them and stay in the saddle. This was a spectacle that provoked not a little laughter from Sir Thomas's servants until their master reprimanded them for it, and it gave equal pleasure to the townspeople who despite the weather had come outdoors to watch the proceedings.

Fuller, sitting very heavily on a horse Matthew thought much too small for the load it bore, seemed happy to be in command. He was dressed in a long black cloak of beaver on which the falling snow had created little white splotches, and his face was unmuffled and ruddy, as severe in its expression as though etched in stone, although Matthew didn't know whether Fuller's firmly set mouth demonstrated grim determination or an effort to control chattering teeth. He disposed his troops behind him with an easy confidence, giving orders in short bursts of speech that went generally unheeded, such an air of excitement there was. At his waist was a sword in a scabbard and a belt of fine-tooled leather that Matthew surmised must have cost a great sum.

A trumpet sounded, and Mildmay started out with his company. The crowd watching cheered wildly; then Fuller gave an order for his own men to move, pointing his hand in the direction they were to go, and another great cheer went up, but many of the wives and daughters of those in the two companies seemed struck with grief.

Among these was Joan. Matthew spotted her as he passed by his shop. She was standing with the door open looking out and the cold air coming in, watching him as he rode by. He raised his hand in farewell and smiled as much as he could bring himself to, but Joan only nodded. Elizabeth, her arm around her mother, waved and smiled back and called out to heaven to spare her father and the company. Joan made no gesture and spoke no words at all. She just stood there with a stricken look, as though she were frozen solid, letting the cold in and the heat out and not seeming to care a whit.

The sight of Matthew wrapped up almost beyond recognition in his heaviest cloak and his face muffled like a Saracen moved Joan to more than pity. He was in the thick of the troop, which rode three abreast; for that reason she almost missed seeing him.

The troop blurred in her vision. Her husband seemed so small atop the horse. Men and their mounts fused into a single black body moving through the town like a great beast, the rattle of their trappings and the hoofbeats of the horses muffled on the snow-covered cobbles. She did not cheer with the others, did not call out as the other women had done to their men. Everything she had to say she had said before—the admonitions, the vows of love—and now it was more than she could do to restrain the tears, which would surely have frozen on her face were her cheeks not earlier warmed by the fire. That husband could not tell wife when he would return was hard; worse still was that he could not be sure whither he was bound. Vernon and his men vanished; it was if the snow had swallowed them up and would not deliver them forth again. Yes, she thought, that was the worst of it.

She had brought with her to the doorstep much of the heat of the fire and though dressed more lightly than her husband, still she did not feel the cold as much, except that in her imagination she saw the snowy waste through which he must travel, he and the other men, and she knew that although the troop would meet no resistance from the fugitives, there was grave danger in this weather. For this thrust of nature was not the usual damp of the season or dusting of white, but a blast many times more frigid and malign. The snow was heavier than she could ever remember having seen it, and in its blinding thickness calculated to frustrate the will and lure the unwise into disaster. Joan saw now that the circle of evil that had brought about the murders at Crookback Farm was still widen-

148

ing, that there might well be more victims dragged within its cruel circumference.

The cheering died away as she shut the door, only then beginning to feel a cold more profound than the elements. She looked at Elizabeth, who was smiling.

"Father will be well," Joan's daughter said in that low and melodious voice that every day seemed to grow more like her mother's, or so Joan's doting husband had observed. "Don't worry, Mother. Trust God to bring Father home again."

"Well may I worry in such foul weather," Joan returned, moving beyond the wide-eyed replica of her own girlhood, who followed after. "A man can die in such cold as easy as not, and go to heaven if he has been just and good. That may be God's will, yet it is not mine, and that's what matters now. I have heard of it, what happens to those that die in the cold. Their bodies harden like wood. Their bones crack like twigs. They thaw only in their graves."

These words spoken, Joan would have fain retrieved them: turning on the threshold of her kitchen, she saw at once the effect they had on Elizabeth, whose cheery disposition—an inheritance from her father—was no match for so grim a picture of mortality. Elizabeth seemed frightened now too.

"But you are right," Joan said, forcing herself to smile. "All will be well, as you have said. Your father sat most confidently upon his horse. He showed not a whit of fear in his leave-taking. Did you not see him, and were you not as proud as I? Shall we be less courageous than he?"

"You did not cheer when he passed by," Elizabeth said, tears welling in her eyes. "You did not wave at him or bid him Godspeed."

"All these I did in my heart, daughter," Joan said. "And when the heart speaks it speaks more loudly and with greater eloquence than the tongue."

Elizabeth approached and embraced Joan, and as the girl's cool cheek was pressed next to her own Joan could feel the wetness of her tears. She looked into Elizabeth's eyes that were her father's eyes, as much as the oval face was Joan's.

"You are a dear daughter to me, Elizabeth," Joan said. "And a good friend too. Trust in God, your father will return safe and sound."

Alice had been instructed not to return to the house until the snow had stopped and melted, so Joan now occupied herself in the kitchen, while in the absence of Peter, Elizabeth was charged with opening the shop and setting out the goods, which were arrayed on three long trencher tables that occupied practically the whole main room of the house, together with a little table at which Matthew was wont to sit and keep his accounts.

"Who will buy cloth on such a day, Mother?"

Who indeed? Joan thought, not answering, too lost in ever present fears.

She set about to bake bread, good mind-dulling work that would allow her to make use of her time and dispel her darker imaginings. There were after all two mouths to feed, and Matthew would not be helped by his family's starving in his absence. But she could not rid her mind of the final image of the horsemen disappearing into the whiteness as deep in its own way as the dark of night. How must her dear man feel now? He could not be a mile from town, and yet in such weather that mile must seem a hundred. She imagined the troop strung out along the road, which would be beyond discernment save for the hedgerows. She imagined the exhalations of the horses forming steam even whiter than the snow and the breathing of the men in and out and the anticipation that must quicken their pulses. All this she imagined as though she were astride a horse herself, encased in the unnatural cold and near blinded by snow.

And this thought occurred to her in a moment: If the wretched, underdressed man and boy sought in the storm were innocent of the hideous murders, was the real murderer in the company that sought them?

Elizabeth came into the kitchen to announce she had set all the cloth upon the tables but that she doubted anyone would come. She sat down on the stool by the fireplace and asked

Joan about the fugitives. She had slept under the same roof with them, and the thought of that degree of intimacy frightened her.

"They are just a man and boy, cold and frightened," Joan said as her strong fists pummeled the dough.

"Then why are they being sought?" Elizabeth asked. "Surely Sir Thomas knows what he is about. Would he hunt them down if they were innocent?"

"Pray God no," Joan said. "And yet even a knight may err, his knightliness notwithstanding. No man knows all truth, nor woman either."

Matthew had told Joan everything he had learned the night before about the accusations now made against Adam Nemo and Nicholas Crookback. They had spoken of these things until long after ordinarily they would have been asleep. But they had not discussed the murder with their daughter, although after her presence at the table the night before and her exposure to all Sir Thomas's theorizing, Elizabeth had formed her own views. She was, after all, old enough to wed and bed and give birth and govern a household and, by God's bodkins, to say what she thought and to whom. She was, in a word, a true daughter of Joan Stock of Chelmsford. Let England beware.

Joan told Elizabeth about what she and Matthew had found at Crookback Farm. Elizabeth listened intently. When Joan had concluded, Elizabeth said, "Then you think that if revenge was the cause, Adam Nemo would have acted before, and that Nicholas was too dutiful a son to raise his hand against his father, mother, and siblings?"

"So I believe," Joan said, pausing from her labors as much to emphasize her conviction as to rest her arms. "This blaming of Adam smacks of the wish for an easy solution. Sir Thomas wants to tie the matter up neatly, have the town go on about its business. I know how men think. They love nothing better than the stone house of certitude—even when it is founded on sand. Women, now, are different. They do not hurry in their reasoning. They look all about them and make a shrewd face, building slow but sure. Besides," she said, returning to the main point, "that Adam is a culprit does not square with his behavior after."

"When?

"When he brought the news to church," Joan said. "Why would he trouble himself to do that, he that is thought to be so cunning, since it would only fix him with surety at the scene of the murders? To my way of thinking, were he guilty he would have fled and let the devil find the bodies at his leisure. He would have let the blame fall on the surviving son, who, loving Adam, would hardly have incriminated him even if he had the wit and the voice to do so. It was Adam who led Matthew to the well. It was Adam who prayed him look down. Believe me, daughter, I was there when the bodies of those unfortunates were brought up on William Dees's back; I saw Adam Nemo's face, and Nicholas's too. May I never live to see my grandchildren if those two are guilty of this thing."

"Then who killed the Crookbacks?" Elizabeth asked, leaning forward on her stool as though she were about to rise.

Joan admitted she did not know. "He may be among the hunters, but he is not one of those that are hunted. Perhaps it was he who set things about so that it would be thought Adam and Nicholas did it."

"Oh, Mistress Profytt, you mean?"

The question slipped from Elizabeth's lips. She looked at her mother curiously. Joan knew what Elizabeth thought of Agnes Profytt; Elizabeth and Agnes had never gotten along, even when both were virgins.

"No, I don't think Agnes did this either."

Elizabeth looked almost disappointed. She said, "Nor their husbands, who wanted their wives to inherit the land and hated Nicholas because he would do so?"

"No," Joan said, slowly, because something was forming in her mind, something large and certain, though there was no proof she could offer but her own intuition that it was true. This thing had no physical shape; it offered no picture to her eyes. But it was real and true and somehow the feeling of it clarified her mind.

"By someone who knew John Crookback years before," Joan said. "By someone who may have sailed with him on Captain Frobisher's ship."

The image of a great vessel in a high sea passed before Joan's eyes. A tall man stood at the helm, surrounded by his crew. Then the ship sailed on as quickly as it had appeared. She had recognized no faces among the ghostly crew.

"But why, after all these years?" Elizabeth wanted to know. She looked at her mother appealingly, as though the answer to her question were as essential to her life as was the bread that Joan now set by the hearth so that it might rise and assume its proper shape.

They had walked all night, blinded by snow and often foundering in the drifts. With the day and a lighter fall of snow, Adam could see how little progress they had made in the confusion of the storm. He had lost his bearings. They had not gone in circles; but neither had their course been true. They stood in a field; one he knew; one that in another season would be green with barley and rye but now was as flat and barren as any waste in his own country. Only a distant row of hawthorne broke the monotony of the landscape, and that could hardly be seen.

He no longer had to lead Nicholas, who seemed finally to have grasped their peril. Nicholas struggled alongside Adam now, his breath condensing in a fine mist, seemingly impervious to the cold, although having given his gloves to Nicholas, Adam now found his own hands so numb as to be past feeling.

If indeed it was the field he remembered, he knew there was a manor house somewhere near it that lightning had struck and burned the most of, leaving half standing and the rest all charred timbers and rubble. Having fallen into other misfortunes, the owner had sold his land to the highest bidder, and Adam had heard his master complain that the present owner had no use for it except for the sheep he grazed upon it in summer, which sheep he valued above the house.

Beyond the decayed manor was a forest of some extent that

his master had hunted in with much pleasure. Adam had once accompanied Burton there, holding his master's horses as the man and his companions gutted the huge buck the brace of greyhounds had brought down and squabbled over who should have the antlers. The forest was a deer park gone to ruin like the house nearby, with many trees fallen and a great many thornbushes and other unruly vegetation, and the fallow deer and wild deer, Adam had heard, had now all been slain by poachers because there was no gamekeeper in his lodge and hardly a soul to complain of the thefts.

After a mile the snow ceased and the sun began to emerge weakly in the pale sky, so that Adam could see the manor rising up above the plain on a knoll, all tumbledown as he remembered it but more bleak and desolate in the snow and ice. He could see the part of the house that still stood and knew there would be shelter there and an ample supply of wood from the old fallen timbers. So they should have warmth and rest before he determined what to do next, and there would be hares, conies, and other creatures at least in the deer park, even if the deer were gone. Adam knew how to fashion a snare out of twigs and branches, placing it over the creatures' burrows to entrap them when they emerged. He could strip the skin from the still quivering body of the creature and have it roasting almost before the little heart had stopped.

He was not certain that they were being pursued, but he thought it likely, given the mood of the crowd outside Matthew Stock's house the night they left. He looked behind him from time to time, relieved that the snow covered their tracks within a few minutes, but then the snow had turned to sleet and the hard crust that was formed thereafter left clear imprints of their footprints. He could do nothing about that, but he hoped it would snow again, or the sun would come out and melt it all. Somehow he knew neither was to happen.

*He had become conscious of the men some time
before they appeared, coming out of the sea in their
little craft, which rode high and proud upon the water*

154

and which they caused to advance with flat-ended sticks they pushed and pulled with their hands. When he saw them, he stopped and waited while they approached, curious, even fascinated by their appearance. They were the tallest men he had ever seen, with skins that were pale like the undersides of fish and their upper lips, jaws, and necks covered with hair like beasts. They made barking noises with their mouths, sound without meaning, and their eyes seemed full of confusion and anger. He had not accepted what they offered in their outstretched hands, knowing somehow it was dangerous to do so. Among his people gifts were to be accepted with caution. A man never knew what was expected of him when a gift was given.

The English had made the first sudden move, but his own response came before he had had a chance to plan it. He was running over the ice, the cold air searing his lungs, he running faster than he had ever run. He would not have been caught had he not lost his footing. And then he was on the rock, with the man pressing his knee into the small of his back, pinning his arms and grinding his face into the rock The man started to pound him on the head and shoulders. Adam endured the blows without crying out, but his eyes were full of tears and he could taste blood in his mouth and feel a searing pain in his cheek. He was powerless to free himself from the tremendous strength of the Englishman, who kept screaming the sounds that conveyed nothing but rage and whose body and mouth smelled vilely, a strange odor Adam had not smelled before.

And then the man who was their chief, he who was called Frobisher, ordered Adam's attacker off, making the noises Adam could not understand. Adam's face had been bloody; his back and shoulders ached where he had been repeatedly struck. They had taken him into their boat and then into the larger craft, larger than any he had ever seen, the length of the village of

*his people and with almost as many men but none of
their women.*

In his mind's eye he saw the attacker's face—the image suddenly came to him, in every detail, the face he had not been
able to remember but which now was as vivid in his memory
as though the incident had happened a few moments before
and the field of snow through which he passed was the very
icy slope on which he had been captured twenty years before.
Yet he still could not remember the words, which had had no
meaning to him then. Was he ever to know the thing Frobisher had said to Ralph Hawking to keep him from killing the
savage beneath him?

Chapter 11

ה

After about an hour's march, during which by Matthew Stock's reckoning the company could hardly have proceeded more than two or three miles from the town, the snow ceased and the morning assumed a startling, almost impudent clarity. But if anything it became more bitter cold and the forced merriment that had characterized the company's departure vanished with the realization that this hue and cry was no holiday sport, but a hardship to be endured and a mission with mortal consequences. Japes, gossip, and bawdry gave way to complaint, and then to a grim silence, as the men bent forward to preserve the heat in their bodies and the horses struggled to maintain their footing in the snow, which was covered now by a thin layer of ice.

Then Fuller called the column to halt, saying the animals needed rest. He ordered William Dees and Sawyer to dismount, remove the faggots borne by the two packhorses, and set about to build a fire beside the road. This the two men did with dispatch, and soon Matthew stood with the rest of the company around the fire, watching it spread from the kindling to grow into a generous bush of flame. The woodsmoke caused his eyes to burn, he stood so close. He took solace in the crackling and snapping of the dry wood, in the opportunity to give his poor buttocks a rest from the saddle. He breathed a prayer of relief for the reviving heat and thought of Joan, hoping she would have the wisdom to stay indoors, to lock the house, to keep safe until the actual murderer or murderers were found.

Sir Thomas's servants had brought wine in leather bottles, and the bottles were passed around the group, who, warmed both inside and out, now became more companionable again. Some of the men talked of what they would do when the fugitives were caught, but most refused, talking about the weather and how unusual it was, as though even to mention the danger to those they'd left behind would have the effect of making it more grave. There was a general agreement that this was the worst snow they had seen. There was much discussion of what it portended, oddities of nature not being without their meaning.

During their rest, Matthew talked to Hugh Profytt and then to William Dees, and then to both together. Nothing was spoken about the murder or the men accused of it; rather the talk was of their horses and their relative merits. It was a strange conversation, Matthew thought, under the circumstances, this talk of horseflesh when somewhere ahead of them—or behind, who really knew?—there were two poor wretches, hungry, cold, and surely frightened to the quick, and there was the danger to the families in town.

The men warmed themselves and talked, but not their general. Fuller remained aloof, stiffly conscious of his command. A bulky figure and bearlike wrapped in his great shaggy cloak, he remained a little farther from the fire and drank none of the wine but seemed to be concentrating on some issue in his own mind, screwing up his brow like a mathematician considering how a fortification should be laid out. After a while, beckoning him to his side, he asked how Matthew did with unwonted friendliness and then how he thought the other men were bearing up.

"I think they do right well, Master Fuller," Matthew replied, casting his eye over his companions, some of whom were standing so close to the fire as to be practically aflame themselves.

Then Fuller asked him whose land they traveled by. They were on a rise, and Matthew pointed out each farm and where Master Burton's land lay to the north and west.

"That's this Adam Nemo's master, is it not?"

Matthew said that it was,

"It's not unlikely then that Nemo will run for cover in a place he knows. Where must he have better knowledge than on his master's land? Although he be a savage, yet he is a cunning devil. If I mistake not, he will know every tree and hollow, if there be caves or other hidingplaces. Every inch must be covered."

Matthew said he thought that was right. What better place to find refuge than where one knew the lay of the land?

"Time's come to spread the men out, like a net," Fuller said, holding his hands out and spreading his gloved fingers. He looked at Matthew with a slightly raised chin, as though appraising Matthew's ability to understand and follow orders. "Since there's but two of them and thirty-odd of us, there will be little contest if we go forth in groups of five. I'll want you to lead one of the groups, Master Stock."

"As you wish, sir."

"Choose four of the company to go with you. I'll have Vernon and this stonemason Dees to choose their four. I will take four of my own and five other men will follow the road."

Fuller now turned aside to give these instructions to the whole company. He spoke in a resonant, calm voice, like a master directing his manservant to find his shoes beneath the bed. The leaders stepped back from the fire and did as they had been ordered, each taking turns at selecting who would accompany them. Vernon, who was offered the first choice because he was a gentleman, chose first not a townsman but one of Sir Thomas's servants, while Matthew chose Peter Bench, his apprentice, and Martin Grubbs, a cobbler. He chose the grocer, Abraham Pierce, too and would have had two other of his closer friends from the town had they not been selected first by William Dees and Fuller. Toward the end the selection was small, and he took Hugh Profytt, consoling himself with the thought that at least the choice would dispel the sense that he had anything against Agnes or her sister.

When the company was divided, Fuller indicated in which direction each group should search, and there was some dispute when Vernon was ordered to cover a range of ground that looked especially difficult to travel in the snow, while Dees, a mere stonemason, was given a flat field with hardly a rock or crevice upon it. Vernon said it was a great shame that he should be treated with such scorn and Fuller said that no scorn was intended and so he was right sorry that any offense had been taken. The condition of the land had nothing to do with the choice, he said.

No one seemed to side with Vernon in this dispute, not even the men in his own group, who like the entire company looked rather sullen-faced and joyless at the prospect of leaving the fire and setting forth again. The dispute was quickly put aside however, when one of Sir Thomas's servants shouted that he had seen what he thought were the fugitives, momentarily, on a distant hillock.

Before Fuller could command, the men rushed for the horses, Matthew with them. The fire was left burning with alongside a dozen good unused faggots, and within minutes the whole company was spread out on the smooth field that was William Dees's assignment and making for the hillock, with Fuller, a heavy burden for his poor mount, following the company and Dees, who was a good rider, in the lead.

The excursion proved to be futile, however, for the company came to the top of the rise and saw before them another stretch of snowy terrain, and nothing to be found there except a row of trees in the distance and a wide field no fugitives could have crossed from the time the alarm was sounded until the present, nor were there any sign of tracks.

Now the men all heaped ridicule on the servant who had given the false alarm, but Fuller silenced the criticism with a sharp reproof, reprimanding them all for moving forward before he had commanded it. He said that at the very least the servant, whose name was Hopkins, had been alert, which was more he said than was true of those who were drinking wine and warming themselves by the fire with such indifference to their duty that a host of fugitives might have passed by without their observing it.

This rebuke was delivered with such sternness that all in the company fell silent. Even Matthew felt himself reproved. A greater melancholy than before seemed to fall upon them all, as Fuller sent Hopkins back to the fire to retrieve the packhorses and the good faggots remaining and then repeated his instructions as to who was to go where. Afterwards there was an undercurrent of grumbling among the men, who had found Fuller's reproof too stinging for their comfort.

Joan had told Alice to stay home that morning. Why risk life and limb by walking the slippery, treacherous street, or exposing herself to the menace of murderers? she had said. But Joan herself felt free to go where she pleased, and sometime after her conversation with Elizabeth she bundled up and set out to visit Alice, which is to say, she went to find Alice's husband, Richard.

Assuming that he would be home protecting his family rather than in some alehouse carousing with his friends. Assuming that even if he were home he would satisfy the curiosity of a mere woman, he having been so recently honored by gaining the ear of great gentlemen of the county and London for what he knew of a distant cousin now murdered.

Alice and her family dwelt in the poorer end of the High Street in a small house no bigger than a kennel. It was a kind of tenement where the door of one abode was almost within a handspan of the next and each house had one miserly window to let in the light and there were two houses to every chimney. Joan had visited on other occasions, generally when her servant was ill, and so she knew she would herself be well received. As for the husband, she knew Richard on sight but couldn't have spoken more than a dozen words to him in as many years. Once a soldier, Richard had but one good leg and had lost an arm and eye in a battle with the Spaniard in Flanders, the details of which Alice had shared with Joan and Matthew on numerous occasions to their great pleasure, for Alice was quite good in re-creating the sights, sounds, and smells of warfare, having lived with a relic of its horrors. Unable to work because of his disabilities, Richard spent his time in alehouses, where his devotion to the grape often caused his dutiful wife considerable grief.

As it turned out, Joan found both wife and husband at home. Alice embraced her employer and expressed surprise and a little concern that she should have come, the weather being what it was, and Joan said she had come to talk to Alice's husband. Richard was sitting by the hearth nursing a cup of what smelled to Joan like chicken broth. The aroma was savory and when Alice offered Joan a cup she did not refuse it.

The husband, who had not been overly distracted by Joan's arrival, seemed more interested when he learned that he was the cause of Joan Stock's visit. Using his crutch, he struggled to his feet out of respect for her who was the source of his family's maintenance.

Joan urged Richard to sit down again, for she could see with what difficulty he stood upright. He was a man of rather heavy, cumbersome build, prematurely aged because of his infirmities. Joan remembered that Alice had said her husband had received his injuries when a cannon he was firing exploded; the left side of his face retained the bluish tinge of the gunpowder that had taken his eye. The right side of his face, however, showed that his features would not have been unpleasant in his youth, when he and Alice wed. His speech was rather slurred, and Joan was uncertain whether this proceeded from his war injuries or from some early morning imbibing, which she had heard was his habit.

Richard sat down again with difficulty on the edge of the

162

hearth, and Alice ushered Joan to a stool but remained standing herself. Joan said she had heard Richard was a cousin of John Crookback who was murdered, and Richard, smiling a little, said by God he was in truth. He seemed neither surprised nor reluctant to have the topic broached by another, although Joan imagined he had told this story many times over since John Crookback and his family were discovered slaughtered.

Joan's surmise was verified by the ease with which Richard Hull described the complicated connection between him and the deceased farmer, but she found his explanation difficult to follow. It seemed all a tissue of uncles and nephews and their children, going back several generations where the names sounded strange even to Joan, whose family, from what she understood, had been the first to lay one stone upon another in Chelmsford. Joan listened patiently, although family connection was not what she was curious about, and when it appeared that the former soldier's account was complete, she said with artful casualness, "I am told John Crookback was also a soldier in his youth."

"Nay, no soldier, but a mariner," Richard answered, turning his lips up in a rather ghastly grin as though happy to correct this fundamental error. "For he never trudged a mile nor bore a pike, as I have done in my time, but sailed with Martin Frobisher. Frobisher is now dead, I am told, but was then a great admiral upon the seas."

"John Crookback told you tales of his adventures?" Joan asked.

"Not to me directly. We had little to do with each other. Yet I heard of them." As he said this, Richard cast his eye down to where his thigh ended in a stump, as though to ask what a hale man like John Crookback would have had to do with an old crippled soldier of the wars. "From others I have met over the years, and I have met not a few who sailed with Sir Francis."

"Do you mean Sir Martin?" Joan said.

"By the mass, is that not what I said?" Richard Hull looked befuddled for a moment, glanced up at his wife, and then stared at Joan again with his good eye, the bad one being so mutilated by the explosion that it was hardly more than a small hole above the ruined, bluish check.

The man then launched into several anecdotes about his cousin's life at sea, one of which placed him in a very hot clime rather than in the frigid wastes where Joan had been given to understand John Crookback had served. She wondered about the accuracy of these accounts. Was Richard Hull simply confused, as he had been about the names of John Crookback's commander?

"Did you and John play together as boys?" Joan asked, trying herself to remember the boys she had known as a girl and feeling disheartened at her failure. What a devious trick time played. Had she ever known John Crookback herself? A baker's daughter, she had dwelt in town, not five houses from where she now lived. John Crookback had lived on his father's farm. No image of a youthful John Crookback crossed her mind that was not mixed up with with other youthful figures of her childhood.

"Oh we never did much together," said Richard, shaking his head as though this was one of the great sorrows of his life. "He was older, you see, by enough years that we had different friends. The truth was that in those days I hardly knew we were cousins at all."

Richard gave a short snort of laughter at this irony, glanced up at his wife as though seeking her permission to continue with this line of thought, and then turned his attention to Joan again.

"When did you find out you were kin?" Joan asked.

Richard thought for a moment, scratching the beard that grew only on his chin. "Marry, I think it was after he had come back, after he had inherited his father's farm. He had run off to sea, you know, as a mere boy. He and the father did not see to eye to eye on matters." Richard nodded his head sagely, and Joan asked what were the matters on which the father and son had differed, but Richard said he did not know. Just matters, he said, such as those that regularly divide sons from fathers, making life difficult.

"Were there other heirs?" Joan asked, although she already knew the answer to this question from Sir Thomas's report.

"Nary a one," Richard said promptly with a kind of satisfaction, "although the farm is a fine one. Would that I had been closer in kin, and we should not live in such a condition of wretchedness as we do today. I should have been a farmer rather than soldier—marry, I should have kept leg and eye and my better face. Yet he owed me much, for when he came home it had been so long since he was gone some wondered if it was he at all or some other."

"How was that? Joan asked.

"No one had seen John Crookback for a dozen years or more," Richard said. "I was one that went to take a solemn oath before him who was then magistrate that it was John Crookback indeed, and that he was rightful heir, although in truth I remembered him only as a boy who was older than I and played roughly and had yellow hair. John left with nary a hair upon his chin and returned with a full beard. Yet I swore it was he, and believe so still, and others did the same."

"Did what?"

"Why, swore it was he and not some other," Richard said, opening his good eye widely. "There was an inquiry before the will was pronounced good and John Crookback named the true heir. Witnesses were brought forth and they affirmed it was he—that is, the true son. All of which gave me courage of my convictions that boy and man were the same and no other."

"Who were the others who verified he was the same man?" Joan asked, never having heard that there was any question of John Crookback's identity when he assumed his father's land.

Richard considered this, his fingers finding their way to his beard again. He scratched slowly with the one good hand God had left him, and Joan thought, he searches for fleas, or cannot think but if he scratches. But uppermost in her own mind was the question, does he speak truth or merely tell a good story?

"I don't remember," Richard said finally. "It has been twenty years after all since my cousin returned from the sea. My memory is not as good as it was."

165

No, she thought, it was true indeed. And she could hardly fault Alice's husband for failing to remember, given his experiences, when she was faulty in that regard herself.

Joan listened with only half her attention as Richard proceeded to tell her how his memory had failed. She was thinking about beardless boys and the men they became and how a face changed with the years and how difficult it was to discern the boy within the man. Age played the devil with a man's face, replacing the smooth flesh of childhood with wrinkles and coarseness and the disfigurements of disease and the scars of war. With women it was no different. She thought of Elizabeth, the child she had been and the woman she now was, and could hardly believe they were the same and yet she was Elizabeth's mother and knew they were. How might John Crookback's maturity and hardships at sea have changed his countenance? A man's bristling beard was like a mask.

Some things, of course, changed not: The color of eyes and hair, tricks of speech, the slope of shoulders and the line of a jaw betrayed the lineaments of a man's parents. But these details were not always well remembered.

Joan resolved to ask elsewhere about John Crookback's return. Joan herself had been unaware of that event then; but her head had been full of other things. She took no particular notice of a sailor's return to inherit a farm. But perhaps someone lived still who remembered what had evidently made little stir almost twenty years before.

She thanked Richard Hull and Alice for their time and for the broth, upon which she passed a judgment pleasing to Alice, and was on her way home again when she remembered who might recall what she had never known.

Joan was glad she remembered when she did, for the house she now sought lay between Alice's and her own and she supposed she might as well stop there as not, there being so little to do on a day when she was almost the only one to brave the streets except for a group of boys who had ventured out to hurl snowballs at each other.

Thomas Barber was an ancient man who for many years had

166

been clerk of Chelmsford and therefore master of all records. Nearly eighty, he rarely left his house, Joan knew, but his mind remained keen for a man of his age and he had known Joan's father well when her father still lived. She was certain Thomas Barber would not mind a visit and was soon proven right. After much knocking and Joan's assurance that it was she and not some murderer with blood on his mind, the door was opened by the old man's granddaughter, a plain, rather sad woman named Dorothy who had never married and had devoted herself to taking care of her grandfather.

Unlike Alice and her husband, Thomas Barber lived in a condition of modest prosperity, the fruit of his labors, for he had been a busy scrivener as well as town official.

Joan found him seated by a blazing fire, covered with a lap robe. He looked up with a quick, startled expression, as though her entrance had awakened him from his nap.

Joan told him who she was to save him any embarrassment, but in fact he remembered her very well and immediately began to tell a story about her father, who had once been involved in a complicated legal transaction with the town. Joan listened with amazement as the old man recalled the most minute details—details that she herself had never known, since all this happened when she was a child.

She interrupted his reminiscences to ask about John Crookback's inheritance. Master Barber had heard about the murders, he said, nodding his head as though the event confirmed his worst suspicions about the human race, and the business of Abraham Crookback's will he remembered. "I remember the father. Abraham was old when he begot his son upon Mary Wood, who died shortly thereafter; he had but one son living when he died himself and no other close kinfolk that I recall."

"Was there a question then as to whether John Crookback was indeed the rightful heir?" Joan asked.

"Abraham Crookback's will was as clear as could be writ. It was not the conditions of the will but the identity of the man that was in question. No one had seen him in years. He had run away as a boy because his father used him poorly, or perhaps only because he wanted to see something of the great world beyond. We wanted him to prove himself, and so he did."

"What evidence did he furnish?" Joan wanted to know.

"Witnesses to his identity, and of course knowledge that none could have save it was he and not some other."

She wanted to know what witnesses, and the old scrivener thought for a moment and then beckoned to Dorothy, who all this time had been standing in the corner watching her grandfather with a concerned look on her face. Dorothy went to a cupboard in the corner, where she opened a drawer and withdrew a book. This she carried to her grandfather with a kind of reverence. Without a word he took it from her and began thumbing through the pages.

"The town has records," he said. "At least it should if they have not been burned or destroyed by mice. But I kept my own. Habit I suppose. I was always a record keeper, ever since my youth, when my father taught me to read.

It took the old man several minutes to find what he was looking for. "Yes," he said, drawing the single syllable out, "here it is. In the matter of the will of Abraham Crookback, farmer. The heir designate was his son, John Crookback, mariner."

"And the witnesses? Are they named in your book?"

"Yes. There was Philip Vernon, William Dees, Stephen Clarence, Richard Hull, and Dorcas Millichap."

Joan had known Vernon and Clarence. Both were dead now. Vernon was the father of the man who was now coroner, a gentleman of some weight in the neighborhood. Clarence had been the father of the woman who would become John Crookback's second wife. Only Richard Hull and William Dees remained alive. But what of Dorcas Millichap, of whom Joan had never heard?

"Who was Dorcas Millichap?" she asked.

"A woman who once was a servant in the father's home," the old man answered promptly. "Each of the men affirmed that it was John Crookback who presented himself."

"Even though they had not seen him in years."

"As I said, John Crookback answered questions sufficient to satisfy all of them. Here, I will read it to you myself." The old man held the book close to his eyes, straining to read the script. " 'Sundry persons presented themselves to question the heir and were satisfied by his answers, which showed a most, a most . . .' " He peered at the word. "Yes, 'a most sufficient knowledge of his father's character and habits.' "

Joan asked. "Was there anyone at the inquest who challenged John Crookback's identity?"

The old man thought for a long time, then he said that there had been a challenge, someone had doubted the man was Abraham Crookback's son. But as to the question that had been debated, he finally admitted he could not remember what that question was. There had been so many questions over the years, so many witnesses, so much testimony regarding so many things. The scrivener seemed almost ashamed at his failure.

Dorothy then said that her grandfather was weary, and Joan understood that she had overstayed her welcome. She left the house with a distinct sense of unease. She felt she had learned something of value from Thomas Barber, but was unsure what it was. There had been some doubt obviously as to whether the man presenting himself as John Crookback was indeed he; had it been otherwise, there would have not been a hearing. Someone had contested his identity. Who? For what reason? She felt she needed to know more and resolved to ask William Dees and Master Vernon upon their return. Surely Dees would remember the hearing, and Master Vernon, who had been too young to remember the actual event, might recall something his father had said.

Adam Nemo built a small fire, having found amid the ruined timbers an ample supply of kindling that had survived when the house had burned. In his imagination he dreamed of a tower of flame, radiating such warmth as to melt the snow that

169

had drifted in through the paneless windows and where the wall of the manor had crumbled under the intensity of the earlier conflagration, but to make too much smoke would not be wise; its trace would be seen readily in the sharp, clear stillness that had emerged since the snow had stopped.

He and Nicholas sat close until feeling had returned to Adam's hands and feet. Then he motioned to Nicholas his intent to find something for them to eat. The boy, still listless, seemed to understand and even smiled thinly. Adam wondered what scenes of carnage were passing before Nicholas's eyes as he sat in his silence, scenes making hunger and terror of capture lesser concerns.

Within a short time he had built and set several traps, and one had yielded a hare of sufficient size to feed them. But he had left tracks in the snow, and his efforts to cover them did not appear to him very successful. If snow fell again, it would be well for them; if not, it would be otherwise. He constantly surveyed the white fields below him, but for all he could see he and his friend might have been the last men on earth.

Solitude did not bother him as it did the English, who were unnerved by it. In his own land of ice he had hunted larger prey than hares and often alone, moving nimbly over the rocks and ice. Alone, he had thought about his gods, sometimes sensed their presence in the sky and sea. The English had snatched from him the deities of his birth, so that he hardly remembered their names, as they had taken from him his own true name. They had replaced them with their own god, who was one, not many. The difference did not seem to be as important to him as it was to them.

But he did not hurry back to where Nicholas was. He found pleasure in being alone in the snow. He was remembering what he had forgotten, regaining what had been taken. He said his true name aloud and he remembered the name of the god of the winter sky and said a prayer, hoping that his neglect would be forgiven and that both his god and the god of the English would understand.

He was climbing up over the breached wall when he remembered something else—the thing that Frobisher had said when he called the brutal sailor off, and in so doing spared Adam's life—*Crookback!* Frobisher had cried. But surely the memory was wrong. And yet as Adam thought of the event it was as if he could hear Frobisher's hoarse voice snap, *Crookback! Let him be. You'll kill him, you bloody devil.*

Adam heard the words as clearly as though they had been spoken not a moment before. But they made no sense. Crookback had been in the boat. Crookback had treated him kindly. Crookback had never thrown him to the ice and beaten him.

For a moment he wondered if he had been deliberately deceived. Perhaps his gods were indeed angry, perhaps they too had played with his memory. He had, after all, forsaken them for so many years. He shuddered, not so much because of the cold as from fear of the gods. He was a divided man now, neither English nor of the people. What was he? How could he supplicate his gods, and what did the false memory mean?

Chapter 12

ה

Matthew led his men to the edge of a field and then alongside a low stone wall, only the top of which could be seen for the snow. They rode in single file so that the horses in the rear could take advantage of the tracks of those ahead, moving very slowly; Matthew told them there was no hurry. No one talked during this time. Then they came to a break in the fence and crossed over to a neighboring field. The ruin of the manor house rose above them, and not a soul stirring for anything that Matthew could see.

It was Hugh Profytt who suggested the fugitives might be hiding in the ruins. The other men who heard the comment agreed that the manor would make a fine place of conceal-ment. Part of the house retained its roof and walls. The manor gave a good view of the surrounding countryside, elevated as it was. Matthew thought that was the trouble. If the two men were within the ruin, would they not see Matthew and his men approaching? Would they not flee in the opposite direc-tion? Was the effort it would take to ride up the hillside worth the trouble?

A heaviness of spirit swallowed him up. He wished that like his timid neighbor he had pled illness as an excuse to stay home.

Hugh Profytt said he thought the manor was worth a try. The red-faced young man looked at Matthew with a critical expression. "But I suppose you think otherwise," he said.

"Well," Matthew said, "we have little to lose."

Profytt was plainly surprised by Matthew's agreement. "I thought that because you have been defending the two from the beginning you might be reluctant to pursue your duty, Master Stock."

"I am not reluctant to pursue my duty, Master Profytt. I know my duty and have my instructions and intend to carry them out, with God's help." Matthew said this very stonily. He looked at Profytt and then at the other three men. They were clearly made uncomfortable by the sudden tension, especially Peter, whose mild, good nature was ever disturbed by discord.

Profytt said, "Four dead and murdered is a grim harvest to go unheeded. You seem to care little for that fact, Matthew Stock. You would have us all home and warm while these miscreants range the countryside. God knows who they will murder next, and if our own families are safe."

That said, Profytt urged his horse forward, as though he were assuming command, but Matthew reached out and grabbed his arm.

"If we are to advance, we should do so in good order," Matthew said in the same stern voice, but his teeth chattering a little. "Master Fuller put me at your head. Will you dispute with his choice?"

Profytt looked at Matthew for a moment with baleful eyes, then swore an oath under his breath. He looked at the other men, and finding no support in their expressions, he drew his horse back and made an exaggerated gesture of obeisance. "As Your Worship commands," Profytt said.

Matthew decided to ignore the insolence but now was sure Hugh Profytt was his enemy. The young man was thoroughly of his wife's party, just as Matthew feared, but why should Matthew have supposed it might be otherwise? Were not man and wife one flesh? Profytt would be watching Matthew's every move. Matthew's actions would be reported in Chelmsford—or more probably, misreported; his judgment would be accounted evidence of an undue sympathy for the accused men. That's how it would be, he was sure of it. Matthew was glad to have Peter in his company, and Abraham Pierce. Pierce too could be trusted to tell the truth.

Matthew motioned for the men to advance, warning them in a whisper to keep as quiet as possible. The snow would muffle the horses' hooves, but the human voice would carry even farther in the stillness. If Nicholas and Adam were hiding in the ruin, they might not see the approaching band, but they certainly could hear them. Matthew prayed the fugitives were not there. He also prayed that if they were, there would be no bloodshed in their taking.

When Joan returned to her house, she sat for a long time in the kitchen in a brown study. She recalled every word that had been spoken in her two conversations of the morning, recalled them all twice over, and had the unshakable feeling that she had taken in something important but wasn't sure what it was. From time to time she interrupted these meditations to think of Matthew, where he might be and how cold and forlorn in the cruel snow. But she also thought of Nicholas and Adam and felt pity for them too, for nothing she had learned had removed from her heart the conviction that the two men were falsely accused. And yet she knew too that the murders had something to do with Adam, his strange origins and even stranger existence in a land not his own.

After about an hour Elizabeth came down from upstairs, and mother and daughter talked. Joan told Elizabeth she had set out to see Richard Hull and the old town clerk, Thomas Barber. Elizabeth expressed dismay that her mother had gone abroad, and what was worse, in express defiance of her father's orders.

"Your father does not order," Joan said. "He admonishes."

"Is it not the same, Mother? I fear for you. The town is not safe."

Joan looked into her daughter's concerned face. "An admonishment," Joan said slowly, "falls some deal short of a command. It is counsel. Which may be heeded or not, as long as it be considered. And I did consider it."

"And chose to do the contrary," Elizabeth said,

"I did. I do not deny it. I had good reason."

Elizabeth wanted to know what the good reason was, but she did not ask skeptically. Joan told her what Richard Hull had said and what she had learned from Thomas Barber. Elizabeth listened intently but confessed confusion at last; she wanted to know what these ancient matters and disputes had to do with murders that had happened within the week.

"I don't know," Joan admitted. "Something. I have yet to learn just what."

"I think Father follows the truer path," Elizabeth observed, making the face she made when she was trying to be wise. "For he tracks the men accused. Even if they are innocent, as you and he believe, yet may they have knowledge that will reveal all, making these dark matters plain."

"I don't know that that is so," Joan observed, nettled a little at her daughter's taking an opposite stance. "Men are strange, foolish creatures. They follow routine as though there were no other way to accomplish a thing. A man is accused of a crime and flees, men give hue and cry and pursue. The flea doth bite and the dog scratches; it is as simple as that. Yet it is not so simple, this ferreting out of truth. It is not so simple."

Elizabeth went to the window and looked out. She observed that the sun had begun to melt the snow. "The men will have an easier time of their search if the snow melts," she said, turning to look at her mother. "They will have full advantage of their horses. Nicholas and Adam Nemo will be on foot. They will be quickly taken. Neither man can likely disguise himself, being as they are both strange and curious."

Yes, Joan agreed in her own mind, the two would be more readily taken if the snow melted. But what then?

175

Elizabeth left her, and Joan returned to her somber meditations on the past and how its heavy hand might have left its imprint on the present. She recalled what Elizabeth had said about the fugitives. They were a queer pair—a foreign-looking man and a boy who could neither hear nor speak and who was a seeming idiot. In her mind's eye she imagined how they might disguise themselves and could think of nothing that would not in set them just as much apart from the ordinary run of Englishmen. If Adam and Nicholas had been of that breed—having English features and complexions, and without infirmity—the outcome might be different. They might lose themselves in any crowd, and no pursuer would have been the wiser. A thousand disguises would have offered protection from discovery.

But it could not be so for these twain.

Then she thought about John Crookback. Maturity—which altered voice, face, and stature—had conferred upon him the best of disguises. The sheer forgetfulness of his neighbors had been an ally in the effort, for his reappearance would not, she reasoned, have occasioned any question about his identity as the true son of Abraham Crookback had someone not perceived a difference between the man and the memory of the boy. And even so, four or five had remembered and claimed it was truly he.

Was the objection raised by some heir presumptive? Master Barber and Alice's husband had affirmed that there was none. Or was it some busybody with a grudge against the son? Yet he left as a boy. Who would bear a grudge against a mere youth?

And what, she thought further, if the John Crookback who returned from sea was a false John Crookback? Were these honest witnesses to his identity liars then, or merely deceived by an imposter who resembled the true prodigal and had acquired by some means a store of knowledge to verify his identity? Crookback Farm was a valuable property, even in those earlier days. Its soil was rich, its prospect of the surrounding countryside fair, and the house and barn were soundly built.

And yet even if this vision of things were true, what had it to

176

do with the murder of the same man and his wife and children twenty years later?

Why, it might not have anything to do with it at all.

She had reached this point in her conjectures when there was a knocking at her door. Rising to answer, she heard the familiar voices of several of the men who lived in the street. They were the watch, they said, wanting to know if everything was well within the clothier's house. They had been appointed to go door to door, given that the murderers were afoot.

"All is well in this house," Joan announced, not wanting to open the door for the cold.

But she realized it was not so when they had gone on. All could not be well in such confusion of mind and heart as she found herself in, worried for the two men who had been guests beneath her roof and whom she still believed innocent, and concerned at the same time for a husband who pursued them.

She went back to her kitchen, surrendering herself to the thoughts that plagued her and would let her accomplish no meaningful housework. She knew she was but a wife, no officer of the law or member of the watch, and yet she felt compelled to dig into the mystery herself. She resolved to speak to William Dees upon his return. Perhaps the stonemason would remember something from that old dispute that even the prodigious memory and records of Thomas Barber had not contained.

Something had awakened Adam. The same dream as before, a dream as puzzling to him as the Crookback murders, and dream and murderers were somehow associated in his mind in a way he did not understand. Had he not awakened, Adam would not have seen the men until it was too late to flee. He had gotten up from beside his friend and in standing he had seen beyond the ruined wall to the white plain below him, seen the black specks that were surely men, not cattle, for what cowherd in his right mind would have been driving his charges on such a day? That is how Adam Nemo knew they were men—men on horseback, and men who must have no other intent than pursuit, for if the road was perilous for cattle, humans could hardly be eager to travel it, save their travel had some desperate purpose.

He drew Nicholas up from the little fire, where he had been crouched on his haunches, to show him the men, then extinguished the blaze with snow. After a few minutes the men were close enough to count. There were five, and they had left the road and were riding across the field and up the slope that led to the house. Adam recognized the man in the lead: It was the clothier Matthew Stock, Adam was sure. Which left the issue of the purpose of this little company in no doubt.

"They shall not take us," Adam said aloud for them both. He grabbed Nicholas's wrist and headed toward the wood.

While Matthew had seen no smoke, yet he smelled it, and for the first time since setting out, he felt there might be something to Profytt's instinct that the ruined manor was inhabited by the fugitives. Matthew was concerned, however, when he saw Profytt draw the pistol he had been issued from the interior of his coat, and he broke his own rule of silence to admonish him to put it away. He felt sure the men they sought were not armed; there would be no need of pistols.

"They are desperate murderers, Master Stock," Profytt said in a loud whisper. "I will take no chances with them. If they be within, they shall surrender. If unarmed as you say, then that's all the better, for our task will be the more speedily done."

Profytt having now ridden too far away for this dispute to continue, Matthew motioned to his remaining men, Pierce and Grubbs, and he urged his horse onward. On the slopes of the rise the snow was not so deep, and in places enough melting had occurred so that now the earth appeared, together with rocks that glistened in the sun. Matthew shielded his eyes against the glare and sucked in gulps of the icy air. His lungs ached. He knew now that Master Burton's servant was concealed in the ruin and the Crookback boy with him but was not sure how he knew, for other than the whiff of smoke from a fire that might have been made by some other poor wretch in the storm, he saw nothing but the blackened timbers and what remained of the walls of that part of the manor house that had survived the fire.

When they reached the house itself Matthew signaled Pierce and Grubbs to dismount, Profytt and Peter Bench now having disappeared from sight around the other side of the ruin. Matthew led the way through what had been the door into the roofless interior, careful of his footing, since the floor of the house was covered with fallen timbers that were half buried in the snow. He wanted no broken limbs to testify to his hardihood. The house seemed deserted, as far as he could see, but then he heard Profytt's voice call out for him and he moved forward around another half-fallen wall and saw Agnes's young husband pointing down at his feet and looking at Matthew with an expression of triumph.

"There's been a fire here," Profytt said, "and not but a quarter hour before our coming. See, Master Stock, he who made it tried his best to conceal it with fresh snow. Yet I found it out."

Matthew went over to have a look. Profytt was right: Beneath a thin veneer of snow were the remains of a fire. The burned wood was still warm to the touch.

"There's footsteps too," Profytt said, nodding at them. "They've tried to cover them up, but it is plain that there are two of them. So who must it be but the murderers we seek?"

Matthew nodded in agreement and told Pierce and Grubbs to fetch the horses and bring them around to the rear of the house, where Profytt said the tracks led.

"Had we marched forward with greater speed we would have had them," Profytt said, staring at Matthew accusingly.

"Greater haste would have put us at too great a risk in this weather," Matthew said. "Besides, if it is Nemo and Crookback, they would surely have seen us at whatever speed we approached."

"Do you doubt it is they we seek?" Profytt asked incredulously. "By God, it must be they. Who else could it be?"

Matthew did not bother to answer the question. He regretted having further provoked the hotheaded young man with an expression of uncertainty he might well have kept to himself. The truth was that he shared Profytt's conviction that the tracks were made by the fugitives; he simply did not want to give Profytt the satisfaction of an easy victory. But he saw too in the expressions of Pierce and Grubbs that despite his friendship with these neighbors, they would have preferred Hugh Profytt to him as leader of their band. Even Matthew's own apprentice, when he came up to where the other men stood, seemed impressed by the evidence Profytt had uncovered.

The tracks led away into the wood that had been its late master's deer park, a tangle of thistles and oaks that commenced within a stone's throw of the house. Even without the leaves of summer, the wood looked thick and treacherous. Matthew was no forester, but if Nemo and Crookback had taken refuge within, then he supposed duty bade him follow, although he had no stomach for it, for the tracks seemed to lead perversely into the thickest part of the forest.

"Why do we wait?" Profytt asked as the men stood looking. "Our delay only allows them time to achieve a greater distance or to conceal themselves the better."

Grubbs agreed. "Let us move forward, Matthew. It will be a great honor if it is we who bring them home again."

They left the horses at the edge of the wood, tied to trees. Profytt said someone should remain with the horses. "If they come around behind us, we may find our labors within are futile and the two fugitives handsomely mounted."

This practical advice further raised Profytt's stature among the little band, and Matthew was now humiliated by having to second orders given by one under his own command. He told Grubbs to guard the horses, but Grubbs objected. "Why must it be I, Matthew? Have I not as much right as you or the others to take the murderers?"

180

Profytt agreed with Pierce. "Abraham has shown himself well in our pursuit, Master Stock. You choose him unwisely—and over your own apprentice, who would appear by his dull eye and trembling to have little stomach for the chase."

Everyone turned to Peter. "I shall do what Master Stock bids me," Peter said.

Matthew had wanted his apprentice, the only one of the group he now trusted, by his side, and he resolved to stand fast to his order. He felt himself losing more and more ground to Profytt, and his dislike for Agnes's husband surmounting his dislike for the wife herself. He reminded the men that he had been put in charge of the group. But Hugh Profytt stormed, "You were so charged because Master Fuller believed you to be capable. You have called into question that capability by your halfhearted pursuit of the murderers of your own townsmen. Were Master Fuller here he would choose another in your stead. Of that I am sure."

"You mean yourself," Matthew said.

"At least I do not dawdle," Profytt said hotly. "And it was I whose judgment was confirmed about the house and I who found the fire and the tracks."

Matthew started to answer this but was interrupted by Peter, who volunteered to stay by the horses himself.

Matthew was not pleased by his apprentice's well-intentioned offer, but he realized that further discussion was not only futile but that it undermined his authority the further. He wished more than anything now that Fuller had not divided the company. He would have much preferred to be part of the larger group; at the head of these four he felt vulnerable, and he half agreed with Profytt's assessment of his capacity. He knew he had not shown himself well. Profytt had been right about the manor as a place of concealment. The energy and purpose of the younger man was obviously superior to his own; within the forest, he would undoubtedly offer further proof of his superiority.

"So be it," Matthew said after an uncomfortable silence. "Peter will remain with the horses, since he will have it so. The rest of us will follow the tracks as far as we are able."

Without waiting for further instructions, Profytt led the way into the woods, and the other men followed, as though without a formal declaration the mantle of leadership had been transferred.

The park had been abandoned along with the house and, untended by any forester, had been overrun by a riot of brush and briar. It was difficult to move with any speed, and their efforts at keeping quiet were frustrated by a constant crackling of dead branches that seemed to carry for a league or more. The tracks were soon lost, and so was Matthew. He looked about him. In every direction there seemed the same bare branches of winter grown so thickly together as to be a kind of net. He was thankful now for Profytt's own boldness, for the young man remained in the lead, moving forward as though he had a compass in hand, although he was no better equipped than the other three men.

Matthew was very tired and heartsick. He was sure now that his failure would be as great a piece of news in Chelmsford upon his return as would be the capture of the fugitives, if they should accomplish it. Agnes Profytt and her sister would be delighted, as would a number of his neighbors who were jealous of Matthew's success in his trade. But above all he felt the humiliation of being lost.

Suddenly the forest opened into a clearing, and as suddenly the tracks of the fugitives reappeared. It was Pierce, not Profytt, who found them, and he cried out for joy so loudly that Matthew was forced to remind him of the need for a silent pursuit.

This admonishment given, Matthew's attention was then drawn to another cry, this time from Grubbs, who had been bringing up the rear and had fallen behind. "There they are!" Grubbs cried, pointing to the other side of the clearing.

Matthew looked and saw the men. He did not recognize the first, but the second was definitely Nicholas Crookback. They were disappearing into the woods again. Profytt had seen them too and began to bound across the drifts of snow. Matthew and the other men followed after, but Profytt had reached only the middle of the clearing when he suddenly cried out and tumbled headlong. When Matthew and the others reached him he was sprawled in the snow, bawling and cursing that he had broken a leg or worse.

Coming up to where Profytt lay, Matthew could see what had happened. A small stream transected the open space in the forest and it had been obscured by a snowdrift. In his headlong rush, Profytt had ignored everything but the image of the fleeing fugitives and had stumbled over a rock in the streambed. Now he was in real agony, beating his fist into the snow until he had smashed through it to solid ground, his red face contorted in pain.

Profytt stopped screaming long enough to sputter out appeals for help mixed with admonishments that the other men continue their pursuit. Since Matthew realized there was nothing that could immediately be done for Profytt, he motioned the others to follow, and watching his own footing, he directed Grubbs and Pierce to where he had seen Adam Nemo disappear into the trees.

The part of the forest into which they now entered was if anything more dense than what they had already come through. By Matthew's reckoning, the deer park could not have consisted of more than several score acres, but so overgrown was it that they might wander back and forth for days without emerging into the fields again. Then he saw the fugitives, about a stone's throw ahead—if a stone could have been thrown in such a thicket. He cried out, ordering the two to stop, but his warning was to no avail. He ran faster after them, moving through the undergrowth with great difficulty and his heart pounding with such force that he thought it might break from the exertion.

For what seemed a hour but may only have been a quarter as much, Matthew continued the pursuit, now seeing his quarry, now losing sight of them. Grubbs followed after Matthew, but Pierce with his long stride and stronger heart moved ahead and to the right. Then suddenly Matthew saw a thinning in the trees, and blue sky beyond: the end of the deer park.

*　*　*

Man and boy ran until they came to where they could see the forest end and the fields begin again and looking back, saw their pursuers. Then Adam heard shouts from a new direction. He looked to the right and saw other men, on horseback, their mounts struggling in the snow toward him. Trapped between those behind and those in front, Adam stopped for a moment in confusion, and the delay was long enough to give the pursuers the advantage. He recognized the stonemason first. William Dees leapt from his mount and ran at them, flinging himself upon Adam and wrestling him to the snow, while another man whose face Adam did not recognize fell upon Nicholas.

For the next few minutes all was pain and confusion, but despite his struggling, Adam was no match for the stonemason's superior strength. The man's hot garlicky breath was on the back of Adam's neck, his curses in his ears. A hoarse excited voice cried the order to fetch Master Fuller and Sir Thomas. Someone else cried that the murderers had been taken. Blinded by the pain of having his arms pulled nearly from their sockets and twisted behind his back, Adam could think only of that earlier time when Martin Frobisher saved his life by calling out the name Crookback as though the two syllables were an incantation with sufficient power to stay his attacker.

But there was no Frobisher to save him now.

Chapter 13

ה

The men of the *posse* were transformed by the actual possession of their quarry. It was as though the cruel deaths of man, woman, and children had been but half believed before and only now had the full enormity of the Crookback murders come home to them. Men Matthew had never seen enraged were now voicing the most uncharacteristic opinions about what should be done with the captives. Some wanted Adam and Nicholas executed on the spot, either by hanging or the cutting of their throats. Others urged that the two be taken back to Chelmsford first so that the whole town could witness the executions.

Matthew spoke against this, doing what he could to restrain the violence directed against the fugitives, which now consisted of taunts and random blows, wrenching of their arms, and the most vile threats, although it was clear that neither Adam nor Nicholas intended, or were capable of, further resistance. Finally, Fuller and his little troop arrived and shortly thereafter Sir Thomas, and with the arrival of the magistrate a calmer spirit prevailed.

Sir Thomas, who appeared more than a little disappointed that it was not he who had captured the fugitives, first congratulated William Dees for taking the two men and then Matthew for having flushed them out of the forest. "You have acted with courage at considerable risk to your own lives," Sir Thomas said, looking at where Hugh Profytt lay on a makeshift litter. Profytt had been brought out of the forest about a half hour earlier and was now being prepared to be conveyed back to the town, with much discussion among his friends as to how to lessen his discomfort.

Then the knight settled the matter of what was to be done with the prisoners in a way that was no surprise to Matthew. He said the men would be bound over for the next assizes, when they would both come to trial for their crimes. He said he hoped justice would be done and that the whole town might witness a lawful hanging. "This is not a place for private justice," he said, "but for the full measure of the laws of England. Let us have no more talk then of precipitous action. We shall return to Chelmsford with our prisoners. Let notice be taken of how speedily justice does her work when the laws of God and queen have been flouted."

After this speech, Hugh Profytt's litter was raised and suspended between two horses, one of which was Matthew's. It was thought a more comfortable method of conveyance than to drag the litter behind, where it might bump against rocks. Profytt was in a great deal of pain with his leg, his shank bone having broken through the skin, but he continued to curse the accused men as though they had not only murdered his father- and mother-in-law but personally inflicted the agony he was now experiencing. It was clear from his baleful expression that he blamed Matthew for his humiliating injury as well. Sir Thomas told Profytt to bear his pain like a man, and after that the young man swore the less but wept a good deal, so that the tears froze on his face.

The return of the *posse comitatus* was heralded by several of its members who were directed to ride on ahead and alert the town. So by late afternoon when the expedition returned

186

the townspeople were waiting in the streets despite the bitter cold, cheering and waving as Sir Thomas led the company of men up the High Street toward the Sessions House. As for the prisoners, they had been bound and seated back to back on one of the packhorses and were subjected to much railing and cursing from the townsfolk, who threw cobbles or tossed nightsoil from their windows above the street, some of which landed upon the heads of the members of the *posse,* to their great annoyance. It was difficult for Matthew to tell whether the response of his neighbors evinced anger at the prisoners or relief that the danger had passed.

At the Sessions House the *posse* was formally disbanded, but not before Sir Thomas delivered another speech about the majesty of the law and the evil of those who commit murder upon their parents. His speech went on at such length that some in the crowd slipped off to their homes before its conclusion to get themselves warm and have a good supper. Then the magistrate announced that the prisoners would be taken to his own house for the time being and later be conveyed to the jail in Colchester. He thanked all members of the *posse,* mentioning the leaders of each of the bands of searchers by name, and after each name a cheer went up from the members of that band. When Matthew's name was mentioned there was less enthusiasm, except from Peter Bench, Matthew's apprentice.

Hugh Profytt had been taken directly to his house and a physician sent for. As happy as he was to be home again, Matthew suspected he had not heard the last of the incident in the deer park.

He had listened to the magistrate's speech with a heavy heart, both because he was weary beyond measure from the day's efforts and because he remained convinced that the accused men were innocent. However his neighbors might celebrate their liberation from danger, he resolved to keep his own house as tight as a fortress until he was persuaded that the true malefactors had been taken.

Joan had watched the returning troop with joy and had wept despite herself at the sight of her husband alive and well, for she had seen the litter on which Hugh Profytt lay first and had dreaded that the taking of the prisoners had been at the cost of human life. Of course she had feared the worst, that it was her husband who was so distressed and borne. Then she saw Matthew, seated upon his horse, riding only slightly to the rear of the magistrate, and she was filled with more pride in the man she married than she had ever felt before.

When she saw the prisoners, however, she was filled with a great sadness. These were her former guests; now they were bound and mortified, destined, if she was any judge of her neighbors' disposition, to meet a speedy and cruel death. Some of the foul matter aimed at them had found its mark, and both men were not only shivering with cold but also covered with stinking filth, as was the poor horse that carried them. She did not join in the curses flung at the accused men but went indoors again after they passed and directed Elizabeth, who had been gawking at the spectacle from the upstairs window, to come down and help her with supper, for her father would be as hungry as a bear, she said, after his adventure.

The meal—brown bread and butter and a round Essex cheese, a well-cooked capon and cup of steaming broth to go before and make the belly, she said, accommodating to the rest—was all upon the table when the master of the house returned. Joan greeted her husband with a warm kiss and a firm embrace and then helped him off with his cloak and gloves and boots. But she had also supervised a fire of such happy fury that he was soon himself again, and even as he ate he related all that had transpired during the day, omitting not a detail nor sparing himself the embarrassment of relating how inadequate he had felt as a commander, even in the presence of Elizabeth, who hung on every word of her father's report.

"Agnes Profytt is an evil-tongued shrew. She will grow old before her time and live to be cursed by her children," Joan pronounced with unwonted bitterness. "It is no surprise that she has a husband who is no better. How dare he usurp command when it was given to you by Master Fuller? If that young hag makes one remark about the event and I find it out, it will go ill with her. I shall gouge out her eyes, so help me God."

Matthew joined Elizabeth in laughing at this outburst, but Matthew deeply appreciated his wife's loyalty. Of milder temper himself, he nonetheless had benefitted from time to time from Joan's more forthright disposition, for despite her charges against Agnes Profytt, Joan could hold her own in any tongue-lashing, although their own marriage was nothing if not cordial.

When it was clear he was finished with his narrative of his long day's events, she related her own activities.

"I asked you not to go abroad. The murderer remains at large and unidentified," he said sternly.

"I went only to Alice's house, a journey of no great extent."

"A sufficient distance for danger to befall you. You might have been seized in the street, dragged into a house before you were aware, and your throat slit for your pains. In your absence the house might have been invaded and Elizabeth attacked. You will not have a dog for the fleas that breed, so without me here there would be little help."

"The watch did its duty," she said. "I felt I was in no danger."

"What am I to do with you, Joan?"

She gave no answer but smiled sweetly, and Elizabeth laughed a little to ease the tension. Then Joan deftly sidestepped the thorny issue of her disobedience by reporting all that Alice's husband had said about Abraham Crookback's will and the hearing about whether John Crookback was the true son and heir of the father. "Alice's husband was there, as was William Dees, to affirm that the John Crookback murdered yesternight was John Crookback in truth and not some other."

"No one said otherwise?" Matthew asked.

"There was an inquiry," Joan said. "Someone must have doubted."

"He had been gone to sea for what, fifteen years? What is more natural than that his identity be confirmed by witnesses, persons who knew him?"

"As a boy, Matthew," Joan said, "not as a man."

"You are thinking that the John Crookback we knew was not the true son of his father but an imposter?"

"So I think."

"But your proof is a slender reed," Matthew said. "Fifteen years absent, there would be naturally a question, but that does not mean that John Crookback was any other than he claimed to be. Besides, this controversy as you call it may have no bearing at all on the murders, no more than do the black stones and the Italian assayer and Martin Frobisher's voyages."

Joan considered this. She looked at Elizabeth and could tell from her puzzled expression that she shared her father's doubt. What ground, after all, was there for her growing conviction that the roots of the murders went down so far as the question of John Crookback's identity? Nothing more than a feeling. She had had such feelings about things before; sometimes, as Matthew reminded her, the outcome had not verified them.

She told him she had spoken to Thomas Barber too. "It was he who presided at the inquiry into Abraham Crookback's will."

Matthew looked at her with new interest. "Marry, Joan, you have rubbed this sore raw, have you not? And who else in town did you query about these matters?"

"No one else," she said, somewhat defensively. "It was Barber who told me all that had happened in that time. Despite his great age, his memory is most complete. And he read from a book he kept wherein he noted all the facts pertaining thereto, who testified and to what."

"Well, then, if Master Barber was satisfied that John Crookback was who he claimed, why should you dispute it? Barber is as honest a man as there is in Chelmsford, nor is he well known for having committed errors in the carrying out of his duties. His judgment is enough for me."

"And for me as well," Elizabeth said, who all this while had listened intently and only now had ventured to give her opinion.

At this Joan thought it prudent to change the subject, feeling that she was doing little if anything to persuade husband and daughter that she was right. But she resolved not to let the matter drop. Men's lives were at stake, and also her pride. She would prove her intuition was no idle speculation but a true insight into the murders.

Agnes Profytt was first frightened to learn that it was her husband who was carried on the litter, moaning as if he were at death's very door, then relieved that his injury was no more than it was. She sent for Martin Day, physician, who pronounced the shank bone broken cleanly—as any fool could see, she muttered to a neighbor who had come to her house to commiserate. Agnes scolded the physician for the manner in which he reset the bone, causing her husband such excruciating pain that he fainted despite being well-liquored in preparation for his ordeal. She saw that her husband was fed, cleaned, and put to bed, and then she went as soon as it was possible to her sister's. Agnes had heard the circumstances of the misfortune from her husband, his friends in the *posse comitatus,* and from Master Fuller himself, who had brought Hugh to the house expressing the warmest sympathies on behalf of himself and Sir Thomas.

None of which honors lessened her anger when she understood that her husband had fallen under the command of Matthew Stock. She no sooner entered Mildred's house but she began to heap as much abuse on the clothier—and his wife—as she could. These charges Mildred gave ear to for some time with kindly patience before she asked what Agnes intended to do.

"We are most relieved to have the murderers of our father and stepmother taken," Mildred said. "But what of your dear husband, who would not have been injured had Matthew

Stock not ordered him to rush headlong into disaster? A prudent commander would at least have enjoined caution. Poor Hugh was doomed."

"He was doomed," Agnes agreed, nodding her head vigorously and glaring at her sister as though she were somehow an accomplice in the fiasco. "And now my husband's leg is in grave danger, or so says the physician. We shall starve, while the clothier, who is much to blame for all this, feeds his belly and prospers. Is it not enough that our beloved father and stepmother have been killed? Is it not enough that Stock tried to dissuade our honorable magistrate against pursuing the murderers? Has justice not been frustrated in this?"

Agnes's last question was so shrill and quarrelsome that Mildred had to remind her that after all, she was not an ally of the clothier or his wife but a true sister and as much a hater of Matthew Stock and his works as was Agnes.

Miles Carew came in the door, bringing a blast of cold air with him, for which indiscretion he was immediately reproved by his wife. The young man seemed to ignore the chastisement, however, and greeted his sister-in-law and wife as though he had never committed an offense. He sat down at table with them, reaching for the flagon of wine at its center, and said almost casually, "The clothier's wife has been to see Richard Hull, who sits all day in the tavern and tells stories about the wars."

"And what of that?" asked Mildred.

"Only that she has been asking him about your father, that's what. About his voyages and about his inheritance."

The two sisters exchanged glances. Agnes pressed her sister's husband for more information.

"Many of the men with Sir Thomas and Master Fuller are at the tavern, still talking about the pursuit and exchanging monstrous lies," Miles Carew said.

"As men will," Agnes said sourly. "But Richard Hull wasn't with them. How is it he offers his story when there are better to listen to?"

"Hull holds forth with the best of them," he said. "When

one man finishes his account, Hull steps in with his own story. He's a big man now, since he is distant cousin to your father and yourselves."

"By God's good grace, a very distant cousin," Mildred said with distaste. "This wretched man trades upon our grief. It is monstrous. I pray, husband, you had the wit to tell him to say nothing of me or of my father. My family's business is none of his. And I would not have my reputation sullied by association with such as he is, a notorious idler, braggart, and tosspot."

During Mildred's remark, Agnes had sat very quietly, resting her long chin on her fist and screwing up her face as she did when she was concentrating. Her eyes were as hard as stones. Then she said, "So this is what she would have, is it?"

"Who?" Mildred asked, turning from her husband to her sister.

"Why, Stock's wife," Agnes said. "Richard Hull is kin, but she is not, and I am more angered by her snooping than his bragging. Why should she take such an interest in our father were she not bent on finding some means to excuse our brother and his minion from blame?"

"Perhaps she hopes to uncover some scandal, some gossip to defame us," Mildred offered.

"She shall not," said Miles Carew. "By God she shall not."

Mildred looked at her husband, her lips curling with scorn. "Be careful what you resolve, husband, for I shall hold you to it."

"And so will I," Agnes said.

Mildred looked at Agnes, her scorn fading. "What shall we do, sister?" she asked anxiously. "Shall we tell Stock's wife to mind her own housewifery and leave these murders to those appointed to look into them."

"We might do so," Agnes said. "But I doubt it would do any good. Joan Stock is beyond such admonitions. She's a self-willed harlot of a wife. Her husband is nothing more than her simpering servant, a uxorious ass. Or so I have heard it said."

Mildred said she had heard the same thing about the Stocks. "The husband is horribly henpecked, for he has more blood on his face from her pecking than remains in his whole body. I warrant she plants horns upon his head as well, pleasuring herself with his pasty-faced, bean pole apprentice, him they call Peter Bench."

They all laughed at this joke, and Mildred's young husband the hardest of the three. Then he said, "Give me a domineering wife and I will show you a cuckold of a husband. May their horns grow long and tall as the members that engendered them."

He laughed again at his own wit, but Mildred chastised him roundly for the indecency of his comment, saying it was too bad an honest woman could not enjoy the privacy of a little conversation with her own sister but some man spoiled it with the crude, filthy language of the tavern.

"I will not have that woman nosing around asking questions about my father," Agnes said in a quieter voice than she had used before. "I will not have her working to free the murderers of my father and stepmother."

"And our dear stepbrother and stepsister," Mildred added piously. "Oh, how shall we proceed, sister?"

Being as it was not as cold as before and the snow almost melted from the cobbles, Agnes Profytt took her time walking the quarter mile to her own house. She engaged along the way in as many conversations as acquaintances she met, for she was a woman only content when she believed nothing of import was happening beyond her notice. From such familiar intercourse she heard more accounts of the search for the fugitives. She also encountered Dorothy Barber, who was sweeping snow off the doorstep of her grandfather's house with a broom whose handle was taller than she, and learned to her dismay that Richard Hull was not the only person the clothier's wife had spoken to about John Crookback's obscure history.

"And I suppose Stock's wife learned everything she came for?"

"Oh, I don't know why she came," Dorothy said, furrowing her brow so that she seemed even more homely than usual. "My grandfather told her all about your own grandfather's will. And about the inquiry when your father came back from the seas, and the names of all those who testified on his behalf. You would have been so proud, Agnes."

Agnes said she would be proud indeed. "I never knew about the inquiry," she said. "Tell me who the persons were who testified on my father's behalf."

After struggling to remember, Dorothy told her the names.

"That's most interesting," Agnes said, wishing Dorothy well and hurrying on her way.

Now Agnes was nearly beside herself with curiosity and rage at this newest discovery of Joan Stock's nosiness, so much so that she forwent the next five opportunities to talk to her neighbors and went straight home to confer with her husband, whom she hoped had come sufficiently to himself that she could have the benefit of his ear for the plan she had in the making.

Before arriving, however, she had one final encounter that put the finishing touches to her design. The weather having caused virtually all business to cease, the taverns had become the gathering place of most of the men of the town, who if they had not had the distinction to be part of the hunt were taking vicarious delight in hearing about it from the mouths of the actual participants. Among the most sought after witness to the events of the day was William Dees, whose capture of the fugitives had made him more celebrated than had his good fortune in finding the bodies of the murder victims.

As her luck would have it, Agnes encountered Dees, whom she accounted a friend and ally for his hostility toward her stepbrother and Master Burton's servant, as the redoubtable stonemason was making his way from one tavern to the next. He greeted her with a cheerfulness that both flattered Agnes and assured her that the tale of his exploits had been well received at the establishment from which he had just come.

"A very good day to you, Mistress Profytt."

Blushing at this courteous salutation from a man who on other occasions could hardly bring himself to nod, Agnes responded in kind.

The stonemason expressed his sorrow at her husband's injury and asked how he did.

"As well as any man might, given that his poor leg was almost yanked off and there was a deal of blood. The physician said he had never seen so pestilent a break of bone in his life."

Dees murmured sympathetically and made a movement suggesting his intention to continue on his way, but Agnes prevented it with a hand on his arm. "One question, if you please," she said.

Dees looked annoyed at being detained but Agnes ignored that.

"I understand you were a witness for my father when his inheritance was disputed."

The stonemason's face showed his amazement at this knowledge. "Why, I was indeed. But how should you know that? You were hardly more than an infant in those days."

"Very true," Agnes said, bowing a little at what she took to be the stonemason's flattery and thinking him a more handsome man than she had remembered. "Then I understood little of my father's business, other than that we had come to my grandfather's farm to live. Matters of law were beyond my comprehension. No, it is from Joan the clothier's wife that I had this news, for she has been looking into the history of my family."

"And why should she do that?" the stonemason asked.

"What but the curiosity of a woman, I suppose," Agnes said.

"Curiosity? Surely there are other matters to be curious about," Dees said.

"There are in fact," Agnes said, curling her lips into a smile. "But you know neither she nor her husband are persuaded Adam Nemo and my stepbrother murdered my family. I think she would point the finger of guilt elsewhere."

"Oh, would she," said Dees. "Where would she point the finger?"

"I can't begin to imagine," Agnes said. "But surely her long nose will make trouble for someone. And i'faith, I think it a great shame that your worthy service in this cause should come to nothing, as it undoubtedly will if it is proved you have brought in them who are innocent."

She let this point settle in the stonemason's mind for a moment before proceeding, and to good effect, she thought with great satisfaction, for Dees said nothing in response but stood there, his large, whiskery face a mask of confusion and vexation as he stared down at his boots.

"Now if some man were to speak to Sir Thomas . . ." she offered.

The name of the magistrate brought the stonemason out of his reflections. He looked up quickly. "Speak to Sir Thomas?"

"You know how men are, Master Dees," Agnes said, moving a little closer to the stonemason and adopting the sweet voice she reserved for wheedling and temporizing. "They give heed to each other but to a woman's complaints not at all. If, on the other hand, some prominent man of the town—"

"If you mean me, Mistress Profytt, I am hardly a prominent man of the town, but no more than a simple—"

"Why, it was you who brought the fugitives in," Agnes said, drawing even closer to the stonemason and peering up at him, for he was a tall man and she a very small woman. "If, I say, some prominent man were to let the magistrate know how hurtful it is to the cause of justice that Stock's wife should go around stirring up old grievances and controversies and disputing Sir Thomas's actions. Especially since the mystery has been resolved and the malefactors are in his charge. Does it make much more than trouble where trouble has been eased?"

Dees agreed that it made trouble, this nosing around in family histories not one's own. "For what has it to do with anything?" he said, his eyes flashing with a sudden anger. "If Stock's wife is fishing for gossip, she shall not fish in my stream."

"Or deprive you of any honor you deserve," Agnes added.

197

"Trust me, I'll speak to Sir Thomas," Dees said. "And he'll talk to her husband straightway, I am sure of it. For Sir Thomas wants the matter done and over with."

Agnes expressed her gratitude to the stonemason, and continued on her way, speaking to three other men of the town before reaching her own house and declaring to each that Joan Stock had been asking questions about his family history. She told them as well that the clothier's wife disputed the consensus of the townspeople that the true murderers of John Crookback and his family were now held prisoner by the lord of the manor. Each expressed a predictable dismay at the invasion of his privacy and resentment that a hue and cry so happily and heroically concluded should be disputed by one who thought too well of herself as it was.

The manor house of Sir Thomas Mildmay was larger and grander than the house of his own master, but Adam Nemo had little opportunity or inclination to admire its masonry or number its bristling chimneys. Exhausted, bruised, and terrified even more than before his capture, he wished the assizes finished and his sentence given and the rope burn on his neck. His innocence mattered nothing to him now. He had little sense left of the injustice of the charge against him and less hatred for his captors and detractors, but only a desire to be finished with the English and their ways. If he could not return to his own land the way he had come, he would return perhaps in death. His immortal soul would sing among the crags and ice, sail upon the wind and dive to the green depths of the sea. It would be free of the insanity of his present life.

Dusk came as they arrived at the house, under heavily armed guard and bound as they had been when they were brought into Chelmsford and paraded before the townspeople. Their warders, a half dozen of the servants of Sir Thomas, treated the prisoners roughly, cursing them and spitting at them, and on one occasion threatening to cut off their manly parts, but then he who was chief among them called the others to order and the threats ceased. Adam and Nicholas were roughly ushered through a side door of the house and then immediately conveyed to a dark cellar, where they were shoved into a cramped, windowless cell and their manacles were removed. These unpleasant surroundings assured Adam that for all the impressiveness of the manor house his present accommodations amounted to nothing more than a prison, where he would languish along with his companion at the magistrate's pleasure.

This impression was no sooner formed then qualified, however, for shortly after being placed in his cell he heard an exchange of orders, and then the servant who had been in charge of their imprisonment returned, seized Nicholas, and bore him away, with Adam too exhausted from his flight and bruised by his capture to protest or question the man as to where his friend was being taken.

After that he sat a long time in the darkness, cold and hungry, but neither candle nor food was brought to relieve his distress. In addition, the blows administered by the stonemason in his capture caused him considerable discomfort, and had he been of a womanly disposition he would have wept.

Instead, he drew into himself, pulling himself up into a ball, as much for consolation as for warmth. He thought of Nicholas. Why had he been removed from the cell? Where was he now, and in what wretched state of loneliness and despair? The thought of his friend and his circumstances was as great a pain to him as his own miserable condition, and he would have cried out to one of the gods—either him to whom the English prayed or to one of the deities of his own people—but in his exhaustion and despair he could not find enough faith in anything to utter a word.

Chapter 14

ה

Matthew slept like the dead all the night, so exhausted he was, but Joan tossed fitfully and had horrible dreams of impenetrable woods and the savage beasts that dwell there. Toward morning she had a nightmare of such vividness that she came awake with a start, trembling like poor Jack Potts, who often sat begging at the market cross.

It was a dream about Adam Nemo, in which she saw him twisting about on the hangman's rope, his face all swollen and his eyes bulging and his black swollen tongue protruding like an eel's head. Then Adam was cut down, cut down by the boy Nicholas, who in the dream could not only speak but sing. The voice he had was like her own husband's sweet tenor, a rivulet of pure sound.

In the dream Nicholas sang all the time while he was removing the corpse from the gibbet. Then at the terrifying end of the vision, Nicholas placed the body on a platform that Joan realized was an altar and said the words the parson used when he administered the holy communion: *Take and eat. This is my body and blood which was shed for you.*

She awoke in such a frightful state she could not remember Nicholas's song, only the words he spoke above the body: *Take and eat.*

She could hardly wait for Matthew to awake so she could tell him of the dream and ask him what he supposed it to mean. For were not all dreams of some significance? Were they not a means by which either God or the devil conveyed dark truths to the dreamer, warning of things to come or revealing that which is obscured in the waking life? Who, Joan considered, believed otherwise? To dispute the purpose of dreams was hardly better than atheism, to her way of thinking.

But she could hardly begin her account of her dream when Matthew compelled her to hear the dream he had had, despite his appearance of dreamlessness, which had some of the same horrid features as hers.

"I was never so thankful as to find myself awake and in my own bed," he said, rubbing the sleep from his eyes and beseeching her to light a candle, for it was not yet dawn. "I was again in the snow, but you were with me, riding on another horse, a black, sweating gelding with fiery eyes. Yet you managed him well, sitting very proudly, dressed in your green gown with the embroidered front, while I was bundled up against the cold."

"Was I not shivering to be so dressed in such weather?" she asked.

"It might have been midsummer for all the discomfort you displayed. You rode boldly forth. In the dream we were seeking Adam and Nicholas, but there were only the two of us. Then we came upon a forest, larger and darker than the deer park, so that it seemed impossible to find a way therein. We rode round and round about."

Joan said that the dream did not sound as fearful as he had claimed.

"But the worst was yet to come. Against my counsel you rode into the forest; all of a sudden you did, and I never saw an opening at all. The trees swallowed you up, and I could hear your horse's breathing and hear your voice beckoning to me to follow but could see nothing but the trees, which as I have said grew so closely together as to be woven into one solid fabric."

"And this made you afraid?" she asked, rather hoping that Matthew had revealed the entirety of the dream, for his account was beginning to make her flesh crawl and she was now more than ready to forgo this exchange of dreams and rather bury the memory of them in the clear light of day. Getting out of bed, she lit a candle. The timorous flame did little to dissipate her melancholy. She crawled back under the covers, drawing close to him.

"You called for help," he said.

"Was I in danger, then?"

"You were."

"What, of being lost?."

"You weren't lost. You had been attacked."

"By brigands? By Adam or Nicholas?"

"No."

She heard the tremor in his voice and knew that he was not finding it easy to convey his dream to her. It was no wonder, given it was a dream of the forest. The forest was no place of refuge or repose, but of confusion and isolation and the terrors that went with them. Satan, it was said, dwelt in the forest, which was why witches congregated there to practice unspeakable rituals.

She patted his thigh and said, "It is better to tell me than to keep this thing in your heart. Fear not, husband. It is a dream you speak of, not reality."

Matthew hesitated; she waited. Then he said, "You called out that you were attacked by dead men."

"Dead men!"

"Men without flesh upon their bones."

Joan felt a great fear when he said this. Matthew's dream had been truly terrible. What could it mean? For a few moments she made no response. Then she said, "You are right, then, husband. That is the most grisly dream, if I was so used, that ever I heard."

"And you told me their names."

"Which were?"

"John Crookback, you said, and Ralph Hawking."

"John Crookback we know," she said, "and yet I trust his body, having been buried within the week, is not yet so rotten. But who is this Ralph Hawking? I remember no such name."

"Nor I, and yet you said Ralph Hawking in the dream. I recall it as though you said it no more than a few minutes ago."

"How did the dream end, Matthew? I trow you came to rescue me like a good husband."

"I would have done so, had I been able, Joan," Matthew said. "That was the worst part. I could not find a way into that dismal wood. Yet you called out in full voice. Then your screams became the weaker, like the twitter of birds. I tried the harder but to no avail."

"That was the whole of it? The dream, I mean?"

"Is it not enough?"

"I suppose it could have been worse," she said, thinking of her own dream but now firmly decided to save the telling of it for another occasion. To herself she prayed for light to come to dissipate her gloom.

"I suppose it could. Yet it was bad enough. I woke with my heart pounding and was never so happy when I reached out and found you in bed beside me," he said again, "safe from dead men and dismal woods."

"Yes," she said. "Better a warm bed than a dismal forest any day. I would be spared the dead men, too."

He did not respond as she hoped to her attempt at wit, which was, she realized, a feeble effort, meant to revive her naturally buoyant spirits. That both she and her husband could have dreams of similar character only convinced her the more of their prophetic purpose. The question in her mind now was whether they proceeded from heaven or from hell—whether they were shadows of things to come or clues to the mysteries of the past.

"Let's pray, husband," she said just as the room began to grow light, "that God in heaven may dispel the melancholy that these visions of the night have wrought and save our souls from whatever evil they may portend."

"Yes, let's do," he said. They knelt beside their bed. First Matthew prayed and then Joan and then Matthew again.

It was market day. After breakfast Joan got her basket, and with Alice as her companion she went out into the street and headed toward the market cross. This widening of the cobbled street made of the Sessions House a little island and on Thursdays tradesmen and farmers of the shire sold their wares from booths set up for the occasion. Since it was winter, both booths and customers were far apart indeed, although there were some neighbors walking amid the stalls. As she passed by she greeted most, for she was well known in the town, but was surprised to find her friendly greetings were not returned with the warmth to which she was accustomed. Instead she detected an aloofness in the response of several of her friends that mystified and disturbed her mightily. She gave Alice instructions as to what to look for among the stalls and returned home.

Midmornings Matthew spent in his shop, often working at his accounts or helping customers to select from among the rich store of cloth, for which Essex was famous. As she entered she found him sitting upon his high stool, his big ledger open and Peter Bench at his side. Matthew was explaining something to his apprentice, and ordinarily Joan would not have interrupted, but so upset was she from having been shunned by persons she had known all her life that she could not refrain.

"Matthew, something has happened."

Matthew looked up suddenly, and seeing her expression was troubled, he sent Peter off to the rear of the house to fetch some cloth stored there. He regarded Joan with a mixture of curiosity and concern and led her into the kitchen, where they sat down at the table across from one another. Matthew took Joan's hand, taking off the gloves she had neglected to remove in her haste to report whatever it was she had to report.

"Why what's the matter, Joan?" he said, rubbing her hands in his own to warm them. "Is it another murder? Are our friends dead?"

She assured him that to her knowledge neither of the catastrophes he mentioned had occurred. She said, "I was walking in the market, among the booths, and saw Sarah Bright and Jane Dale and greeted them both."

"And what if you did?" Matthew said, a puzzled look upon his face. "That's no new thing. The two women you mention are so much about, it would be a wonder if you did not see them."

"They said never a word, neither one."

"Now for those two that is a wonder," he said, smiling.

"This is no jape, Matthew," she said.

"I see it is not, but I still do not understand what you are complaining of."

"I greeted the twain with a friendly wave, such as this." Joan made a little wave Matthew recognized as a distinctive gesture. "Neither responded with word or wave but turned quickly away, shunning me as though I were a leper."

"Are you sure they saw you?"

"Of course I am sure," she said impatiently. "I am not blind. My eyes are, if anything, better than your own."

Matthew acknowledged that her eyesight was superior to his; she had proved it time and time again. "If you were shunned by acquaintances of such long standing I cannot begin to comprehend the cause. What offense have you committed to be so treated, or I?"

Their discourse on this topic was now interrupted by the arrival of Alice. This followed so quickly upon Joan's own return that she was amazed, for Alice ever loved good gossip and might be depended on to stay two hours or more in doing what might have been done in a quarter of the time.

"Back so soon?" Joan said as the cook came into the kitchen, put the basket on the table, and placed her hands on her hips in an attitude of exasperation and dismay. Joan knew at once that something was amiss.

"I have been given an earful of fresh news," Alice said, "that sticks in my craw like a fish bone. You, Mistress Stock, are a part of the tale, as is my shiftless husband. That he should be preyed upon by idle minds is hardly beyond his deserts, for he wastes time in a tavern rather than seeking work within his ability. But that you should be so used . . ." She shook her head.

"How have I been used?" Joan exclaimed, hardly able to wait until Alice would bring out the substance of her report.

"By Sarah Bright, who said you pried into her business, inquiring of sundry persons regarding scandals in her family."

"Which thing I never did!" Joan exclaimed, amazed that such a lie should be told of her.

"And from Mistress Dale I heard a similar tune: that you did peek and poke about in the town, at every door. And that you thought the murderers caught were never such, but that the real murderer was one of them, She advised me to leave your employ—she asked that I come cook for her."

"The shameless hussy," Joan said. "These are base lies and the work of an enemy of more wit than Jane Dale may boast of, for a sheep has more good sense than she. It is doubtful this mischief was given birth in her addled brain."

"Did either woman say who did tell them these tales?" Matthew asked.

"They did not, Master Stock, but would say only that they were mightily offended by your wife's suspicions, that they were as blameless as could be, and that neither would ever speak to Joan again, nor would they make purchases at your shop but would off to some other clothier to satisfy their needs."

"You are right; this is serious business, Joan," Matthew said.

She nodded and turned back to Alice, who was still breathing heavily from the haste of her return. "I don't suppose either of my erstwhile friends made mention of Agnes Profytt."

Alice thought for a few moments and then said, "Why I believe Jane did. Yes, she did mention Mistress Profytt's name, and the name of my husband and of Master Barber, the old man who lives at the end of the street."

"This is Agnes Profytt's doing," Joan said, looking at Matthew with dangerous eyes. "Don't try to tell me it is not. And do not say you told me so, that this trouble would not have come if I been Mistress Compliant and stayed home. I have the right to walk the streets of my own town as I please and when I please, murderers or no, and to ask reasonable questions of my neighbors in matters in which I have some interest. And what of greater interest than my husband's very life? I mean the dangers you faced in the hue and cry."

Matthew agreed that she did, but his agreement did little to pacify Joan. She could not restrain her anger. "This woman is hardly better than a witch, for while she may not call upon the powers of darkness yet her malice knows no bounds. This is not grief for her dead father and siblings that moves her—all the world knows how she regarded him, and her stepmother the more. Where there was such a deal of resentment before, why should anyone find a blooming love now for those poor murdered wretches? No, I say, husband, this is not about grief. It is about greed, and jealousy, and boundless envy and pride, and God knows what other vices of the heart."

"Whatever it is about," Matthew said, "she must be stopped, or we shall have no friends nor be trusted in our own town. Her tongue is a flaming organ; it will set all Chelmsford on fire."

"You should go to the magistrate," Joan said. "Sir Thomas will set things right. These women need to know that I have made no inquiries regarding them and hold no suspicions of their probity. And Sir Thomas must know that you do not work to undermine his authority or his actions."

Joan was now so wrought up by this malicious gossip against her and Matthew that she could no longer sit at table. She stood and began pacing the stone floor of the kitchen in a fury, while Matthew sat very quiet, thinking, and Alice remained where she stood, her arms still akimbo and her normally cheerful countenance glowering over the offense done her beloved mistress.

"My husband is also a target of these whisperers," Alice said.

"How so?" asked Matthew.

Alice's expression changed. She seemed reluctant to speak.

Picking up the hesitation of her servant, Joan stopped her restless patrol and urged Alice to answer the question Matthew had put to her, for she said she wanted to hear all the unsavory accusations made, whether against her and Matthew or against Alice's own husband. "Let us have no secrets between us," she said. "We are all defamed. We must join together. Fear to tell us nothing."

Alice nodded, gulped some air, and said, "It is said that he makes lies on Mistress Stock's commands."

"What lies?" Joan asked.

"Lies about John Crookback, and what went on before."

"Before what?"

"Before—in the old days. When John Crookback returned from the sea to take up his inheritance. It is said these lies are shaped to put into question their inheritance because the Stocks would have the land for themselves."

"A foolish slander," Matthew said. "What possible claim could we have to Crookback Farm, even if the rest of these libels are true?"

"It is said that if the claim of the Profytts and Carews is doubtful, then my husband may lay claim, which claim he intends to share with you. It is said that you are planning to accuse the daughters of the murders, for no murderer can inherit his victim's goods."

"So may the law decree," said Joan, "but I still do not understand how Matthew or I should benefit from your husband's inheritance any more than another citizen who urged your husband on."

"Sarah Bright said she understood that you and your husband and my shiftless one and I were all at one in the conspiracy. That you were working to clear Nicholas and Master Burton's servant from blame and to shift suspicion to the Profytts and Carews."

"Still that would not accrue any benefit to us," Matthew reasoned. "We have no connection to the Crookbacks, nor does anyone think it that I know of. Free of blame, Nicholas Crookback is the true heir as the sole surviving son of John Crook-back."

"Sarah Bright said that it was all a conspiracy, that you would find a way to make my husband the heir. Why, she even said to me she hoped I would remember her well when I came into my newfound wealth, although she warned me to beware of my husband's love, for she said when men became suddenly wealthy they often tired of old wives and sought out new. I am healthy as a horse and plan to live until I am old, said I. But she said, men have ways to bring good women to an early grave."

"This is all confused and malicious gossip," Matthew said with disgust. "It makes no sense at all. Surely a reasonable person would see that we have no way of benefitting from the Crookback inheritance. I am no farmer, but a clothier, and no more relation to John Crookback than to the queen."

For a while Joan had been silent; Matthew looked up at her, as though to ask if her fury was spent. "I am thinking," she said, "that something of these calumnies is truth."

"What, for heaven's sake?"

"Well," Joan said, regarding her husband with a shrewd expression she reserved for occasions when she was thinking very hard about something, "my queries do undermine the claims of the Profytts and Carews. If John Crookback that appeared to be was some other person only posing as the heir, then his claim was fraud. Nor would the imposter's daughters—or for that matter his son, Nicholas—have a valid claim. Another heir must be sought, and as far as is known, Richard is the only living relation of old Abraham Crookback."

Matthew thought about this, then said, "Marry, so it may be that this assumption of impostership undermines their claims. Still, it is not true we have accused Agnes or Mildred of murder."

"We have made no charges of that kind," Joan agreed, "but consider this. What if their father was not John Crookback, mariner, but some erstwhile companion of the real heir, who, having learned the circumstances of the true John Crookback's youth, then returned upon the true heir's death—or heaven forfend, murder—pretending to be John Crookback?"

"Go on," Matthew said.

"Then toward his life's end, this same imposter of whatever true name remains yet to be discovered, is called to account by conscience, informs his family of the truth and his intention to confess all that he may find a place in heaven. The children of such a man would be disgraced. More to the purpose, they would lose all, the farmstead as well as their reputation."

"I cannot believe patricide would proceed from such a motive," Matthew said. "Agnes and Mildred are the daughters of the dead man."

"A man that rumor held was much detested by the same daughters, and the stepmother and her brood held in less esteem by these children of the first wife. It all fits, Matthew, like hand in glove. The Profytts and Carews are of modest means. Their shares of Crookback Farm would enhance their wealth considerably, just as the silence of their father about his true identity would spare them disgrace. There may indeed be things that even the greedy will not do for money, but the desire to avoid the contempt of one's neighbors may be an even stronger motive to break God's laws and man's."

For another hour she developed her theory, until her husband claimed he was persuaded that there might be more truth in it than imagination. "But you must do more than conjecture," he said. "Proof must be furnished, of which precious commodity we have little at present."

"At least it's a beginning," she said smiling pleasantly at him, grateful for this modicum of support, for she was not perfectly sure of her theory herself, and not unhappy at the vision of Agnes Profytt or Mildred Carew—or perhaps both—dangling from a hangman's rope.

By the end of the afternoon the absence of custom in his shop had made Matthew even more worried about the damage done by Agnes Profytt's malice, if indeed she was the source of the calumnies. He also had second thoughts about Joan's account of the murder, which he believed not so neatly woven as she had argued with such vigor. In the first place he wondered why, if the murders were the work of the daughters and their husbands, Nicholas Crookback should have been spared. By all accounts, the daughters hated their half brother, finding him both obnoxious and an embarrassment to them. Why should he not also have been slain and dumped down the well? Unless of course Nicholas was an ally against his own father, which thing Matthew could hardly credit.

And in the second place, he thought the preventing of the false John Crookback's confession would not require the murder of his wife and other children. Unless Crookback had told them and they too knew the truth, which thing Matthew thought possible but unlikely. No, to Matthew, the breadth of the slaughter suggested revenge, not a desire to suppress a dangerous truth. Master Fuller's view that Adam Nemo murdered the Crookbacks had this to recommend it, that a savage bent on avenging an old wrong might according to his benighted reasoning kill his enemy and all his relations too. That made a kind of sense. Joan's explanation did not.

He was mulling over these matters when the door of his shop opened. He looked up expectantly, hoping to see one customer at least, and was surprised to see the very man of whom he had been thinking. But Fuller was hardly alone; with him were Sir Thomas, William Dees, and Miles Carew. All the men looked very serious, and when he welcomed them to his shop Sir Thomas responded with a curt God save you, and they all came in and stood around very awkwardly, Matthew thought. He asked if this worshipful company were there to buy cloth, but no one answered or seemed to appreciate his humor.

Having heard the shop bell ring, Joan at the same time came in from the kitchen and now stood wiping her hands on her apron. Before anyone could say another word, she was asking Sir Thomas and Master Fuller if their worships would have something to eat or drink, for it was late in the day, she said, almost suppertime. And she looked at Matthew too, as though to ask if more light should be fetched, for it was near four in the afternoon if she had counted the last peal rightly.

"We will not stay long enough to partake of your hospitality, Mistress Stock," Sir Thomas said solemnly, and then he turned to Matthew and said, "We have heard some things we like not, Master Stock."

"What would those things be, Your Honor?" Matthew replied, feeling that he already knew and shifting his own gaze to meet that of Miles Carew, whose smug expression convinced Matthew that he was right.

"I will not mince words," Sir Thomas said. "I have heard that you and your wife have been asking questions touching upon Miles Carew's late father-in-law and have been casting suspicion among your neighbors, so as to throw into doubt the guilt of Nicholas Crookback and him they call Adam Nemo in that same person's murder. I would know if what I have been told is true, and if it be so, what proof you have to offer."

Matthew exchanged glances with Joan, who was standing very still, her hands still caught up in her apron. In the dim light of the window her face seemed gray and immobile.

"I admit, Your Honor, that I have my doubts about the guilt of the two persons you have named."

"And your proof?"

Matthew again looked at Joan. Her dark, watchful eyes gave him no signal of reassurance. Looking back at the magistrate, Matthew shrugged and admitted that he had none, not an iota.

"I see," said Sir Thomas, frowning. "So you have no proof at all."

"Yet that either my wife or I have cast suspicion upon any other persons is a malicious falsehood spread by I know not whom," Matthew said.

"We have heard otherwise, Master Stock," said Fuller, stepping forward a little, so that his imposing form seemed to fill the room. "Miles Carew here claims you told Sarah Bright that his wife was no true descendent of Abraham Crookback, and that both he and his wife might have had good reason to see

212

her late father brought to his grave sooner than the natural course of things allowed. To me that is nothing else but an accusation of murder."

"And I am falsely accused, and my wife as well," said Miles Carew, lifting his chin defiantly behind Fuller.

"As God is my witness, I have made no such accusations," Matthew said.

Now Joan spoke, declaring that she too had never said any such thing and hoped heaven would spare whoever had claimed otherwise, for it was a damnable lie and false witness.

"Moreover, there is a wealth of evidence proving the two prisoners guilty as charged," Fuller said, looking around at the other men for support of this proposition. "Who but a heathen would have committed such a monstrous act? Who but a simpleton could suppose that decent Christians such as none may doubt the Profytts and the Carews to be would risk damnation to kill their very parents. It's a monstrous thing just to think it."

"Well," Joan said, "Nicholas is their son and he is accused. Why is it less monstrous to accuse the son of killing the father than to accuse the daughters?"

Fuller regarded Joan contemptuously. "Why, what are you thinking, woman? This Nicholas is no ordinary boy. His affliction is a curse of God—for some evil done either by him or by his parents. Were it otherwise, he would be whole. In any case, he cannot be considered to have the same moral impulses as a normal child. He cannot be trusted to have within his heart the law which makes patricide unthinkable."

Joan had no answer to Fuller's speech. He was a learned man; she was a simple housewife. What did she know of moral impulses or patricide, whose daily concern was the care of her husband and the rearing of her child? And yet Joan knew in her heart what Fuller had said was neither right nor true. Whatever a moral impulse was, she was convinced it was as much a part of Nicholas's being as it was of her own. She had looked into the boy's eyes; she had seen no evil there. And while she might not know a fig of philosophy, she knew right from wrong, goodness from its opposite. If anything, Nicholas's affliction was a blessing from God, setting him apart from his neighbors, surrounding him with the aura of sanctity. But she did not put these thoughts into words. She merely bowed her head in apparent submission, praying that Fuller would now be satisfied that his point was made.

But then Matthew answered on her behalf. "The accused men are no strangers to this town," he said in a calm, confident voice, looking straight in Fuller's eye. "Adam Nemo has lived among us for twenty years, since John Crookback brought him here; Nicholas Crookback all of his life. Were either imbued with the evil you suggest, sir, surely it would have manifested itself earlier. But it did not so. No one has complained of Nicholas's behavior. No one ever feared Adam Nemo's vengefulness, nor even detected it. No one thought anything but that Adam was a foreigner, like one of the Dutchmen who labor in our trade, and for that reason strange in appearance, and strange of speech. It seems wrong to me that he should be condemned for a moral fault simply because he is not English—as it seems wrong Nicholas should be likewise regarded because an accident of birth left him deaf and dumb. Surely God understands the words of his heart, and if indeed this is so, then we do him wrong to call him evil whom God has heard in silent prayers."

For a moment Fuller made no answer to Matthew's statement. Joan held her breath. The room was deadly quiet.

Then Fuller said, "I see, Master Stock, that what is said of you in the town is true, that you think a great deal of yourself, for how else should you presume to contend with me over matters of philosophy? Have you been at the university, then, and studied these matters, or do you have your learning from some other place?"

"I have no learning, sir," Matthew said, "above what I have acquired in my trade and in our school here, and precious little in the latter."

"Then you speak presumptuously and foolishly," Fuller said. "Take my advice. Seek not to counsel those whom God has chosen to place above you."

"Master Fuller speaks wisely, Matthew," said Sir Thomas. "He has studied the nature of humankind for many years and has traveled among the savages of America. He knows their practices and their disposition. As for the good demeanor of this Adam Nemo, it is not unusual for these savages' true natures to rest obscure for many a year, only to burst forth when they are least expected. Is that not so, Master Fuller?"

Fuller said it was.

There was another awkward silence, during which Joan was so fearful that she wished she might sink through the very floor. She looked at Matthew, whose face was ashen, but whose eyes still burned hotly with what she recognized as suppressed anger.

"I am heartily sorry if I have overstepped myself," Matthew said. He looked at Joan and then made a low bow in Fuller's direction. "And I beg your pardon, Master Fuller. Of course I do not presume to know more than you about philosophy or human nature. I am a clothier, a simple man."

"Well then," said Sir Thomas, "let us have no more contention about these accused persons. Let the queen's law take its course. At their trial all evidence will be heard, and at that time I trust justice will be done and with great satisfaction we will watch these two hanged."

There were murmurs of agreement from William Dees and Miles Carew at this. Then Miles Carew said, "What about the slanders against my wife and family, Sir Thomas? Should Stock not be admonished to desist?"

"I do admonish him, Miles Carew," Sir Thomas said, looking directly at Matthew. "And his good wife as well. The town has been more than troubled by these murders. Let those troubles not be added upon by malicious rumor, nor a decent family who has lost much in these horrors be vilified by groundless suspicions. John Crookback's claims to his father's farm were duly considered, with honest witnesses coming forth, such as our good William Dees who knew John Crookback from boyhood on and acquitted himself so bravely yesterday. The matter is settled once and for all. Let us not dig up old controversies that have been laid to rest. Is that understood, Matthew?"

Matthew said it was. Their visitors departed without further word, and husband and wife stood looking at each other and not saying anything for some time.

That morning Adam's jailers brought him breakfast—a piece of moldy bread and a thin gruel in which he found nothing afloat. The gruel was cold, tasteless as brackish water. But it was all one with him who had no appetite at all and had determined not to eat. He spent his time listening, and he would have called out for Nicholas if calling out would have done any good. The smell of his own excrement, unremoved from the leaking chamber pot left for him, was so disgusting as to bring on an awful nausea. This he endured too, waiting now for the end of his misery.

He was contemplating that end, and it was worrying him not at all, when he was startled by the ring of a pistol shot from somewhere nearby. His heart failed him for fear—not for himself, for had he his choice he would have preferred a ball in the head or heart to a broken neck, or worse, slow strangulation upon the gibbet. But what of Nicholas. Had they killed him outright, without waiting for the trial?

Only a short time later Adam heard several sets of footsteps approaching. The door was unlocked, and then it swung open; three men—one of whom was the near giant, he who had escorted Adam roughly into his narrow cell the day before—stood outside.

"There he is," said the big man, his face as round and pocky as the moon. "Take your look and do not say I asked too much for the honor."

The other two men, who were evidently household servants such as Adam had been, smooth-faced and neat in their liveries, looked in hesitantly. One made a face of disgust and complained of the stench.

"Oh that's as much him as his shit," said the big man in

216

response to the complaint. "The savages all smell that way. Master Fuller says as much. But does he not look like the very image of a murderer?"

The servant who had voiced the complaint said it was so, and the big man said all savages were murderers at heart and that no honest Englishman would be safe until the miscreant before them rode upon the three-legged mare, as the gallows of St. Giles was called.

"Pray God he ride soon," said the third man, who had flaxen hair so soft a woman could have been proud of it and a clear blue eye and red lips. He looked at Adam as though he were a dead, bloated dog rotting on his doorstep.

"Oh he will ride soon enough," said the big man, "for the evidence is weighty against him, though he has the gall to deny it. His companion, the dummy, is another. He's English, but of the same heathenish stripe, for he cannot speak nor hear, as you saw when I fired my pistol next his head."

The men all laughed nervously, and Adam was somewhat relieved to learn that the explosion he had heard had not heralded the death of his friend.

"Can he speak in his native tongue," said the servant with the womanly face and hair.

"We shall see," said the big man. He walked into the cell and, seizing Adam under the arms, lifted him off the ground as though he weighed nothing. Adam's heart lodged in his throat.

"Speak the tongue you were born to, you monkey-face," the big man commanded through clenched teeth. His breath was very bad, and the man's body odor was almost as foul as the chamber pot. "Do not deny me, or you'll be sorry."

"Did Sir Thomas give you permission so to use me?" Adam managed to say.

The big man's eyes glared at this. He lowered Adam slowly to the ground but did not release the pressure on his sides, which was as painful as it was humiliating.

"I suppose you'll tell him, will you? If you do, you'll be sorry. You'll wish you were hanged yesterday and already buried. I'll make what little is left of your life so miserable you'll wish you were never born in that godforsaken country whence you came.''

The big man squeezed more tightly, and Adam feared his chest would be crushed.

"Speak your savage tongue," he said, "so that my friend here can have joy of it."

Adam tried to remember. No words would come to mind. The big man squeezed harder, and now Adam knew he could not speak even if he had willed it. He had no breath. He felt the sudden sharp agony of a rib snapping. The intense pain dissolved into blackness.

In that blackness he felt no more pain but heard voices, English voices raised over a field of ice.

Crookback, let the man be!

Chapter 15

ה

"Husband, what shall we do?"

Matthew sighed heavily and sat down on the stool. He rested his forehead in his hand. "Grow old and die before our time," he said, and then he laughed a short bitter laugh that was half a choking sob and had not a whit of humor in it. He looked up with tears in his eyes.

She went to him and put her arm around his shoulder and pulled his head to her breast. "I pray you, do not lose your faith, husband," she said, "or fall victim to these melancholy thoughts of death and dying. You have done no wrong in this matter but have had wrong done unto you. God forgive me if I have been the cause of some of it. I should have obeyed. I should have stayed at home yesterday, or at least kept my doubts to myself. Yet you will win Sir Thomas's trust again, I know you will."

"You are not to blame, Joan," he said, straightening a little. "This is Agnes Profytt's doing, just as you surmised. If I weep womanishly, it is not out of guilt but frustration. My hands are

219

tied. I am slapped in the face. Your inquiries must cease. We must have naught to do with the Profytts or the Carews or even with Alice's husband, for we shall be watched now, and the first breach of Sir Thomas's command will bring punishment on our heads. As it stands, my business may be ruined by these vicious tales of Agnes's."

"God forbid it comes to that," Joan said. "Of Essex clothiers you are prince. No one knows his trade better than you, or is more deservedly praised for honest dealing. These troubles will pass."

"The town has a long memory," Matthew said.

Joan could not deny it. The town did indeed have a long memory. Old scandals were remembered for generations; old wrongs were righted by the victims' grandchildren. Master Fuller had condemned the savages for their vengefulness; how were so-called Christians any better, after all was said and done?

"Besides, your theory stands more to reason than it did."

She wondered at this; her husband had seemed only half persuaded before. Now, when he had more reason to disbelieve, he had become converted. Why? she wanted to know.

"My dream of yesternight," he said. "The one that put such fear in me. It came to me when the gentleman were here, all of a sudden."

"You dreamed the dream again?" she asked, marveling.

"No, the name that neither of us could remember having heard before, the name of one of your attackers. John Crookback was the one, and the other name was Ralph Hawking."

She nodded, remembering that he had told her this.

"While Master Fuller spoke of the savages and their ways, I remembered where I had heard the name. It was the letter we found in Crookback's chest. Ralph Hawking was he to whom the letter was sent; the assayer assured him that the black stones contained gold."

"Why yes, so it was. It was so plain the letter must mean something, concealed as it was."

"But Sir Thomas dismissed its importance, convinced as he was that Adam Nemo and Nicholas were the murderers."

"We should have kept it for ourselves, for all the good it did. Sir Thomas thought nothing of it."

"Yes, when the name came to me, I thought, why should I dream of it were it not of some strange meaning, as we first supposed? John Crookback threatens you, because his murder plagues us. My dream yoked the two men together. They are both threats, and now I believe as do you that the explanation of these murders is found in the past—in Frobisher's voyage and in the bringing of Adam Nemo to England and then to Chelmsford—and in John Crookback's inheritance."

Joan said she was glad beyond words to have her own opinion shared by him. "You asked what we must do before, and now I know," Matthew told her.

"And that is?"

"We must sort this riddle out ourselves, for it will not be done for us. If I am ever to regain Sir Thomas's trust and vindicate our name, it must be shown that we have been right all along—that Adam Nemo and Nicholas Crookback are innocent."

"Do you dare disobey Sir Thomas's command that we have no more to do with these matters?" she asked.

"I must," he said. He told her a plan.

After supper Joan pointed out that if they went their separate ways they would attract less attention. Matthew wanted to visit Crookback Farm again; Joan was bent on finding out more about the witnesses in the matter of John Crookback's inheritance and had concocted an excuse to visit William Dees and his wife. "I can go now and carry her some fresh bread for herself and her children. She is sick, I have heard. My visit will be construed as nothing more sinister than a mission of mercy. Her husband may tell us something about this Ralph Hawking, for William knew John Crookback in those old days."

"And I will go to the farmstead," Matthew said. "It has been deserted since the murders. Who would prowl around there at night? I want another peek at John Crookback's bedchamber. We may have overlooked something."

"What would that be?" she asked, because he spoke as though he already knew.

"Something that tells us more about this Ralph Hawking. John Crookback possessed his letter; is it not possible he had other things of the man's?"

William Dees and his family lived at the other end of town from the Stocks; his house was more modest, and his shop in a shed attached to the rear. The stonemason had married somewhat late in life, and Joan did not know his wife well, since she had come from another town and was rumored to have been a harlot before her repentance. A slight, pale woman with thin arms and legs and the doleful expression of one who has been forewarned of an early death, she seemed to have been sickly all the days of their marriage. In matters physical, then, she was a stark contrast to her large, muscular husband, who was the very image of health even though his age surpassed hers by a dozen years or more. Joan knew that at an earlier time Dees had been fond of Susanna Crookback, and yet he and John had been friends and often companions, proving to her satisfaction that old enmities did not always endure.

The stonemason answered the door when she knocked and seemed more than a little surprised to see her.

"I have come to pay my respects to your good wife, if that is not displeasing to you," Joan said. She showed him the basket she carried, told him it contained bread and sweetmeats for their supper.

"Why should it be?" Dees answered, He motioned for her to come in.

I thought that perhaps after this morning—"

"Oh think nothing of that," Dees answered agreeably. "A little misunderstanding. Exaggerated by the those who should know better. I bear you no grudges, Mistress Stock, nor your good husband, who gave decent service to us during the hue and cry."

Relieved that he had no resentment toward her, Joan went in and found his wife, whose name was Esther, sitting on a stool by the fire. At her feet slept one of her children, a little girl of four or five. Joan could hear the other children, two older boys, in an adjoining room.

Dees shut the door to the room where his sons played and said to his wife, "Esther, Joan Stock has come to see how you do. She has brought a little present."

Esther Dees was wrapped in a heavy if threadbare cloak; only her small, round face peered out at Joan. The woman's eyes were so pale as to be almost colorless. She tried to smile in response to her husband's introduction, but her attempt amounted to nothing more than a slight parting of the lips. That she was seriously ill was obvious, and painful for Joan to behold.

Joan bent over to take the woman's hands, which despite the fire in the hearth were as cold as ice. "How do you do, Esther?" she said, "I heard you were sick and now see that the report is true."

"It is true," she said. "Thank God my good husband is here to take care of me and the children, else we would perish this cruel winter."

Joan looked up at Dees, who was standing behind his wife protectively. The fire whose heat had failed to warm his wife's hands had so warmed him as to cause him to sweat, for rivulets ran down his forehead into his thick beard. Looking at his massive chest, and sturdy legs, she wondered if William were still using Esther as a wife, or if he had forgone his privilege. The man must be immense, she thought, and the wife seemed such a frail thing, hardly able to bear the weight of her own body, much less his upon her. Joan had not heard that Dees frequented the brothels of the town, of which there were a disgracefully large number.

A little bench also stood before the fire. On this Joan sat while Dees remained standing. For a few minutes Joan chatted about the weather, avoiding the subject of the murders for fear of betraying her true motive for the visit.

Then, addressing Dees, "I was most happy to see you in Sir Thomas's company this morning," she said as airily as she might.

223

"Why is that?" Dees said.

"So that my doubts might be laid to rest. It's true I wondered whether John Crookback might be Abraham's true heir, but when I learned you were among those who swore it was so, my doubts were satisfied, since I know you to be an honest man."

"The matter was settled nearly twenty years ago," Dees said with sudden bitterness. "John Crookback was my friend in my youth. He remained so until the day he was murdered by his idiot son and that savage that Master Burton kept as a servant. No one knew John Crookback as well as I, not even his wives."

"I understand he had an old friend who also testified," Joan said.

"I would not call Richard Hull an old friend, if that's he of whom you speak, Mistress Stock," said Dees.

"Oh, I meant Ralph Hawking," Joan said.

Dees started at the name and then said, "I do not know anyone of that name, Mistress Stock. If John Crookback had such a friend it was in the days when he was at sea, not in Chelmsford."

"Marry, I think it was at sea," Joan said.

"How did you come by the name?" Dees asked.

"My husband found it in a letter of John Crookback's when we searched the house at Crookback Farm for Sir Thomas. The letter was addressed to Ralph Hawking; because Crookback kept the letter along with other personal things, Matthew supposed that the two men were friends."

"That might be, I don't know," Dees said. "What personal things might those have been, if you don't mind my asking?"

Now Joan was not sure what she should say and indeed wondered if she had said too much already. Her greatest concern was to stand clear of any talk of the Profytts and Carews, talk that might create the impression that she possessed a desire to incriminate either family. She decided that she could afford to be direct.

"My husband found a chest in which your friend kept his private papers. It was there he discovered this letter from an assayer addressed to Ralph Hawking, and your friend's will."

"Where is the chest now?" Dees asked.

"Still at the farm," Joan said. "Unless Sir Thomas has taken it for evidence.

"As I say, John may have known this Ralph Hawking while he was with Frobisher," Dees said.

There was a note of finality in the stonemason's voice that suggested to Joan that she had asked too many questions, and that were she to ask more the true purpose of her visit would be too obvious for her host to ignore. "Well," she said, rising and looking down at Esther. "May God bless you and make you soon well, and your good children too."

"The children and I are well," Dees said. "Only my wife is sick."

There was so much pride in his assertion that Joan felt a sudden dislike for the man, who before had always seemed an agreeable sort.

When Joan returned home she recounted to Matthew her visit to the stonemason's house, describing the lamentable condition of the wife and reporting every word that William Dees had said in response to her questions about Ralph Hawking.

"He denied ever having known such a one. He suggested Hawking might have been a friend from Crookback's days as a mariner."

"Which may be the absolute truth," Matthew observed.

"So my expedition came to nothing," she said. "Dees was most forthright. He irked me only in being so proud of his radiant health when his wife is sickly. I like not that quality in a man—no, nor in a woman either."

"If the John Crookback we knew was not the true son of Abraham Crookback, it is quite possible that Dees was as much deceived as was Richard Hull, or any of the others who affirmed him to be who he claimed to be," Matthew said.

She asked him if he still intended to go to Crookback Farm, and when he said he did, her feelings were mixed. How safe was it to travel the distance to the farm, much less to search it in the dark? "The murderer is still at large," she said.

"And he will remain so if we do nothing. Sir Thomas is content with his present understanding. Certain it is that he will remain so until we can give him cause to believe otherwise."

Mildred Carew had sent her husband on an errand after dark, and he had stopped on the way back at a tavern to drink with his friends and regale them with the story of how the upstart clothier had been humiliated by Sir Thomas. It was a good story indeed, and in the retelling, Miles had magnified his own part in the mortifying proceedings to such a degree that it was now he who had denounced the clothier and wrought his abject apology for having cast aspersions on the Carews and seeking to question the magistrate's conclusion. It was proving a popular story among the rougher crowd of the town, who generally envied the merchants, but even the more respectable of the tavern's patrons found the story absorbing, and all were wanting something of interest to talk about since it now appeared the murderers of John Crookback and family were identified and imprisoned.

It was on his way home that Miles Carew saw a figure come out of the clothier's shop and almost immediately dart into an alley. Suspicious, he followed a little ways until he was convinced the figure was the clothier himself, and Miles surmised by his furtive movements that he was up to something he wished to conceal.

He was almost relieved to have discovered this, for he badly wanted a new tale with which he might divert his wife's predictable anger at his lingering at the tavern. He reported what he had seen as soon as he walked in the door, before Mildred could lash him with her tongue for his tardiness.

"Where was he bound, do you think, and at this time of the night when all are indoors?" Mildred asked.

"I have no idea, but he walked as one careful not to be seen," her husband answered, relieved that the issue of his delay had been overlooked. "Like one up to no good. Like one sneaking into some chicken coop for a free supper."

"That doesn't sound like our clothier. He is an ass, yet honest to a fault."

"Honest?" exclaimed Miles Carew. "Why just this day you railed at him for his lies against your father?"

Mildred looked at her husband from under heavy lids. "The child stirs within me, husband. Pray don't contradict my words," she said in a flat, threatening voice.

Miles said nothing but stared moodily into the fire.

She then asked him why he had stayed so long on his errand. She told him she could smell the wine upon his breath when he entered and asked did he think for one minute she was fooled by his idle tales of Matthew Stock's sinister comings and goings?

Miles Carew looked at his wife's shrewish expression and her bloated body and uttered an uncharacteristic curse and condemnation of the married state. Then he bolted from the house before his wife could have the last word.

Matthew carried a little brass lantern beneath his great cloak but did not light it until he was long past the town. There was a moon rising, and the light of that whimsical orb reflected off the patches of remaining snow in the desolate fields. Some time later he saw the shadowy outline of Crookback Farm, and in its solemn presence he began to wonder about the wisdom of his plan. The spirits of the murdered were said to walk the places where they died, and Matthew had some concern for that. His other worry concerned the living—whoever it was who had cut and slashed the bodies of the Crookbacks and then stuffed them down the well so heartlessly. But he saw no sign of life, nor any spirits either, only the looming farmhouse and the barns. The silence was so profound that his own footfalls seemed to profane it.

The door of the farmhouse was open, as though the house had stood waiting during the days since the murders for someone to come in and take care of it. Matthew raised the lantern and entered.

He was not surprised to find that little had changed, nor were there signs of anything having been removed. Even the bloodstains remained on the walls of the chamber in which the slaughter had occurred. He went at once to the upper part of the house and into the bedchamber that had been Crookback's and his wife's. The chest in which he had found Crookback's will and the letter to Ralph Hawking was where he had left it, at the foot of the big four-poster bed, although the lid was open and he was sure he had left it closed. Perhaps, he thought, Joan had opened the chest after he had left, or maybe someone else had been in the room. Doubtless Agnes and her sister, bent on harvesting every last item of value to leave nothing for thieves.

He placed the lantern on the floor next to the tall cabinet against one wall of the chamber and opened the cabinet's doors. He pushed Susanna's clothing aside to expose the back of the cabinet and thumped upon the wood, listening for an echo indicating a cavity behind. The wood seemed solid. Further inspection of the cabinet, including some artfully made sliding shelves, which revealed nothing more than the stockings of both husband and wife, handkerchiefs, other small items of dress. All disappointing. Matthew began to wonder if his expedition had really been worth the trouble when he might have been home in his own bed.

He set his lantern down and pulled the cabinet out from the wall to reveal beneath it fistfuls of dust and mouse droppings and in the pale wattling behind it a long, gray water stain stretching from the ceiling to the floor. He stood there looking at the stain, breathing deeply, for the wardrobe was solid and heavy and he wondered how it had ever been carried up those narrow stairs. Then he noticed the planks of the floor, how they were irregularly configured in this place with short pieces and long side by side, unlike the rest of the floor, where the planks were a good six to eight feet in length, and uniform. He thought that the wardrobe might have been positioned to cover the irregularity and was about to push it back into its place when it occurred to him that it might be a trapdoor rather than bad carpentry.

He raised the lantern to have a better view and then got down on his knees in the dust. Running his fingers over the planks, he found a widening of the grooves between them, which allowed him to take hold of a section of the planking and lift it.

Revealed was a shallow cavity the length and breadth of a small coffin, constructed between the rafters of the room below and the floor of the present chamber, and from its exact conformity and neat fit, built by design rather than occurring by happenstance. Inside was a folded cloth. Matthew reached down and drew it slowly aside, his heart beating with anticipation.

He was almost relieved at what he found, for after all that had happened he feared to find something as gruesome as what had already been discovered at the cursed place. Instead, he saw a small arsenal, which John Crookback—for he assumed it was he and not his old father before him—had carefully preserved against dust and the depredations of rats and spiders. There was a sword in its scabbard, a brace of pistols, and two leather bags, one of which proved to contain powder and the other balls for the pistols. There was also a pair of knives, a dagger and a poniard. The poniard had a jeweled pommel and must have been worth something, but the dagger, which was a common piece such as sailors wore, had carved in its haft the initials R.H.

Ralph Hawking, Matthew thought.

Matthew held the lantern more directly over the hiding-place to determine if he had missed anything and had concluded he had not when he heard the creak on the stairs. He held his breath.

Footfalls.

Had he had more time he might have used Crookback's sword to defend against the sudden rush that came out of the darkness too fast for him to identify or repel. He felt a great stab of pain in his left shoulder, and then a blow to his cheek so savage that he was blinded by it, and then another blow to his head, which sent him reeling against the wall and into an unconsciousness as deep as death.

* * *

The big man with the red hair and brawny arms was to be Adam's warder. He came three times during the day, bringing water and sometimes food. The chamber pot was never emptied, so the stench continued to nauseate. The big man taunted him about it, telling him to drink deep of the pot if he could not abide the food, but when Adam's food came it was meager fare and half eaten already. It was obvious the big man was eating it, more out of malice than hunger, Adam reckoned, given the man's robust condition. He looked fed quite well enough as it was.

"Your darling will not eat now," said the man when he came to Adam's cell past dark, Adam thought, although in the windowless, stinking room it was hard to tell. "He cannot hear, he cannot speak, and now he cannot eat."

The man said this in a singsong voice, grinning malevolently. The voice made Adam's flesh crawl. He resolved not to eat either; he and Nicholas would die together. Powerless against their enemies, they could at least exert power over their own bodies. If the Christian god did not understand, then perhaps Adam would find compassion among the gods of his own people.

He thought much about Nicholas, more fearful for his friend's fate than for his own, and the longing he felt to see and touch the boy was almost more than he could bear. Sometimes, however, his thoughts would find their way from Nicholas to his own earlier life, and he would wrestle with the mystery which plagued him. *Crookback, let the man be.*

Why had Frobisher called out Crookback's name when it had been Hawking who had been the attacker, more vicious in his assault than a mad dog. And why had Hawking responded? In the excitement of the moment had Frobisher confused the men who looked so much alike they might have been brothers?

Then of a sudden it came to Adam—what he had been struggling to remember and comprehend since the Crookback murders had disturbed his long forgetfulness. Frobisher had not called out the wrong name on the day of Adam's capture. His brutal assailant had in truth been John Crookback. And Adam's benefactor had been Ralph Hawking.

For a moment the image of the two men merged, then divided into two again. Unaccustomed to English faces and hearing only the gibberish of a foreign tongue, Adam had of course confused the names and the men too, both tall and well-muscled, with golden beards and faces raw with wind and cold. So alike they might have been brothers.

The rest of the story now followed with a sharp clarity that left him almost breathless at its audacity and larcenousness. It had been Crookback, not Hawking, who had died in London in the tavern brawl of 1576, his skull crushed like a muskmelon. Hawking, not Crookback, it was, who had gone from London to Essex, assuming his friend's identity and thereby inheriting a prosperous farm; Hawking not Crookback who had been encumbered with two simpering babes who were his own flesh, not Crookback's, and a dark youth from *terra incognita* still too mind-boggled by the strangeness of scene and ignorant of English to discern or expose the imposture. It had been a curious retinue designed to make Ralph Hawking's imposture all the more probable, since it was well known in the town that Crookback the boy had run off to sea and sailed with Frobisher. Adam and the two girls must have been authenticating evidence, presenting the would-be heir as an honest widower and a charitable guardian of Frobisher's savage. Why should he have been thought other than he seemed?

And thus Ralph Hawking had commenced a new life as John Crookback; married Susanna; fathered three more children, had grown old; had been murdered; had been buried under the Crookback name, and of his true identity none in Chelmsford had been the wiser.

Except perhaps one, Adam thought. There had been one who was wise, as the devil is wise, one who had known the truth, one who done wickedness because of what he knew.

Chapter 16

ה

Elizabeth, anxious, had asked where her father had gone. Joan told her only that he had gone to visit someone at the end of the street. On some business, she said, looking away quickly so that the daughter would not catch the deception in the mother's face. Joan had been vague as to the details, not wanting to get into a lengthy explanation of Matthew's theories about the murders, not all of which she shared.

But Joan's reticence only piqued Elizabeth's curiosity. Elizabeth asked who it was he'd gone to visit, and Joan had avoided a lie by changing the subject to a chore that her daughter had neglected. They quibbled about that, mother and daughter, and Joan had resolved the dispute with a sharp reproof that brought tears to Elizabeth's eyes.

Afterwards, they made peace between them, and Elizabeth went to bed, but Joan sat still in the kitchen waiting for Matthew to return and feeling guilty. Why had she not told Elizabeth the truth? Why had she spoken sharply over an inconsequential oversight? Elizabeth was the best of daughters, the only one of her children who had survived birth. Joan sighed heavily and felt a deep remorse. She prayed for Matthew's safety, for his venture out into the night seemed now to have been made with reckless disregard for common sense, which dictated that a cold, dark night was no time for excursions into the countryside.

She hadn't realized how tired she was, and after a while, the kitchen being so amply warmed by the fire, she dozed.

Joan came awake with a start, almost toppling from the chair. She was chilled to the bone, so much so that she had to put on the vest she had removed earlier because of the heat in the kitchen, but even that did not help. Her cheeks and forehead were clammy and cold. She stoked the fire, and it grew large and generous in the grate, and still, although more than warm enough before, she could not get warm again.

A shadow passed before her eyes, clouding her vision. Joan feared she was about to faint. She heard Matthew's voice.

Somehow she knew her husband was not in the room with her and yet still the voice was unmistakable, proceeding mysteriously out of the thin air. The voice was weak and far away, more a whimper than a cry, and it spoke her name, repeating it again and again.

"Matthew?" she said aloud. "Matthew?" But there was no one to hear.

Her knees buckled beneath her, and she sank to the floor, feeling colder than ever, her head swimming and her vision blocked by the shadows that kept passing before her. She tried to wave them away, rubbing her eyes; she slapped her face to restore her vision. Nothing helped. She continued to hear the voice.

And then there was silence.

She knew what had come upon her. All her life she had been subject to such seizures. She called them "glimmerings," waking dreams. They warned her of danger to herself or to others, and it was to her husband's credit that, informed of them, he never belittled their significance or disputed the interpretations she gave of them.

The glimmering had passed. Her vision was restored, and she felt her flesh grow warm even as she noticed this transformation. She knew what the glimmering meant: The voice she had heard, with its mute appeal for help, left little doubt in her mind.

She went straightway to wake up Peter Bench. She was shaking him into awareness when she heard the clamor of the church bells.

The plunge into space was what revived him, a splaying of limbs his salvation from further descent. That and the miracle of a purchase on an irregularity in the otherwise smooth shaft of Crookback's well.

So he was not to be drowned like an unwanted kitten, but by grace saved, preserved a little while longer at least, to suffer cold and starvation, and the slow agony of loss of blood, for he could feel it in his hair, warm and moist.

He was pendulous like a bat, bent nearly double and pressed against the cold, hard stones, struggling not to lose his grip, every muscle in arm and leg aching and taut as a bowstring. He groaned and struggled to get himself upright, stifling his sobs and remembering now what had happened.

Who had done this to him but the very murderer he had sought—a truth he felt now in his racked bones, even as he felt the agony of his fear? It had been a man by the strength of him, for no woman had flown at him with such maniacal fury, or hit him with such brutal force. And no passing stranger had carried him unconscious to the well to stuff him where the other victims had been obscenely stuffed, their bodies all bloody and left for the water to disfigure beyond what the knife had done. What had the murderer been doing lurking about at the scene of his treachery? Perhaps, Matthew considered, he had been followed to the farm. An easy task on such a night. Matthew had been discreet in leaving the town, not so much after he had hit the high road, lighting his lantern and moving along swiftly, not looking behind him, this being no casual amble through the darkness but full of purpose and anxiety.

He was not sure but that his assailant waited above at the well's brim, listening for sounds of life below. Hearing them, would he then throw stones or some heavy object to give quietus to this new victim? Matthew waited what seemed a very long time, listening himself. In his cramped position, with his head bent back and but a few inches above the water he could not see above him to that aperture that opened to the night sky, the few dim stars, and what remained at this hour of the crescent moon, although he longed for such a hopeful view. He wondered if it would be obscured by a face, looming above the hole like a second moon, malevolent and eager to realize completely an evil intent.

After a while, hearing nothing above, feeling the blood pounding in his head and finding the cold most efficient in numbing his extremities despite his gloves and boots, Matthew struggled to improve his situation. At least he could try to get himself upright and not remain in so torturous a position. The maneuver was not easy, and he could not now stifle the cries of pain as he drove his fingers into the slight crevices of the slippery stones, which were round and smooth as masonry, and that he remembered from a brighter and happier day were as wondrously black as obsidian.

Adam was already asleep when Faulkborne, as Adam had heard his companions call him, brought supper. The hulking jailer bellowed out that supper was served, and Adam awoke to a dish of something lukewarm and stinking thrust beneath his nose.

Faulkborne laughed his deep throaty laugh. "It's the cook's specialty," he said. "Roast of a bull's testicle garnished with his offal."

Adam pushed it away, causing some of the delicacy to drip upon the server. Faulkborne cursed, flung the dish in the corner, and stingingly boxed Adam's ears.

"Sir Thomas shall learn of your abuse," Adam said, getting himself to his feet again, realizing at once that the threat was both useless and dangerous.

Faulkborne glowered. "If he does, it will be your word against mine—the word of a murderer and malcontent against that of a trusted servant. Now which word, miserable monkey, think you my master will credit?"

Faulkborne raised his hand to administer another blow, but he was interrupted by the sound of a sudden cry of alarm in the passage.

The big man turned swiftly to see what it was, and the young flaxen-haired servant with the red lips rushed in, breathing heavily, and by the light of his lamp all pale with fright.

"The dummy has strung himself up," he gasped. "He's as dead as Methusalah."

"Impossible," Faulkborne said, casting a contemptuous look at the younger man. "He had no rope."

"He did it with his hose. He used his hose, he did," gasped the young servant. "The dummy ripped them apart and tied the pieces together and fashioned him a noose and strung it from the beam. Come see for yourself, if you don't believe it. He's naked as a kite from the waist down."

"The devil he did," exclaimed Faulkborne.

"Sir Thomas will not be pleased," said the young servant. "He left the men in our charge. Shall we not answer for this?"

"By Christ, he did leave us in charge," said Faulkborne, "And we've looked after them well but had no expectation of this. If we have to answer for it, we'll say we did our duty faithfully."

"Oh, he's a terrible sight to behold," said the young servant.

Faulkborne pushed past the younger man to see for himself, in his haste leaving the door to Adam's cell ajar.

To Adam the message brought by the young servant, which his antagonist had rushed off to confirm, had the quality of one of the tales Jeroboam used to tell at Burton Hall when the grouchy steward wanted to put the fear of God into the credulous serving girls. Adam did not believe it, refused to do so. But

236

the open door he could see and therefore believe. He sprung to his feet and to the door and into the passage and raced down the same, glimpsing only as he passed the two servants bending over a body with bare white legs he knew as well as his own so that what he had not believed now he could not deny further.

The wail that would have betrayed his passing he suppressed, saying in his mind as he fled, *What I see is not real. It is not real.*

But he knew it was. Nicholas had managed to escape without him, keeping his counsel to the end.

Adam felt the grief gathering about him with such strength that he could hardly breathe. The energy that would have gone into the cry of rage and despair went into his lungs and legs. With a strength incredible to him, given his bruises and his self-imposed fast, he ran out of the house, where looking above him and finding in the heavens the star that signaled north, he set his course.

The fire that had begun in Master Barber's grate and spread so quickly had quite engulfed the old man before he could wake in his chair. Smoke belched from the windows and into the street, filling the starry night sky with cinders and ash and the smell of destruction and death. The fire was observed by the Widow Peters, whose son set the town bells clanging shortly past nine o'clock. Within minutes the whole house was a conflagration and the one next to it as well, that owned by John Gordon. All the men in the town turned out, even those haunting the brothels and taverns, and most of the women, if not to help fight the blaze then to form an appreciative audience for those who did.

Joan and Elizabeth, who was roused from her sleep by the hurly-burly of the alarm and the cries of fire, came to see too. There was a great fear the flames would spread from thatch to thatch and take all the houses on the north side of the street and perhaps the whole town before it was done.

For Joan the fire was a disturbing spectacle, for she was uncertain whether this was the disaster her glimmering had fore-told or she should look elsewhere, perhaps at Crookback Farm itself. Word spread almost as quickly as the flames that Master Barber had been the fire's first victim, and there were many expressions of sympathy for his granddaughter, who had been able to flee the house before the flames reached her and who proclaimed in gasping, half-finished sentences to any who would listen that she had done all a body could for the old man and would have died before she allowed a hair of his blessed head to be singed. But Mistress Gordon was in worse condi-tion, even though she and her family had got out in time. The worthy woman, who had been burned out twice before in her life, wept and wailed and raised a great tumult, crying that now they should be homeless paupers, but Joan, who knew the woman well, consoled her with the assurance that her neighbors would help her rebuild. The important thing now was that the fire be put out before it could destroy more houses.

Water was fetched in pan and pail from every corner of the town and thrown on the fire. Within the hour the flames had died to embers, and those who had braved the night to save the houses of their neighbors stood around shivering and ex-hausted but congratulating themselves on a job well done. Then the women went home, taking their men with them, ex-cept for about two dozen men who returned to the taverns and brothels to celebrate their victory and gratify thirst or lust, or both.

Joan watched all this and yet kept looking into the dark end of the street for Matthew to return. She knew he would not have slipped home, not with the town on fire. He was still at the farm or somewhere along the road, she suspected. And her memory of her vision would not leave her.

Joan and Elizabeth walked slowly home, praying as Joan opened the door that he would be inside. But he was not.

Peter was there, however. The apprentice was extending his hands toward the hearth and looking very weary. She saw he was covered with cinders and realized he had been one of the dark figures fighting the fire. She asked him how he did.

"Oh, I do very well, mistress," the young man said, "but am weary from carrying water all the night."

"You should wash your face," Joan said. "You look like a Moor with all that soot upon your cheeks."

But then she told him the dirt could wait, and begged a favor.

Peter looked up and said, "You may command me in anything, Mistress Stock. You know you can, for all that you and your good husband have done for me."

Mildred Carew hadn't seen her sister at the fire and was curious as to how Agnes could have missed so notable an event. Thus it was that as soon as it became plain there would be no more excitement that night, she made her way down to her sister's house, both to see how Agnes and her poor brother-in-law fared and to complain about her own husband's brutish manners, how he had simply marched out of the house to drink wine until midnight, and she as big as a barn with child, and the whole town in danger of burning down around her.

When she came to the door she saw no lamp or candlelight within the windows, but only the soft glow of the fire in the hearth, which seemed more than strange to her, for she knew Hugh Profytt at least was home, bedridden as he was with his broken limb and, she had heard, a raging fever. Despite the seeming evidence of Agnes's absence, Mildred knocked, and having no answer she assumed a sister's privilege and tried the door. It was not bolted. What should a sister do but enter?

A pallet had been set up in the parlor for Hugh Profytt and by the light of the poorly tended fire she could see his sleeping form upon it. She could also hear his labored breathing, assuring her that the poor wretch, whom she had never liked very much, was still among the living. She was about to leave when she heard strange sounds from the adjoining chamber, where the Profytts normally slept. Here was more breathing of a labored sort, but not sleeping. Approaching she made the noises out to be sighs and groans of pleasure.

Her curiosity now hotter than the fire had been, Mildred

pushed open the door to the bedchamber, where she saw round white buttocks and bare brawny shoulders rocking in her sister's bed, which trembled with these exertions, and slender white arms embracing this muscular, clearly masculine figure.

"Agnes?" she said even before she thought the better of it.

The rocking stopped, and the man raised himself suddenly from his work and twisted around in the bed, so that Mildred could not fail to understand just what labors she had interrupted, and that the workman was the stonemason, William Dees.

"What are you doing here?" Mildred gasped.

Then Mildred saw Agnes clearly enough, her hair all wild as though a rough wind had blown it and her face contorted in a mixture of amazement and anger. She was still panting from her amorous play and her jaw was slack.

"Mildred," Agnes cried, "what is the matter that you do not knock but come boldly in?"

These questions raised between the sisters, Mildred could hardly think of another thing to say. She backed slowly from the room, unable to remove her eyes from the generous display of human flesh before her and feeling somehow that her sister had triumphed again, for how could her story of her own husband's vile conduct ever compete with the story Agnes would tell to explain this bold adultery, and with her poor husband asleep in the next room.

For all his suffering, Matthew was vaguely aware that it was doubtless warmer within the well than aboveground, but that gave him little comfort. His chief cause of agony was the apparent hopelessness of his situation. Satisfied for some time now that his assailant had departed, Matthew had yelled for help at the top of his lungs until no sound came forth but a hoarse croak. His only consolation was the sight of the stars, which seemed in his extremity somehow more brilliant and numerous. These reminded him of the heavenly realm where he should shortly go, and having screamed until his throat was raw and wept, too, he resigned himself to death and prayed for his soul and the comfort of the wife and daughter he should leave behind him, widow and orphan.

It was, he reflected, an earlier death than he'd had any reason to expect. And yet what was he?—thirty-three, Christ's age when Our Lord was crucified, so why should he complain? Matthew had had a good life. There was no denying that. He had enjoyed the love of the best of women. He had fathered a child, who, while no son, was a daughter of superlative qualities. He had enjoyed success and good repute among his fellow townsmen, at least until Agnes Profytt and her party had defamed him. Perhaps it was a good time to die.

But for all these morbid reflections, Matthew felt a disappointment. It would have been good to know whom he had to thank for his fate. If his assailant had only given Matthew a glimpse of himself or spoken a word, so that his voice might be recognized, had only left some clue in his violence. But Matthew searched his memory and could find nothing. Yet he had been lifted up, which argued arms and main strength; had been placed where the other bodies had been deposed, which argued reason. Perhaps, he considered, it might argue sheer insanity.

The moon now rose above the brim of the shaft and a shard of light fell down the well onto his face. Light glistened on the moist stones all around him, and their blackness took on a strange, unearthly sheen. Black stones the well was made of, stones fitted together with great skill, with cement in between to hold them in place. . . .

Black stones.

His memory quickened. Black stones containing gold, the Italian assayer had said in Ralph Hawking's letter, the one which John Crookback had held in enough esteem to retain with his most precious papers all those years. Were these, then, the stones Agnello wrote of? He did not remember having seen the like in Essex fields. Yet if these were the very stones the Italian had assayed, how were they so humbly used in a mere well, rather than stored up in some secret place with other treasures?

But of course, he considered, that was it. What better place to hide the precious ore but in the ground where no one would think for a moment to look for it? Then he remembered what Master Fuller had said: the stones were not gold. The whole thing was a fraud. The investors had lost their shirts, had been up in arms against Frobisher, whom they blamed for the fiasco. Yet Ralph Hawking had been given an assurance otherwise. He had thought them of worth, valued them enough to conceal them.

His thoughts drifted. He was beyond weariness, beyond the exhaustion of labor. Lodged like a bone in the throat of the well, he could not climb, yet neither could he fall. He would have fain slept but his pain was too great. He thought again of death and its advantages, and it almost seemed to him that he could hear Joan's voice calling.

Then he realized he did hear Joan's voice. He shouted as much as he could and was gratified to find his own voice had returned somewhat. When there was no response but silence from above, he shouted again, bending his head back to view the stars, imagining that they could reach down to offer him succor. He shouted again, "God help me, Joan. I'm here. Down in the well."

The stars were obscured by a human face, but not Joan's.

"Peter Bench! Is that you, lad? For God's sake, throw down a rope that I might rise."

Peter's face disappeared and was quickly replaced by Joan's.

"Matthew, Matthew, Matthew! Is it you or some other in the well? We thought your calls a spirit's cry and hardly dared to look for fear of what we might see."

"Have no fear," Matthew called. "I'm no spirit come back to haunt my rescuers. Throw me a rope. Pray be quick. I suffer from this position."

It took them what seemed to Matthew a very long time to find a rope to throw down, and before it dangled before his face he overheard the discussion between wife and apprentice as to how it might be secured, for Joan said she had no intention to offer help that should be none at all but allow her husband to drop into a watery grave.

Then the rope came, slowly. Matthew seized it with one hand, and feeling insufficient strength in doing so he took the rope's end, called for slack, and tied it round his waist.

"You will have to pull me up. I have not enough strength to climb."

Joan helped Peter pull Matthew up. The ascent was slow. When Matthew came to the rim there was a great struggle to get him over, and he lay on the edge of the well taking great gulps of air, every muscle in his body aching. When between the three of them they'd managed to get him completely free and he'd had the chance to catch his breath, he told Joan what she had already surmised for herself.

"So you never saw his face?"

"Nor did I hear a voice."

Her disappointment was palpable. She told Matthew her side of the story, told him about her vision, about the fire, and about the nagging doubt that would not be satisfied unless she came to Crookback Farm herself.

"We'll have you home and in bed in no time," she said.

"Not home, Joan."

"Not home?"

"To the manor house. I must see Sir Thomas."

"Tonight?"

"Tonight."

Chapter 17

ה

Matthew and Joan had been to Mildmay Hall before, on certain high holidays, when the lord of the manor extended his bounty to the common folk of the town, but they had never seen it so turbulent with activity. After the deserted farm and the black well, the hall seemed a little city of light.

Despite the hour, the house was in great commotion, with horses saddled and ready in the courtyard and candles and torches ablaze. Servants rushed upstairs and down. Others merely stood in the high-raftered hall, armed and buzzing. Matthew and Joan found Hubert Selby giving instructions to two other servants. Hubert told them the news: That Nicholas Crookback had hanged himself with his own hose; that Adam Nemo had made a daring escape, and from a warder twice his size and reputed to be a great wrestler; that Sir Thomas was preparing another search party and swearing this time there would be no gentle treatment for the fugitive, who had proved his guilt beyond question by his second flight from lawful authority.

"My master is beyond his wits with choler. He rants and raves at every servant, save for me, who am ever loved by him." Hubert said this with curled lips, as though he were savoring the decline from grace of his fellows. "The hanging of the dummy didn't bother my master so much."

The excited servant did not seem to notice Matthew's disheveled appearance, his badly bruised face, and the wretched condition of his cloak after his ordeal in the well, and it was all Matthew could do to get a word in edgewise. "I must see your master, and this minute," Matthew said. "I have news of my own that will bear on these matters that so concern him."

"Unless it's to tell him where the savage went, I doubt he'll give you his ear," said Hubert. Despite this profession of doubt, he beckoned Matthew and Joan to follow and ushered the two through a quieter region of the house, which was a very handsome one, well furnished and imposing. "At the moment he can think of one thing and one thing only, for he regards the escape as a disgrace to him—for which he punished Faulkborne most severely."

"Faulkborne?"

"The warder he placed in charge of the prisoners. A great dull-witted fellow whose only virtue is the breadth of his shoulders and his sheer altitude. But the little savage outwitted him. Though I love no murderers, yet it did my heart good to hear of it."

They arrived at a heavy oak door at the end of a long passage, where Hubert told Matthew and Joan to wait. He knocked, Matthew heard Mildmay say, "Come," and then Hubert disappeared inside.

Hubert was not gone but for a minute when he appeared again. "It's as I supposed. My master says he's much too busy to talk now. He entreats you to come another time or put your request in writing for his secretary to consider."

"This cannot wait," Matthew said. "Tell him I have discovered the true murderer of John Crookback and his family."

Hubert's eyes grew round with surprise. "The true murderer, you say? Well, then, this is news indeed—if it is to be credited."

"Why should it not be?" Joan said.

"Why, no particular reason, Mistress Stock, other than this is a stale debate betwixt my master and your husband. No, I think Sir Thomas will not tolerate another effort to dissuade him from his present conviction. Even now, Master Fuller is within, and you know what he believes. Neither gentleman will be converted from his previous opinions. Take my word for it."

"Nonetheless, I must try, Hubert. And you must help."

Matthew's plain appeal had its effect. Hubert nodded, but he seemed hesitant to reenter his master's chamber.

"Why do you not go in?" Matthew asked, seeing that Hubert made no move to comply.

"Don't you see, Matthew?" Joan said, turning to her husband and pressing his arm. "Hubert speaks wisely. Such a reason will hardly alter his master's will. It's the same old dispute, which you twain struggled with before. Mildmay is hardly going to lend a sympathetic ear at this point, no matter what evidence you supply."

Matthew looked at Joan helplessly. He realized that she was right. Then he turned back to Hubert.

"Then tell Mildmay that I know where the savage has gone."

Hubert looked at Matthew doubtfully. "You must swear to me that it is so. I will be made no tool to wrench my master's solid opinions."

"I swear it," Matthew said, feeling only a little guilty at the deception necessity had brought him to.

"Hubert says you know the whereabouts of Adam Nemo," Sir Thomas said before Matthew could open his mouth. "How would you know such a thing, given that he escaped within the hour?"

"Perhaps Master Stock is gifted with second sight, Sir

Thomas," Fuller said, his scowl changing to a grim smile. "In which case I wonder that he refused Your Honor of the benefit when we spent so much effort bringing the fugitive to ground."

"I have found out the truth from experience," Matthew said, and then began to speak as fast as he could, fearful that if he stopped the magistrate would order him to be silent or Fuller would make another demeaning comment.

As it happened, Matthew's appearance was sufficient to catch the attention of the magistrate, who had asked him what had befallen him as soon as Joan and Matthew had entered the room, but even when it became clear that Matthew's savage was not the savage Sir Thomas sought, the deception did not arouse the ire that Hubert and Matthew himself had feared. Sir Thomas heard Matthew out, heard him out long enough to cross the threshold of incredulity and consider that they might all have been mistaken. But where the magistrate listened with surprising patience, Fuller mocked.

"This is an idle tale," he said heatedly. "The man has fallen off his horse to receive such bruises. He has invented a story to save himself from ridicule and his friend from the just demands of the law."

"Every word my husband has said is true," Joan said, content until that moment to let her husband voice their shared opinions.

"I would expect a faithful wife to affirm nothing less," Fuller answered, with a nod toward Joan that offended her more than stony silence would have done.

Sir Thomas turned to Fuller and said, "Look, Simeon. We will accomplish little with a hue and cry this time of night. The warders tell me our savage hadn't eaten since he was taken, probably not since his first flight. How far can he go? Who will give him succor? Our good Matthew Stock here gives us a plausible tale, and his appearance gives more evidence that what he says is true. Those bruises upon his face and tears in his clothes do not seem the consequence of a fall from a horse. I believe it is even as he has said."

Fuller looked annoyed at being contradicted but said nothing. He turned and stared into the fire.

Sir Thomas stood thinking for a few minutes more. Then he said, "Well, come. We have little time to wait. Let us experiment upon your theory, good Master Stock, and see if it will hold water or leak."

Matthew had hoped Sir Thomas would provide at least a dozen of his servants to support Matthew's cause and he was not disappointed. In fact, Sir Thomas came himself, and Fuller came too, although Matthew supposed more to see his failure than support his new effort.

"I pray you are not mistaken in this," Sir Thomas said to Matthew as they rode. "I am loath to look the fool to my friends in the county."

"I have not misled you," Matthew said, and he exchanged glances with Joan beside him. "You'll find the murderer you seek within the hour and be lauded for it. No one will think about Adam Nemo's escape."

"Pray heaven they do not, for I feel to blame enough as it is."

It was nearly midnight before they arrived in Chelmsford. Only a few houses showed any light, and the house of William Dees, stonemason, was not one of them.

There was no sound from within for a while at least, and then they heard a gruff masculine voice Matthew recognized as Dees's demanding to know who it was who knocked at such an hour.

"Sir Thomas Mildmay, and Master Fuller," the magistrate called. "Also some of your neighbors."

The men stepped back from the door and waited. It was a moment before it opened, and then but a crack. Dees peered out. Despite the hour, he was still dressed. "What is it you want?" he said, looking startled, as though he had only half believed what Sir Thomas had said before.

"To speak with you. May we come in?"

"My wife is sick abed, Your Honor. My children are asleep."

"We'll speak quietly," said Sir Thomas in the same casual voice.

Dees nodded and opened the door. "May we go to my workshop? It's in the rear of the house. We won't disturb my wife, then. Pray you wait, honorable sirs. I'll fetch a lamp."

Sir Thomas told Hubert Selby and his other servants to wait outside, and he, Fuller, Matthew, and Joan went in. They passed through the larger room where the fire in the hearth was in its last stages and giving off a ruddy glow, which lit the disorder of the home of a man with children and a sickly wife, then through a passage into the shed at the rear of the house. Here there was a great store of stone of every sort, equipment, a variety of monuments, most unfinished, and the smell of rock dust. Matthew had been in Dees's shop before, but he had not realized how much of his business was in gravestones.

They formed a little circle around the lamp. Sir Thomas said, "I see you are still dressed, William Dees. Could you not sleep?"

"There was a fire in the town, sir," Dees said. "I fought it back with the others. You know how it is, sir. After such labors, one finds sleep with difficulty."

"I didn't see you at the fire," Joan said. "I watched from the beginning until it was sodden ash and not a lick of flame. I never saw you."

"Well, I was there," William said. "It was dark. There was much confusion, Mistress Stock. How could you see everyone?"

"And afterwards?" Sir Thomas asked.

"Afterwards I was visiting the Profytts. I wanted to see how my good friend Hugh Profytt did. May I ask the purpose of these questions, Your Honor? I served faithfully in the hue and cry. My honesty in the town is well allowed. Wherefore am I visited at this hour and subjected to these strange queries when I never was so mistrusted before?"

"Master Stock was attacked this night," Sir Thomas said. "He went out to Crookback Farm to look around. Someone came out of the darkness before he was aware, struck him on the head, and then pushed him down the well.''

''If that happened,'' Dees said, turning to Matthew with a sympathetic face, ''I am right sorry for it. But it wasn't I that did it. I was in town all the night.''

''Fighting the fire,'' Joan said, ''and visiting a bedridden friend.''

''So it was, Mistress Stock,'' Dees said, smiling a thin little smile and nodding at Joan. ''Besides, how would I know that your husband was at the farm—a strange place for a man to go after dark, given what happened there?''

''When my wife visited you earlier this evening, she spoke of a certain letter,'' Matthew said. ''I found it in a chest in John Crookback's bedchamber. You knew what letter she spoke of. You wanted to see if the letter remained there. You didn't expect to find me at the same time.''

The stonemason looked around him. His voice trembled a little, and he seemed to stand less erect than before. Matthew noticed these signs and was encouraged by them, for he feared Dees's flat denials would cause Sir Thomas to turn from his resolve.

''I can do nothing more than repeat myself,'' Dees said. ''I never left town. Save when I fought the fire and visited the Profytts, I have been here with my wife and children—to which they will attest if asked—just as you found me. I'd have no reason to hurt you, Matthew, but account you a friend.''

Matthew said, ''Where are your boots?''

''My boots?''

''You're not wearing them.''

Dees looked down at his feet and shrugged. Although still fully dressed he was wearing soft slippers. ''I took them off when I came in. My wife's distressed when I muddy up the house.''

''Let's have a look at them,'' said Sir Thomas in a stern voice that brooked no denial.

When Dees hesitated, Matthew said, ''Surely you remember where you put them?''

"They're in the bedchamber where my wife lies. As I said, she is sick. I hope you won't disturb her."

"We will not disturb your wife," Sir Thomas said.

Dees led the way back into the forepart of the house and into a small, low-ceilinged room with an unpleasant smell. His children were asleep there on pallets upon the floor next to the larger bed that was occupied by the wife, who seemed in so deep a sleep that the intrusion did not even cause her to stir, much less awake. The boots were at the foot of the bed, placed closely together.

Sir Thomas nodded to Matthew, who picked them up and carried them back into the parlor, where they all assembled. He asked Dees, who held the lamp, to hold it over the boots.

"The boots are neither wet nor are there signs of ash, as there would be were you fighting the fire," declared Matthew. "Isn't that so, William?"

Dees said, "I cleaned and dried them after."

"You would have to have placed them near the fire, else they would not dry," Matthew said.

"They were never very wet," Dees said.

"I imagine they were not," Sir Thomas said, eyeing the boots.

"I say only that I was never at Crookback Farm, but in town rather," Dees said.

"Visiting Hugh Profytt and his wife," Matthew said.

"We shall see," Sir Thomas said. "Master Fuller, will you please tell one of my servants to go to the house of Hugh Profytt and bring him and his wife hither that we may confirm the good stonemason's word."

"Profytt cannot come, Thomas," answered Fuller, who up to this point had said not a word, but had been as watchful as a cat. "His leg is broken."

"And so it is. I quite forgot," Sir Thomas said. "Then have my servant fetch the wife. She'll have to do."

The magistrate sat down upon the chamber's one good chair, sighing as he did so that it was the longest night he had ever spent, with so much going on. Joan and Matthew took up seats upon a bench by the hearth, but Dees remained standing, his powerful arms hanging by his sides and his mouth set in fierce determination.

The Profytts' house was only a short distance from the stonemason's, so it was only a few minutes before Agnes Profytt appeared. She wore a heavy cloak and her face had the haggard, disputatious look of someone wrenched unwillingly from sleep. A shrill demand to know why she was wanted at such an ungodly hour had heralded her arrival, but when she saw that it was Sir Thomas and Master Fuller who were the authors of her summons, she made a little curtsy to each of the gentlemen and composed herself.

"I am told William Dees was at your house earlier this night, to visit your husband in his extremities," Sir Thomas said.

The question evidently took Agnes by surprise. For a moment she stood frozen, then turned her gaze from the magistrate to Dees as though she would ask him something but could not speak it. Finally she said, "Whoever says so speaks falsely, though it were my own sister who claimed it. I have been at home all the night tending to my poor husband's needs and whims, as a good wife must. I do not remember when William Dees was last within my door, if he ever was. But it was not tonight."

"Tell the truth, Agnes," Dees said in what was hardly more than a whisper. "It was I who confessed it, not your sister."

"Yes, tell the truth woman," Sir Thomas said. "Let there be no liars here. If the stonemason was in your house this night, I must know it."

"I am a good wife, Sir Thomas, and a virtuous woman," Agnes said, lifting her chin and looking straight ahead as though she were proclaiming this fact to an unseen presence in the room. "I do not keep company with men in my house at night, save he is my lawful husband."

"Oh, Agnes," Dees said, speaking in a normal voice now. "This has naught to do with what we did or did not do, but where I was this night. Speak truth, I pray you. My life depends on it."

A look of confusion passed over Agnes's face. She stood looking puzzled. Then she said. "He was at my house. Even as he has said."

"So you lied before."

"I lied, Sir Thomas."

"Why?"

"I thought it might have disgraced me. After all, my husband is asleep most of the time. All the world knows what he suffered," she said, casting Matthew a baleful look as she said this. "For a man to visit a woman not his wife, late at night— you know whereof I speak, sir. People will gossip. I would not have my reputation dragged through muck. I am no common whore."

"So you lied to save your precious reputation," Sir Thomas said.

"I did."

"You first supposed your sister had claimed that Dees was at your house. Was she there as well?"

"She was, Your Honor."

"And would she attest to the truth of your words?"

"I trust she would, Your Honor."

"So both you and your sister would affirm that Dees was at your house earlier this evening. What of your husband?"

"He was asleep, sir. He knew nothing but what he dreamed."

"Is there other proof? If I find you are lying now it will go very badly with you."

The threat seemed to alarm Agnes greatly. She looked around her and noticed the boots that Matthew still held in his hand. She pointed to them. "Why, William Dees wore those boots into the house. I remember them well. He left filth upon the carpet I lay upon the rushes next my bed, for which I upbraided him, and I had to clean the boots myself."

"What manner of filth was it?" Sir Thomas asked.

Agnes let out a little nervous laugh. "Cow dung. Upon my word, it was indeed. The bottoms and sides of his boots were all beshitten, so that I forbade him to enter before he had cleaned them thoroughly, but he said if it must be done, then I must be the one to do it.''

"But there was no ash.''

"Why, no, sir. He was visiting me while the fire raged. Whoever says otherwise lies in his teeth and I hope he may burn in hell for it.''

Matthew turned quickly from Agnes to Dees to see how he was taking this curse, only to find that the attention of the stonemason had been seized by another. At that moment a rustle was heard, and everyone turned to see that Dees's wife had come into the room. In her white flowing shift and with her pale face she looked the very image of a ghost, and Matthew felt a chill at her appearance.

The woman looked straight at her husband, and seeming to ignore the presence of so many visitors in her house, she said, "What, husband? Have you come back from Crookback Farm already? I dreamed such a dream in which you were hanged by the neck, and I wept and wept but could do nothing to save you.''

A great stillness fell upon the room at this. Then Agnes spoke again, looking directly at Dees. "Five pieces of plate of considerable value were taken from my father's house. I would know if you have them, William.''

"I have them,'' Dees said in a voice quite unlike his normal voice. "They are hidden under my bed. You would have found them anyway.''

"Thank you,'' Agnes said.

Sir Thomas sent Agnes Profytt home, saying he had no more need for her at present but not before chastising her for her lies, of which he said she seemed little repentant. Agnes left as she had come, mumbling and complaining about being awakened, protesting that her reputation was as pure as the driven snow, and that she and the stonemason had done nothing more but converse as honest neighbors might. But at the same time she roundly cursed William Dees as thief and murderer, with more heat expressed at his thievery than at his homicide, if Joan was any judge.

254

When she had gone, Sir Thomas called Hubert Selby and another servant in and said the stonemason should be bound. Matthew and Joan watched all this, careful not to usurp any of the authority that the magistrate was now wielding with such grim determination. The fire had burned very low in the grate, and Sir Thomas ordered it stoked. Joan would have gladly gone home to bed for the lateness of the hour and yet would not have left even if her comings and goings had been under her own power. She felt it was she herself was in a little cell preparing to endure the lash of the magistrate's tongue. But she was determined to stay awake and not miss a word of the confession she knew the magistrate was preparing to extract from the now much humbled stonemason.

Hubert and the other servant bound Dees to a chair. His face was turned away from the fire and toward the bedchamber door, where his wife stood obstinately on the threshold despite Sir Thomas's urgings that since she was in such a poor state of health she return to bed. But now the woman had grasped the direction of things and would not be commanded, continuing to look upon her husband as though he were a man she had never truly known.

"Now Dees, speak the truth," Sir Thomas said. "Your mischief at the farm has been proven by the words of your own wife as well as Mistress Profytt. Explain this letter."

From his cloak, Sir Thomas had withdrawn the assayer's letter. He pushed it beneath the stonemason's nose as though asking him to sniff at it as well as explain its importance.

"I know nothing about this letter, sir," Dees said.

"You would have killed your townsman, Matthew Stock, to have it," said Sir Thomas. He started to read the letter, complained about the dim light, and asked Fuller to read it, which the gentleman did.

"I know nothing of black stones," Dees said when Fuller had finished.

At this denial, Sir Thomas turned to Matthew and nodded. Matthew said, "These stones you are ignorant of are the ones that form the shaft of John Crookback's well. You know this. You laid the stones yourself. I recognized your handiwork."

"How should I remember what stones were used?" Dees said harshly. "That's been twenty years if it's been a day."

"You should remember because you used those same stones in order to hide them," Matthew said, "thinking that they were of great worth and not wishing them to be discovered. You knew John Crookback was not who he claimed to be, but a fraud, the Ralph Hawking to whom this letter is addressed."

"Why would I do such a thing? I am no liar."

"Your conduct this night has proven you are," Sir Thomas interjected. He nodded to Matthew to proceed.

"For a share in the gold, you did it," Matthew said. "Because Ralph Hawking, who was John Crookback's bosom friend and knew the facts of his life as well as John Crookback did, offered you a share of it if you would attest to his identity."

Dees snorted with disgust but said nothing. For a few moments the room was silent except for the pops and cracks of the fire. The stonemason's wife remained in the door of her bedchamber, as though she were guarding it, and Joan felt a great pang of remorse for the poor woman whose fearful dream would soon become a reality.

"Crookback—in fact this Ralph Hawking—kept the gold hidden all those years because he feared Frobisher would find him out. At least that's what he told you who had helped him to his present condition. Then you made a discovery of your own—that Frobisher was dead."

"I hardly knew of the man."

"On the contrary," Matthew said, "you knew a good deal about Frobisher. Hawking had told you the stories, had persuaded you that the stones were of great value. But all those years he knew they were worthless. He didn't tell you that because he depended on you to keep his secret, which revealed would have meant prison or worse for him, disgrace and poverty for his children. Then you heard in some tavern that Frobisher was dead. You went to Hawking. You told him what you heard, expecting him to receive the news joyfully, to dig up the well and have at the gold. You were used, Dees, gulled by your own greed."

Matthew paused. During the last few moments Dees's breath seemed to be coming faster and faster, as though he were struggling to climb a steep hill. Now he suddenly relaxed. His lips curled in the semblance of a smile, but there was no joy in it, only a bitter resignation.

"Hawking was a liar and a plotter," Dees said. "When he came to Chelmsford he came first to me in secret—knowing from Crookback who I was, how Crookback and I had been friends, as boys you know, as close as brothers. He spoke plainly to me, told me Crookback was dead and that he and Crookback had been shipmates; told me that if I swore he was Crookback he'd let me have a share of gold, wealth beyond my dreams, he said. But we must wait he said, wait."

"Wait for what?" Sir Thomas asked.

"Wait for Frobisher to forget or be forgotten, so there'd be no question about whose gold it was, he said. Hawking admitted he stole the stones, you see. He needed a place to conceal them until the furor died down. He said people would forget in time, and then it would be safe."

"Who thought to use the stones in the well?"

"Oh that was my thought, Your Honor. Better than burying them, I told him. For in the meanwhile they would have a practical use. And who would think to look in a well for gold?"

"And you believed all he said about the stones?"

"Every word of it. It seemed to me a most plausible truth. The Spaniards had found gold aplenty in the Americas. Why could not an Englishman have similar good fortune in the northern climes? Is an Englishman not better than a Spaniard?"

"What of the other witnesses to his identity? Did Hawking purchase their testimonies too?"

"I don't think so. I had been his boyhood friend; the others knew him, but at a distance. I told Master Barber that the man claiming to be John Crookback was the John Crookback I had known, both because of his appearance and because he knew things that we twain had done as boys that none other could know save he was Crookback himself. The other witnesses followed my lead like sheep. What did they have but a handful of memories of a smoothfaced boy, glimpsed at work on his father's farm? The man before them was full grown, bearded, his face beaten by sun and wind and hard experience. He insisted he was John Crookback, had information pertaining to his father, the family, the farm. If Hawking hadn't opened his heart to me so I knew the truth, I myself might have been taken in, so great was his likeness to the boy that was.''

''But you were taken in,'' Sir Thomas said.

''He knew the stones were worthless. He used me for twenty years, making me think the stones were of value. He had proved by the letter in your hand, sir. What was his name, Cavello I think? The assayer that wrote the letter. Like a fool I believed it. I mortgaged my honesty, swore Hawking was Crookback, waited for my reward. For years I waited, the more fool I.''

''But why kill his wife too and his children? Surely they were innocent of this wrongdoing.''

Dees stared dull-eyed into the fire as though he were caught up in a trance, as though all his murders he now relived and for the first time he was feeling the full burden of their horror. ''I took care of the dog first—to shut him up. I knew what would happen if I didn't. I didn't mean to kill Hawking at the beginning, only to beat him within an inch of his life. But he fought back, with a strength that surprised me. Before I was aware, my knife was in his chest and he was dead in my arms. We had struggled in his parlor. His wife and the two children came in, saw the blood and the dead man, and started cursing me for a murderer and devil. I was beyond reason then. I had drunk deep before to build up my courage. My heart pounded. I was a crazed man. I slashed about me blindly. Only later did I realize what I had done.''

''Then you put the bodies in the well,'' Mildmay said, ''and got yourself to church.''

''I put the bodies in the well. There was justice in that—at least, I thought so at the time. Also a strategy. I thought to come back later in the day and fill the well in, conceal the bodies and the worthless black stones forever, but Adam Nemo prevented me."

"Why did you not kill Nicholas Crookback too?"

Dees looked up at the knight. "Because I never saw him. I reckoned he was off wandering about the farm somewhere, which he often did. Besides, he was deaf and dumb. Who would believe his report even if he were able to make one? I had no fear of him. When Burton's servant was accused and the boy too, I thought fortune had smiled upon me."

"Fortune will hardly smile on him whom heaven condemns," Sir Thomas said. "You were betrayed, Dees. But your crime was the worse, and your penalty will be likewise."

The magistrate told his servants to untie the stonemason from the chair and to prepare for a return to Mildmay Hall. Joan looked at the wretched prisoner and thought about his confession. She had always thought Dees a slow-witted, choleric man, a man perhaps too devoted to the pot and tankard. But never an evil one. And yet, she considered, was it evil, drunkenness, or just his uncontrollable anger that had turned him into a murderer? It was a hard question, one she felt was quite beyond an easy answer.

Sir Thomas looked at Matthew and said, "You have done more than yeoman's service in this business, Matthew Stock. I promise that it will not be forgotten, either by me or this town."

Joan's heart swelled with pride at hearing these words, and she smiled at Matthew, but there was no smile upon her husband's face, which seemed almost as stony with grief as Dees's; and then Joan was suddenly ashamed that her pride had gone before her compassion, for she knew Matthew was thinking of John Crookback's wife and young children who lay cold in the ground and for whom the magistrate's justice would do little and come too late, and how little it mattered that he had not been Crookback at all, but Hawkins, and a wretch whose greed had overreached an honest mind.

259

Chapter 18

ה

By the same time the next day, few ears in Chelmsford had not heard the sordid tale of fraud, deception, and murder. Matthew's shop was busier than Stephen Satterfield's tavern, with most of Matthew's custom dispensing with any pretense that they were there to do more than gossip about Dees and John Crookback, who had not been John Crookback at all, and Agnes and Mildred, who now appeared to be the offspring of strangers and would have no claim on Crookback Farm. To Matthew were put a hundred different questions about Dees's reasons, and to Joan almost as many. There was great interest too in the black stones. Rumor held that not a few citizens had gone to the farm to dig the stones from their mortar on the slim chance that they contained gold after all, for concerning these matters one could always hope.

In all of this no one seemed to express much sorrow for Agnes and Mildred, who were both now generally criticized for their pride and arrogance, while Agnes's adultery with the murderer having become known—as such mischief will out at last—further disgrace was heaped upon her as an unfaithful wife. Instead, the town's sympathy was reserved for William Dees's wife and children, whom no one thought deserving of such a husband and father. Various persons now remembered other episodes of the stonemason's explosive anger and shared these recollections with their friends. The next sabbath the Parson spoke upon wrath, using Dees's murders as a potent illustration of the baleful consequences of that deadly sin.

Sawyer, beggar turned hero now turned beggar again, left town as soon as he was able, now known for the liar he was. Master Fuller, whom Matthew heard from Hubert was still convinced that Adam Nemo was at least an accomplice of the stonemason, had returned to London and his books; and Nicholas Crookback had not joined his parents and siblings in the churchyard. A suicide, he could not claim burial in consecrated ground, but was buried in some obscure place, although Matthew had no doubt the innocent lad would find more welcome in heaven than many of the so-called righteous who had been his accusers while he lived.

As for Adam Nemo, he was no where to be found to learn that his name had been cleared, even though Arthur Burton offered a handsome reward to anyone who could inform him of his erstwhile servant's whereabouts.

On the third day after the stonemason was taken, the Stocks found Hubert Selby among their customers, but he was there neither to purchase cloth nor to gossip but at the behest of William Dees.

"Dees is being taken to Colchester Gaol even as we speak," Hubert said, getting Matthew into a corner where their conversation would not be overheard. Joan, seeing Hubert, joined the two men.

"He wanted me to deliver you a message. For all the evil he did, he's not totally without some virtuous thoughts. He prays constantly for forgiveness with as much earnestness as a pilgrim. He says he bears you no ill will, Matthew, and is heartily sorry that he tried to drown you."

"I am right glad he's sorry," Matthew said. And Joan declared she was as happy as well that the stonemason failed, for she would be no widow at her young age.

"Dees has a favor to ask of you," Hubert said. "He prays you will execute his will and look to his wife and children."

The stonemason's wish left Matthew speechless for a few moments. He looked at Joan and found her to be similarly astonished.

"He will have no other but you, he says," said Hubert, handing Matthew a piece of paper. It was a testament of few words, written upon cheap, soiled paper. The ink had been frequently blotted to remove errors. The will remembered Dees's wife and children and endowed them with all his worldly goods, along with his request that they forgive him and remember him for the good he had done and not the evil.

"The wretch seems to have forgotten that a murderer's goods and chattels are forfeit to the Crown," Hubert said. "His wife and children will be left with nothing but the clothes on their backs. Dees also asks," Hubert added, "that you see that a monument is placed upon his grave."

"And where would I find a monument for the man, and more, what have carved upon it?"

"Dees said you would ask that question," Hubert said. "And he said I was to tell you to look in his workshop. He has made his own monument and engraved upon it what he thinks fit. He hopes you will find no fault in it."

"Tell William Dees that all these things my husband will faithfully do," said Joan before Matthew could answer for himself. "His wife and children may have nothing of his land and goods but they shall have a monument to his memory."

In the afternoon, the weather now as mild as was typical of the season, Joan and Matthew went to the stonemason's house. Dees's wife, with more color in her face than she had had before and dressed in mourning as though she were already a widow, let them in, apologizing for the delay, for she feared the people, she said, that they might stain her with her husband's disgrace. "He was never a very good husband," she said philosophically, "and more a burden at this moment than ever he was before. Yet he is my husband, and I shall have no other in this world."

"William has asked me to see that a stone is placed on his grave," Matthew said.

Dees's wife nodded and led Matthew and Joan to the shop at the back of the house.

"I know of no monument he made for himself, but if he did, it's among the rest," she said. She left them then, as though being in her husband's workplace caused more grief than she could bear.

In the rear of the shop, amid a clutter of stone rubble, bricks, and lumber, Matthew found a monument covered with a dark stained apron. The monument was of unusual design and composition, made of black stones—the black stones, Matthew was quite sure, that Frobisher had brought back from his famous voyage. Dees had polished them to a high sheen and embedded them in mortar, leaving a flat surface on which he had already engraved his name and the present year and the words REPENTANCE IS NEVER BELATED.

Joan looked down at the monument as Matthew read the words aloud.

"I don't think that's from Holy Writ," he said.

"No, I think not," Joan answered, "And yet pray God in heaven it's true what the words say, for William Dees stands in need of repentance as much as any man since Judas's time for what he did to those innocent children and that wretched woman, their mother."

Then she said, "It is as if he knew he would be found out, or wanted to be. See, Matthew, he has already inscribed this very year of grace. He *knew*, Matthew, oh mark how the man knew he would be found out."

"Hubert was right too," Matthew said. "Dees was a great sinner, yet not without redeeming qualities, though he tried to murder me. Well, when he is dead he shall have his monument. And may his repentance be sincere."

"And may he have his forgiveness too," Joan said. "For I would not deny him that, though he tried to make me a widow before my time."

So far north, snow still lay upon the ground in patches, and at night the stars sometimes seemed as close as his hands. Sometimes now, traveling by night, Frobisher's savage forgot his English name, which was now his old one, and the solitude of his journey quickened his memory and he remembered that which he had been called by his own people. He had said the name a thousand times under his breath until it had seeped into his brain and become one with himself.

He prayed now to the gods of those people, and when he prayed, he prayed not only for himself but for the poor hanged lad who could utter no prayers save those that the heart spoke in silence. He grieved for the boy's loss with such passion that his whole being quaked. He would not grasp that warm hand again or stroke the smooth contours of that shoulder, as white as alabaster, or lay his lips upon that cheek as smooth and hairless as an egg.

He had no idea how far he must travel to come to some coast where he could get an English ship, or whether any ship traveled to where he wanted to go, or whether any would take him, being the manner of man he was. But he had remembered how to build a sealskin craft of the kind his own people made, light as a bird upon the water, as tight-fitting as an Englishman's slipper, and he imagined himself constructing it and setting out alone on the high, fierce waves and coming to the steeples of ice and the seas without bottom and the skies so pale and soulless as to cause the heart to break with the very emptiness of them.